W9-CKS-580

WRIT IN STONE

WRIT IN STONE

Cora Harrison

severn
House

This first world edition published 2009
in Great Britain and in the USA by
SEVERN HOUSE PUBLISHERS LTD of
9–15 High Street, Sutton, Surrey, England, SM1 1DF.
Trade paperback edition published
in Great Britain and the USA 2010 by
SEVERN HOUSE PUBLISHERS LTD

British Library Cataloguing in Publication Data

Harrison, Cora.
    Writ in Stone.
    1. Mara, Brehon of the Burren (Fictitious character) –
    Fiction. 2. Women judges – Ireland – Burren – Fiction.
    3. Burren (Ireland) – History – 16th century – Fiction.
    4. Detective and mystery stories.
    I. Title
    823.9'14-dc22

ISBN-13: 978-0-7278-6812-1   (cased)
ISBN-13: 978-1-84751-176-8   (trade paper)

All Severn House titles are printed on acid-free paper.

Typeset by Palimpsest Book Production Ltd.,
Grangemouth, Stirlingshire, Scotland.
Printed and bound in Great Britain by
MPG Books Ltd., Bodmin, Cornwall

Prologue

The Burren, on the west coast of Ireland, is a land of white stone and dark green-blue sea, encircled by swirling terraced mountains of gleaming limestone, soft fertile grass and hard rock; tiny jewel-bright flowers and wind-torn asymmetrical trees; great pagan stone monuments and small ruined Christian churches and abbeys.

To the north of the Burren, between the mountains, lies a valley, its vivid emerald-green grass neatly segmented into oblongs and squares by low white limestone walls. At the head of this valley, sheltered from north, east and west by the towering hills, sits a Cistercian abbey, dedicated to *Sancta Maria Petris Fertilis*, Our Lady of the Fertile Rock. Now it is a majestic ruin, but from the thirteenth to the sixteenth century it was a prosperous place. Within its peaceful walls monks of the Cistercian order worked, lived and eventually died. Their lives are largely unknown, their deaths soothed by the rites of the church, and their bones now lie among the small humps and hollows outside the abbey.

But at the Christmas festival of the year 1509 a death occurred in the abbey that was not the result of illness, plague or of old age. A man kneeling in prayer beside the tomb of an ancestor was brutally and violently battered to death. And it was Mara, Brehon of the Burren, who had to investigate this secret and unlawful killing.

One

Caithréim Choirdhealbhaig
(Triumphs of Turlough)

In that year of 1317 they came through Burren's hilly grey expanse of jagged points and slippery steeps, a land nevertheless flowing with milk and yielding luscious grass. Then they passed out into the clear land of the abbey, Our Lady of the Fertile Rock, and inside the smooth-walled monastery's stone-fast precinct they bestowed their lifted kine. Themselves, that night, they harboured within the sumptuous abbey's best and most comfortable buildings.

Written by Séan Mac Rory Mac Craith, Bard to the O'Briens, in the year of Our Lord 1459

The church was very cold. The sun had just risen on this the twenty-third day of December in the year of 1509. Clear white light slanted through the three tall pointed windows behind the altar illuminating the finely cut ashlar limestone and the delicately moulded flower heads that decorated the tall columns. The carved vaulting of the sanctuary roof stood out like the skeleton ribs of a long-beached whale and in the chancel the marble effigy of a dead king lay tinged with pink light from the rising sun. All was very quiet and very still.

The day before had been a day of contrasts. Every few minutes strong gleams of pale winter sunshine had slanted streaks of glittering silver across the mountain flanks and then inky black clouds cast shadows over them, reflected on to a gleaming background like insubstantial, wavering goblin shapes. The sky continually darkened and quite suddenly lightened again. The cattle in the fields moved uneasily in and out of the shelter of the wind-torn hedges. Gulls flew in from the Atlantic with raucous shrieks of warning and small brown birds clumped defensively among the gnarled branches of the stunted holly trees.

But a few hours after nightfall, the wind had suddenly died

down and Gleann na Manach (the valley of the monks) had become very still. Then the snow began, not a few blown flakes dancing in the air, but a steady, solid, curtain-thick downpour. By dawn the valley was choked with it, the mountain pass completely blocked, the mountains themselves smoothed and rounded, the fields and lanes filled to wall-height. The Burren was no longer a place of hard, grey stone, but a fairy kingdom of soft dazzling whiteness.

The small church at the abbey was so bathed in bright light that the red sanctuary light in the chancel had faded to a dull glow before the altar. The place was empty except for one man on his knees before the tomb of his ancestor. King Turlough Donn had made it plain the night before that he, and he alone, would take the first hour of the annual vigil to commemorate the death of his great ancestor, Conor Sudaine O'Brien, so no one disturbed the peace of the church. Even his bodyguards stood outside the western door of the church, checking the roads, the snow-filled fields, and scanning the distant mountain passes.

The assassin stood in the shadow of one of the floral-capped pillars and watched the dawn light illuminate the cloaked and hooded figure of the praying man. Nothing was to be heard; the abbot and his monks had sung the office of prime and then had gone back to their beds – the monks in their dormitories, the abbot in his house. The many noble guests who had come to commemorate the anniversary of the dead king and the Christmas-tide marriage of the living king were sleeping within the guest houses. Although the air was cold and chill, it still bore the scent of the incense of the last service.

There was something deeply inhibiting about the silence and immobility of the praying figure, thought the assassin. Perhaps the deed should not be done. Perhaps the wisest, and the best, course of action was to leave the chapel and go back to bed.

And then the kneeling figure sighed, stirred uncomfortably and swept a hand over his forehead. The candlelight brought sparks of coloured light from the jewel-studded ring on the first finger. The assassin knew that ring: the three lions was the symbol of the O'Briens. The sight of it rekindled the desire to kill. The slow fire of bitter resolve, that had begun to subside, now surged up at the sight of this symbol of wealth and power.

The moment of doubt passed quickly. There was a mason's hammer lying at the foot of a pillar. The mason had been working late into the night repairing the decorative stone frieze of drooping-headed harebells before the Christmas festivities had begun and the hammer had been forgotten. The assassin snatched it; swung it. The weight of the mallet seemed to make it take on a life of its own as it swung in a wide arc and came crashing down on the skull of the kneeling man. There was surprisingly little noise, just a sharp crack like the sound from a hazelnut trodden on a stone pavement.

For a second the assassin hesitated. Blood flowed down over the white marble tomb and then on to the grey limestone flags underfoot. Should the murder weapon be concealed? It, too, was coated with thick clots of blood and shards of bone; no, better to drop it. It would be essential to retreat from the chapel before the bodyguards chanced to look in.

These bodyguards watched over the door to the outside, the western door, but the other two doors stood open. One led to the bell tower, the monks' dormitory and to the lay dormitory and the other one to the cloister and from thence to the abbot's house and to the guest houses. The choice was obvious and it was made without a second's hesitation. Within three seconds the church was empty of all living presence: just two dead members of the O'Brien royal family, the one lying within his centuries' old marble tomb and the other on the floor beside it.

Two

Cain Oigillne

'For what qualifications is a king elected over countries and clans of people?' asked Cairbre.

'He is chosen,' said the king, 'from the goodness of his shape, and the nobility of his family, from his experience and wisdom, from his prudence and magnanimity, from his eloquence and bravery in battle, and from the number of his friends.'

Mara, Brehon of the Burren, abruptly sat up in bed. As the cold air puckered her bare skin she slid down again under the covers. But the voices were too insistent and the message they screamed was too strange, too appalling to ignore. Once more she pulled herself up and this time picked her night robe from the sheepskin rug on the floor, slid it over her head and then listened intently. Yes, she had made no mistake. The words were as she had heard them. Already steps were pounding up the stone staircase towards her room. In the case of a violent death then the first person to be summoned would be the Brehon. Her position meant that she would be responsible for finding the criminal and imposing the punishment. Quickly she turned to the sleeping man at her side and shook his bare shoulder.

'My lord,' she said calmly. 'They are crying your death.'

King Turlough opened one sleepy eye and reached up for her. 'Come here,' he said softly.

The voices were louder than ever, and now the abbey bell began to toll. Both of the king's eyes snapped open and he stared at her in bewilderment.

'Stay there,' said Mara warningly, pulling the warm blankets and sheepskin covers over him, even above his head. She took her fur-lined mantle from a peg behind the door and wrapped herself in it, hastily sliding her bare feet into soft leather shoes. Then she opened the door just at the moment that the feet had reached the top landing.

There was a crowd of them: the abbot, obviously hastily dressed, some monks, some lay brothers, even some guests, but Fergal, the king's bodyguard, was first. His was the voice that she had heard calling, but now faced with her calm countenance, he suddenly fell silent. Tears welled up in his eyes and he looked as young as one of her students. He, above all, would know how much the king meant to Mara, Brehon of the Burren. He, and Conall, the other bodyguard, had been a tactful and silent presence at the many meetings between the king and his Brehon, the midnight strolls, the long suppers at her house, the visits. Now Fergal turned helplessly towards the abbot and stood back to allow him to break the appalling news.

'Brehon,' said the abbot, 'something terrible has happened. The king has been killed by an assassin as he knelt in prayer beside the tomb of our great ancestor, Conor Sudaine O'Brien.'

Interesting how he never missed an opportunity to tell the world that he, too, was one of the *derbhfine*, the royal branch of the O'Brien clan. He didn't look too upset at the news of the death of his king, either, she thought angrily. His sharp face, with the high-bridged O'Brien nose, wore its usual expression of sanctimonious self-satisfaction. Mara's agile mind recorded an instant impression of the other upturned faces before her, before turning rapidly to Turlough's predicament. If she could move the crowd from the royal lodge he could get back to his own room quickly.

'I must go to the church,' she said decisively. 'Come with me, everyone.'

The crowd parted, squeezing up against the smooth stone walls as she swept down the stairs. They followed her tall slim figure obediently. At the doorway, she hesitated for a moment, looking out at the thick layer of heavy snow that blanketed the grass between them and the west door to the church. She wished that she had put on her boots, but it was too late to think of this. Only the Brehon, her servants and King Turlough with his two bodyguards had been housed within the royal lodge, the most sumptuous of the abbey's four guest houses. Once she had taken the crowd across the grass and gone into the cloister, Turlough would be able to get back to his own bedroom in privacy.

But who was the man in the church, she wondered, as she walked across the heavily trampled snow of the curving path leading from the guest houses to the west door of the church. She had forgotten until now about Turlough's boast at supper the night before that he would spend the first hour of daylight on his knees before the tomb of his great ancestor. He had probably forgotten it, also, she thought with a small, secret smile. The night he and she had just spent together had not afforded much time for thinking of kingly obligations. For a moment it crossed her mind that Turlough might have gone over to the church before coming to her bedroom last night and played some childish trick by stuffing a bolster and wrapping his own cloak around it, but that was impossible. When the monks rose in the middle of the night for the service of matins they would not have failed to discover the deception.

'He is in here, Brehon,' said the abbot, leading the way through the widely opened doors. 'May God have mercy on his soul,' he added in a slightly perfunctory way. There was no love lost between Turlough and his cousin the abbot, Father Donogh O'Brien.

There was an immense chill within the small church. Heaps of trodden soiled snow lay without melting on the tiled floor of the aisle, the breath of the living rose up in clouds of mist. The sky outside had clouded over with more storm clouds and only the small red light in the sanctuary guided them towards the chancel at the eastern end of the church. The light was enough to show them their way, but the body on the ground was just a shapeless heap. Even in the damp cold air the smell of blood was overpowering.

'Bring torches,' said Mara crisply. 'Stand back everyone until I can see what has happened.'

Fergal and his fellow bodyguard Conall rushed out to fetch torches, but everyone else stood without moving. Mara had been Brehon of the Burren Kingdom for fifteen years and her lightest word was law to the people there. She waited calmly, her hands tucked into the fur lining of her mantle. There was no doubt that someone had been killed here – obviously not Turlough, but perhaps some passer-by had sought refuge from the storm.

But once the torches had arrived Mara gave a gasp – echoed by those around her. For a moment she felt as though she were in the midst of a nightmare – or perhaps that the events of the past night had been just a blissful dream. She bent down and touched the still-warm body. The man on the ground was the king – tall, broad-shouldered, wrapped in a furred mantle, its hood now sodden with blood, one hand flung out with the O'Brien ring sparkling in the torchlight, that ring which only those of the *derbhfine*, the true linear descendants of King Brian of the Battles, could wear.

A heavy sigh came from behind her. She wheeled around to see the emaciated figure of Conor, eldest son of Turlough. His face was whiter than the clumps of snow that lay around them and his large, blue eyes were blank. His thin hand sawed the air in a futile gesture.

'Quick, hold him,' snapped Mara and Fergal automatically stretched out an arm towards his lord's son. Mara's mind registered that there was blood on the bodyguard's sleeve, but her immediate concern was for Conor. He had been ill of the wasting sickness for months and now he looked near death.

'Stand back,' said the abbot authoritatively. 'Give some air to the king's son.'

'The king,' said a low voice from the back of the crowd. It sounded like Teige O'Brien's, thought Mara. Of course, Conor was the *tánaiste*, the heir to his father. If Turlough were dead, then Conor automatically became king. And probably, then Teige, the king's cousin, would be appointed *tánaiste* in his place.

By now, Mara had regained her wits and she could see who lay dead on the church floor before her. Without hesitation, she knelt on the wet floor and swept back the hood from the man's face.

'Conor,' she said urgently. 'Listen to me, Conor. That is not your father. Look at him.'

And yet it was so like Turlough, the height, the shape, the same brown moustache, the same high-bridged O'Brien nose, the ring, the age, everything said it was the king.

But of course, it wasn't. Mara had seen that in a glance and even Conor's white face warmed into a slight flush. Those at the front of the crowd pressing into the chapel saw it also. She rose to her feet.

'I fear, my lord abbot,' she said, 'that your brother, and the king's cousin, Mahon O'Brien, has been foully murdered.' She waited for a few respectful minutes while the abbot approached.

He stood very silently for a moment, looking down at the dead face of his elder brother. He showed no sign of surprise; he did not touch the man, nor did he kneel as Mara had done. He signed himself with the sign of the cross and with a surprisingly steady voice gave a blessing to the dead body and then looked around in a peremptory fashion. A young monk hurriedly approached with the sacred oils and the abbot performed the final service for his brother, anointing the five senses, bending down to touch the eyes, ears, nostrils, mouth and then the hands and feet, and praying for the salvation of Mahon O'Brien's soul. After a minute he straightened up and looked at her. All the piety of his position as abbot was now overlaid by the fieriness of his O'Brien inheritance.

'Who has done this?' he asked and his voice rang out against the rafters of the roof.

'I shall begin my investigations immediately,' said Mara, conscious of her naked feet in the thin shoes. 'But first, could I ask you to get one of your young brothers to take the *mac-an-ri*, the king's son, back to his house and perhaps your herbalist would tend to him. The king's bodyguards and I will go to make sure that the king is in good health and that no assassin has approached him in the night.'

Turlough, she thought, was in remarkably good health when she saw him last, but a return to the royal lodge would give her an opportunity to get dressed and put on some warm hose and boots.

'And the church?' The abbot, she was glad to note, had responded meekly to the note of authority in her voice.

'The church must be locked until I have time to look thoroughly around it,' said Mara, decisively holding her hand out for the large key which the abbot wore around his waist. He gave it to her with less reluctance than she had expected. His brother's death must have shaken him more than had appeared initially. She waited calmly while the crowd dispersed and then beckoned the bodyguards to go ahead of her. She had perfect confidence in her own ability to preserve an air of dignified solemnity, but Turlough, when faced with the anxious queries from his bodyguards, might not be able to resist sidelong glances at her while he declared that his night's rest had been unbroken.

Once everyone had left the chapel, though, she was suddenly seized with a violent attack of shivering. Her feet were cold, but it was not that so much as the sudden realization that this blow was undoubtedly meant to kill Turlough. Everyone, whether noble or humble, lay or monastic, had been gathered in the refectory for supper the night before and everyone would have heard the king's booming voice, declaring that he, and he alone, would keep the first hour of the vigil in front of the tomb of his great ancestor, Conor Sudaine. Mara's knees felt weak and she sank down on the low seat beside her. The smell of blood was making her feel sick, but she tried to ignore it. She shut her eyes and tried to concentrate on the scene the night before.

They had all been there, all the principal members of the O'Brien clan. There was Turlough, of course, in the seat of honour, and she herself on his right-hand side. To his left was Conor, his ailing son, and beside him his wife, Ellice. On the other side of Mara was the abbot, and next to him his brother, the king's cousin, Mahon O'Brien. Mahon O'Brien's wife of the first degree sat opposite and also at the table, to the great amusement of Turlough, was a pretty young girl Mahon had introduced as his wife of the second degree. Of course, Brehon law allowed this. A wife of the second degree was a woman who brought no property and was completely under the control of her husband. Banna, who had brought her husband rich land in Galway, was not looking too pleased at the addition of Frann to her family circle. Then there was Teige O'Brien, and his placid plump little wife, Ciara, from Lemeanah Castle on the Burren. Teige was Turlough's first cousin and a possible choice as the next *tánaiste* if anything happened to the delicate Conor. There were also the other three *taoiseach*s on the Burren: Ardal O'Lochlainn, Finn O'Connor, and his wife, Mona, sister to Ciara O'Brien, and Garrett MacNamara.

Oddly enough, it was Conor, the sickly Conor, who had provoked his father last night. Conor had been ill for a long time, but he had made a great effort to attend the pre-wedding ceremonies, probably, thought Mara, because he knew how heart-sore his father would be at the absence of his other son, the disgraced Murrough. Nevertheless, it may have been some jealousy of Murrough that caused him to make the unfortunate remark.

'People live in the past too much,' he had declared in his thin, breathless voice. 'I don't believe that any man gains a jot of nobility by reason of his ancestors.' Here he was interrupted by a violent fit of coughing and his dark-haired wife assisted him from the refectory, her sharp-featured face impatient and sulky. Ellice and her father, a younger brother to the Duke of Ormond, had thought to make a good match when she was betrothed to the son of the king of Thomond, but it began to look as if Conor would not live to succeed to his father's position.

Turlough had opened his mouth to make an angry retort, but shut it hastily as he saw the red stain spreading across the white linen handkerchief pressed to Conor's mouth. Gloomily he poured himself some more wine.

'A man's ancestors are the most important thing to him,' he said as the door shut behind his sick son. 'Tell me a man's breeding and I will tell you what that man is. My ancestors were great men.' He looked beligerantly around the table and everyone's eyes fell before his. 'Conor Sudaine, whose anniversary we will honour tomorrow, was a man who fought until no drop of blood remained in his veins.' He turned to the abbot. 'We will have a Mass for him tomorrow?'

The abbot bowed his head respectfully. 'At sundown, my lord.'

'I'm not convinced that we do enough to honour him.' The king was in a quarrelsome mood, thought Mara, anxiously eyeing the low level of the flagon of cheap Spanish wine which the abbot had placed before his most important guest.

'Perhaps some extra prayers,' she murmured. The weather was stormy and there would be many young brothers at a loose end tomorrow as farm work would be difficult. It wouldn't do any of them any harm to have an hour of quiet prayer inside the church as a change from the back-breaking toil of digging leeks from the cold wet soil.

'That's it,' said Turlough, crashing his fist on the table and making the platters jump. 'Tomorrow will be a day of continuous prayer, from dawn to dusk, beside the tomb of Conor Sudaine.' He looked around the refectory where every knife was suspended and every eye turned respectfully towards him before announcing dramatically: 'I myself will take the first hour of the vigil, after you have celebrated the office of prime. I will be in the church by dawn.'

'I will be happy to accompany you, my lord,' said the abbot heroically.

'No, no.' Turlough was in a mood to disagree with everyone. 'I will be alone. You, my lord abbot, may take the second hour. Fergal, Conall,' he bellowed over his shoulder, 'I'll rouse you at dawn and we'll go across to the church.'

'Yes, my lord,' they chorused respectfully. They would know the king well enough not to take it upon themselves to rouse him, thought Mara, guessing that by morning, Turlough would change his mind.

So what had made the bodyguards go to the church before Turlough, wondered Mara, rising to her feet and walking quietly down the middle aisle of the church. Carefully she locked all of the doors and then stepped outside. The sky was full of menace, with purple-black snow clouds piling up against the white-capped summit of Cappanabhaile Mountain to the west. The four *taoiseach*s of the Burren stood outside the door to their guest house waiting for her, waiting, like the chieftains from time immemorial, to serve their lord, the king.

'Brehon,' said Ardal O'Lochlainn, coming forward. 'This is a terrible thing. What can we do to help?'

'Could it be one of the O'Kelly clan?' asked Teige O'Brien eagerly. 'He could have crept in and struck the blow.'

'How would an O'Kelly know that the king meant to be in the church at daybreak?' objected Garrett MacNamara. His wife was from Galway and she had distant connections with the O'Kelly clan.

'They have spies everywhere,' said Teige with conviction. 'Everyone heard the king last night. Everyone knew that he intended to be alone in the church this morning. Perhaps they have a spy among the brothers and he managed to get word out. By the mercy of God, it wasn't the king, but only Mahon, who was killed.' Mara had to conceal a smile. There was little love between the cousins, Teige and Mahon. It had been rumoured that Mahon was more favoured than Teige by some of the O'Brien clan, although Teige would be Turlough's choice for *tánaiste*, if anything happened to Conor. Teige's suggestion that an O'Kelly might have come forty miles through a blizzard just because the king might possibly be alone in the church was absurd. It didn't surprise her, though; the outsider was always a popular suspect when it came to murder.

'The bodyguards were on duty outside the west door. No one from the outside could have got in. In any case, no one came or went from this abbey last night or this morning,' said Ardal O'Lochlainn with conviction. 'You have only to look for yourself, Brehon. I've been to the gate and all around the walls. The snow is heaped up and there are no footprints. If an O'Kelly came here last night or in the early morning then he must have flown like a bird.'

'I'll take your word for it, Ardal,' said Mara. She smiled at him. He was a handsome figure of a man as he towered above here; his red hair flamed against the whiteness of the snow and his blue eyes were the colour of the sea. A man of honour and principle, she could rely on his testimony; she knew that.

'I must go back to the lodge now,' she said, 'but, Ardal, perhaps you could make arrangements for me to talk to any travellers or visitors in the lay dormitory. They may have seen or heard something during the last few hours. Just have a word with the abbot, will you? I'll be back in a few minutes.'

As Mara approached the royal lodge she could hear Turlough's voice coming from the king's chamber at the front of the building. Probably the two bodyguards were in there with him explaining the events of the morning. That would give her a moment to get changed. She went quietly up the stairs and into her room. Brigid must have been in during her absence. The room was tidied, the bed covers neat and the charcoal brazier in the corner was filling the room with a welcome glow and on top of the iron bars that covered it was an ewer filled with hot water. Quickly Mara washed, then dressed in her warmest wool gown, pulled on thick woollen hose and her fur-lined boots. A tap came to the door and she opened it.

'I brought you some breakfast. Sit down and eat it now, everything else can wait.' Brigid had been a servant to Mara's father and she had brought up his daughter after the death of his wife.

Sometimes Mara felt irked by her unceasing vigilance, but this morning it was comforting to be mothered.

There was a large round griddlecake still steaming from the hot plate and a wooden cup of hot spiced ale. Mara drank it gratefully, only now fully realizing how cold she had been.

'So it wasn't the king after all, praise be to God,' observed Brigid, seating herself on the window seat.

'How did Fergal and Conall come to make that mistake? And why were they at the church if the king had not gone there?' asked Mara, with her mouth full of griddlecake. The salted butter was incredibly creamy. No wonder the abbey cows were famous for their milk!

'Well, it was I that thought of waking them,' explained Brigid. 'You see we all heard the king the night before – everyone heard him, even the people at the low table at the end of the refectory, they heard him, so when I woke up this morning and I saw all the light in the room, I sat up in bed and I said to Cumhal: "that'll be the rain turned to snow." So he had a look and I was right, there was a great fall of it last night and then I sent him to wake up the bodyguards and get them to make a bit of a path over to the church before the king got up, and that was how they discovered the body with the head beaten in. The king's cousin it was, Mahon O'Brien, is that right?'

'That's right,' said Mara, rinsing her hands in the pewter bowl and then combing out her long dark hair and braiding it neatly. She crouched down by the brazier, holding her hands out to its warmth. Two minutes with Brigid would be enough to give her all the background to what was going on, as well as warming her, she told herself.

'And it couldn't have been anyone from outside,' continued Brigid with a dramatic toss of her sandy-coloured hair, still in its overnight braids. 'Cumhal's been out and had a look. Ardal O'Lochlainn was there when he went. "There's been no one in and no one out, Cumhal," he says. "You're right, my lord," says Cumhal. And it wouldn't have been any of the brothers.' Brigid had a great respect for the monks of St Mary's abbey. 'So that just leaves the people in the guest hall and a few travellers in the lay dormitory.'

'So who do you think it might have been, Brigid?' asked Mara, examining herself carefully in the small silver mirror she had brought with her.

'I couldn't rightly say,' said Brigid, an unusual note of doubt in her mind. Normally her opinions were firm, instant and then unshakeable. 'Perhaps it wasn't the king that was meant, after all,' she continued. 'Who would want to harm him? A nice man like him.' Brigid adored Turlough who lavished extravagant praise on her cooking.

'You think the murderer knew that it was Mahon?' queried Mara dubiously. Unlikely, she thought. And why had Mahon gone to the church at dawn? That was something she had to find out about.

Brigid lowered her voice. 'The word is that wife of Mahon O'Brien was in a great state about him bringing a new wife to the household, and her a girl young enough to be his own daughter. And then of course, I don't suppose that Teige O'Brien was too happy about the last meeting of the O'Briens. Somebody was telling Cumhal about that at the *Samhain* fair. It seems that some of the clans would prefer Mahon to Teige as *tánaiste* if anything happens to the *mac an rí*,' she paused to gasp in a breath and then added, 'God bless and save him, the poor lad; he doesn't look well at all. The wasting sickness, they say it is. Everyone was talking about it last night.'

Mara put down the mirror and gave a last rub of her hands in front of the glow from the brazier and then straightened up. Her quick ear had caught a sound of the door opening from the king's bedroom up a flight of stairs from her own. She went to the door and waited for him.

'My lord, this is a terrible matter,' she said looking up at him, her voice as formal as she could make it. He had dressed, she noticed, and was booted and enveloped in a fur mantle.

'Terrible,' he echoed. He didn't look as shocked as she had expected. And yet, it was surely obvious that the victim was meant to be him. He was a man of war, of course, despite his essential soft and sweet nature. He would have lived with danger from a very early age. Looking at him now, Mara felt her legs unsteady once more. This man, this king, that she had lain with last night to her great pleasure, was still in the utmost danger. Whether it was a murder committed by one of his traditional enemies, or by one of his jealous relations, this was a crime that she had to solve and that had to be solved quickly. If she delayed, then the assassin might make a second attempt and this might result in the death of the man whom, above all others, she loved.

'I am going now to interview the strangers, the passers-by and the pilgrim in the lay dormitory,' she said to him, noting with satisfaction that her tones were clipped and unemotional. He bowed his head.

'I will accompany you, my lady judge,' he said and his tone was as formal as her own and if he squeezed the soft flesh of her arm rather too intimately when he took her by the elbow, then no one but the two of them knew of that.

Three

Brecha Cróliçe
(Judgements of Bloodlettings)

There are two fines to be paid by a person who murders another. The first is called the éraic, *or body fine, and this is paid to the nearest kin of a murdered person. It is forty-two* séts, *or twenty-one milch cows, or twenty-one ounces of silver. Added to this is the second fine, which is based on the victim's honour price.*

In the case of duinetháide, *a secret killing, the* éraic *is doubled.*

A small drifting snowflake stung Mara's cheek as she stepped out from the front door. The storm clouds of earlier had begun to fulfil their promise. The sun had disappeared and the sky was blue-black. No travellers could stir outside the abbey today, she thought, with a quick glance at the snow-clad mountains on all sides of the valley of the monks. The four chieftains, who had been waiting, had moved into the shelter of the doorway to the guest house.

'My dear lord!' It was Teige O'Brien who stepped forward. Mara was moved to see the close embrace between the cousins. He and Turlough were of the same age, had been brought up together and usually the greeting was more of a playful punch.

'God has spared you to us,' said Ardal O'Lochlainn solemnly and the other two *taoiseach*s, Garrett MacNamara and Finn O'Connor, murmured echoing sentiments.

'The wife of our cousin would like to see you and the Brehon, my lord,' said Teige. 'I mean the chief wife, Banna,' he corrected himself.

Probably wants to find out what the division of property will be, thought Mara, but I have to start somewhere and it may as well be with the wife, or better still, the two wives of the dead man.

'You go; I'll wait here for you,' said Turlough to Mara, an

expression of almost comical dismay on his face, but she shook her head at him.

'I think that Banna will wish to see you, also, my lord,' she said firmly. The more people that were clustered around Turlough until the assassin were found the safer he would be. There was no doubt that he was probably the intended victim, she thought. Why should anyone want to kill Mahon O'Brien? Resolutely she took his arm and steered him towards the guest house.

The guest house was a large handsome stone building of two floors high. It had four guest bedrooms on the first floor with rooms for servants in the garret above. The ground floor had a large handsome parlour and a kitchen and washroom with water piped from one of the many spring wells that encircled the abbey. Like the Royal Lodge it was built on the south-west side of the cloisters. It was newly built, replacing a much smaller building, and was unusually large for a small abbey like St Mary's of the Burren. A recent inspection, by an official from a French Cistercian abbey, had spoken rather sourly of the luxury of the guest accommodation, and of the abbot's house, in comparison with the quarters allocated to the monks and to the lay brothers. However, the abbot, Father Donogh, was an O'Brien, part of the royal family of O'Briens. O'Brien money had paid for the original building and O'Brien money paid for the upkeep and the embellishments to the abbey; fitting provision for the kinsmen would be a priority.

'The abbot wishes to see you, also, my lord,' murmured Ardal as they stepped inside the heavy oaken door. 'And he asked me to tell the Brehon that Father Peter is keeping the travellers and the workers in the lay dormitory until she can interview them. If you wish, Brehon, I will accompany you when you have finished talking to my cousin.'

Mara gave him a quick nod and smile as she followed the king up the stairs. She had forgotten that Banna was Ardal's cousin. There wasn't much resemblance between the enormously fat Banna and the slim, handsome Ardal. Not much of a resemblance in temperament, either, she thought with a small, quickly repressed grin, as the king knocked on the door. Immediately loud sobs rose from within and as the maid opened the door, Mara could see Banna sitting on the window seat with a large linen handkerchief covering her face.

There was a slight movement from above and Mara turned to see a young face peering down from the upper storey.

'I'll join you in a moment,' she whispered to Turlough and rapidly made her way up the second staircase.

'Frann,' she said warmly, taking the young hand within hers. 'I am very sorry. This has been a terrible shock.'

'Oh!' The young woman was obviously surprised at these words from the Brehon. Probably no one had thought of coming to condole with her. All attention would have been focused on Banna, the chief wife.

Frann, the newly acquired wife of second degree, was no more than sixteen years old, Mara guessed, looking shrewdly at the smooth face and plump young hands. She was almost young enough to have been the dead man's granddaughter. What had been the attraction, she had wondered last night, peering through the dim candlelight at the slim young figure, to make a man antagonize his wife of over thirty years and scandalize his brother, the abbot. But today, in the fierce white snow-light that streamed through the window of the upper landing, she understood.

Frann's smooth young face had creamy-white skin, the colour of a widely opened rock rose, and her eyes rivalled the blue-green iridescent sheen of a dragonfly in spring. She was slim, but there was nothing childlike in the voluptuously curved line of breast and hip. Her mouth had a curiously lifted and curled upper lip, almost as if it had been moulded from scarlet sealing wax. As Mara looked at her, she saw the girl's pink tongue dart out and moisten the already shining lips; this was obviously an automatic gesture. Frann was well aware of her attractions. She made no other reply to Mara's condolences and showed no pretence of sorrow.

'Come inside out of the cold,' said Mara, taking the girl's arm in a motherly way. 'Come in by the fire. Is this your room, here?'

It was a narrow, bare room, with just a bed and a small, plain chest at the foot of it: more of a room for a servant than for the wife of the king's cousin. There was no heat there; it was bitterly cold and the small brazier by the shuttered window only held cold grey ashes. Beside the brazier stood a basket empty of charcoal. Obviously no one had attended to the room this morning. Banna's servants would have known that, now their master was dead, there was little point in serving this new, unimportant wife of the second degree.

'Come downstairs to the parlour,' said Mara swiftly. 'You can't sit here in this freezing room.'

Frann shrugged her pretty, rounded shoulders. 'I don't mind,' she said amiably, but she followed Mara down the stairs and when they came into the parlour she crouched near to the fire that roared up the chimney and held out her pretty hands to the heat. 'I'm used to the cold,' she boasted. 'I was brought up on the mountains north of Galway. We get real cold there with snow for many months of the year.'

'So what brought you to this part of the world?' asked Mara, heaping some more wood on to the fire. The room was luxuriously furnished with well-padded, carved chairs and cushioned benches and stools. The walls were hung with handsome worked carpets and sheepskin rugs were scattered on the polished flagstones of the floor. This room had been swept and polished this morning, the dead ashes removed and the fire attended to. Mara sat down on the chair by the fire and looked across at the girl.

'My father was a shepherd,' said Frann. Her voice took on a slightly sing-song rhythm as if she were telling an old tale to the sound of a softly played lute. 'We lived in a small cottage by a mountain stream halfway up the mountain. Myself and my brother, we used to climb to the summit every morning to see that the sheep were safe and we used to be able to look across the sea to the magical island of Hy-Brasil. We would stay up there all the days of daylight, looking after the sheep and leading them to places where they could feed from the herbs until evening came . . .' Her strange eyes seemed to be green now, but still held those flecks of blue which gave them that iridescent sheen.

'And in the evening,' prompted Mara as the girl paused and looked at her.

'In the evening,' said the girl softly, 'we used to come down to our little cottage. We could smell the turf smoke and even when the mountain was covered in mist we could find our way home by following that smell. My mother would have our supper cooking on the pot hanging over the fire and then afterwards we would sit around and my father would tell us stories.'

'So that's where you get the gift,' Mara smiled. She had thought so. It was a pretty story and she could see how Frann would have beguiled a middle-aged man like Mahon. He always had seemed a sad sort of man to her, childless and married to a stupid, demanding woman. This girl would have been very tempting to him. 'So why did you leave the mountain?' she asked.

'My father was killed one day in spring,' said the girl and now her rich singing tones took on a deeper, sadder tone. 'He was trying to rescue a sheep and he fell down a crevasse. My mother could not stay there on her own with two children so she took us back to Athenry, the place where her own family came from.'

'And how did you meet Mahon O'Brien?' asked Mara. 'And how did the marriage come about?' The eyes that met hers were clear and intelligent. There was no sense of wasting too much time over stories of childhood.

For a moment Frann looked startled, and the green-blue eyes darted a flashing glance at Mara's face, but then she smiled, a lovely smile, thought Mara, the strong white teeth contrasting so beautifully with the red mouth.

'My mother's father, my grandfather, worked for him,' she explained. 'He was working in the limekiln. He found some work for my brother and me.' For a moment, the girl glanced down at her white well-cared hands and a slight shudder shook her plump young shoulders as if she were picturing those hands raw red, scarified by the lime. 'Mahon came one day and no one was there but me. I told him the story of my childhood and he was very kind to me.'

As I thought, reflected Mara. This is a well-rehearsed story and she is a pretty girl, but I must not delay too long here. This girl had much to lose and little to gain by Mahon's death. There was little chance that she had anything of significance to say.

'So when did you last see Mahon?' she asked rapidly. From above, she could hear Banna's voice rise to a great wail. Turlough would need rescuing soon. He had disliked his cousin and had no love for his cousin's wife, but his sense of duty and his innate kindness would make him offer clumsy attempts at consolation. As far as Mara could hear, he was making matters worse rather than better.

Frann cast down her eyelids. 'I saw him at dinner last night, Brehon,' she said demurely.

Mara allowed a moment's silence to elapse. Mahon, from what she had noticed last night, had hardly been able to take his eyes off Frann. Frann's eyes shot open, surveyed Mara's face cautiously and then, unexpectedly, she giggled.

'Well, he did come to my bed last night,' she admitted and once again she passed her tongue over her shining red lips. Mara's heart warmed to her. At least the girl was honest. She settled herself more comfortably into the cushions of her fireside seat; Banna could wait. From upstairs she could hear the sound of the maid's voice. Turlough should make his excuses and leave rapidly, but in the meantime she would get to know this wife of the second degree.

'So, what did Mahon talk about?' she asked bluntly and smiled when Frann shot her an amused glance. 'I mean did he say anything about going to the church in the morning?'

Frann nodded. 'Yes,' she said in carefree tones. 'He said that he had to save his energy . . .' She shot Mara a sidelong gaze and then giggled again. 'He said he had to save some of his energy because he had to get up at dawn to take the king's place at church. He said that the abbot had asked him to do it and he couldn't say no as he had already refused another favour to the abbot and he didn't want to be on too bad terms with him.'

'So did the abbot come and see him, here in the guest house?'

'No, a lay brother came over when Mahon was just climbing the stairs. I was waiting at the top. I heard Banna start to snore and I guessed that Mahon would come. I had just come out of the bedroom when I saw the young brother give him a piece of vellum.'

'Did you see what was written on it?'

Frann shook her head. 'I can't read,' she said in a matter-of-fact way, 'but that's what Mahon told me.'

'I see,' said Mara. 'And what time did Mahon leave?'

'I don't know. He stayed a couple of hours, I suppose. He went back to Banna afterwards. He said that he wanted a good rest. He got nothing but rest in her bed!' Once again Frann giggled and Mara bit her lip to stop a smile appearing. The young are callous, she thought. Last night this girl lay in Mahon's arms and a few hours later she heard of his brutal murder. Didn't she care? Probably not: he would have seemed a very old man to her.

But what about her future? It was strange that she seemed to care nothing about that. After all, Mahon had rescued her from a life of hard work and poverty where quite soon her beauty would have been ruined.

'What will you do now, Frann?' she asked. 'Will you go back to your mother? How old are you? Fifteen? Sixteen?'

'I will be sixteen in May,' said Frann. 'In May,' she repeated softly. She smiled to herself, a secret happy smile. A slight tinge of rose spread across the shining matt pallor of her rounded cheeks.

'So you will go back to your mother, won't you?' persisted Mara. 'You do know that you have no rights over any property that Mahon owned. This will all go to his wife of the first degree.'

Frann smiled again. She said something, but her words were almost drowned by the scream that came from upstairs. There was a sound of glass breaking and Turlough's voice shouting: 'Mara!' Then heavily booted feet came thudding down the stairs and Ardal's voice calling: 'Brehon!'

Regretfully Mara rose to her feet and went to the door. 'Yes, Ardal,' she said crisply.

She had never seen him look so distraught. Normally he was quietly competent no matter what situation arose. His crisp curls of red hair were standing on end as if he had run his fingers through them, his very blue eyes were wide with panic and he was gesticulating frantically.

'Brehon,' he exclaimed. 'My cousin seems to have gone mad with grief.'

'Mara, come up,' shouted Turlough, appearing above her through the open door. He had a hunted look. His two bodyguards looked as though they wanted to put their fingers in their ears. From behind him came the noise of hysterical sobbing punctuated by a few shrill screams. Mara sighed.

'My lord,' she said raising her voice to be heard over the pande-monium from above. 'I think you should go to see the abbot now. Ardal, will you accompany him? When you return, you and I will go to the lay dormitory to interview the men there.'

Seldom had she been so promptly obeyed by Turlough. He made a quick gesture to Fergal and Conall, clattered down the stairs and wrenched open the front door. For a moment Ardal hesitated, sending a glance up the stairs, but Turlough took him firmly by the arm and pulled him out. The door closed with a resounding thud.

Mara delayed for a few minutes at the foot of the stairs until the four men had left the guest house. She smiled to herself. The wails and screams from above seemed to die down without the audience, she thought as she climbed the stairs slowly. By the time that she had reached the top, only a few hysterical gulps were heard. She pushed open the door and stood there glancing around. Banna had thrown herself on to the bed, her mountainous flesh still heaving with sobs, but the sound was now quite muted. The woman had completely exhausted herself with emotion, thought Mara. A stool had been flung against the window, but luckily only one small, diamond-shaped pane had smashed. Banna's maid was cowering against the wall, sobbing also.

Mara picked up a sheepskin rug from the floor and stuffed it into the gaping hole and then she closed the shutters. The room was now quite dim with just the light from one candle on a side table to illuminate it. Beside the candle was a small flask. She opened it and smelled it. Wine, she thought and poured some into a cup with a steady hand and carried it over to the bed.

'Drink this,' she said firmly, holding it to Banna's lips and the woman meekly swallowed it.

'Cover up your mistress,' said Mara turning to the maid and speaking with crisp authority. 'Make sure that she is very warm. Close the curtains and sit with her until she sleeps.'

The overawed maid dried her eyes and then bustled around taking extra covers from the carved chest at the foot of the bed and gently untying the curtains and closing them around the bed. Mara blew out the candle and put some more charcoal into the brazier. She then went around the room, quietly putting every-thing to rights. After a while she peeped in through the curtains. The hysterical woman was now lying quietly, with just the odd sob disturbing her bulk. The maid sat on a stool beside her, stroking the large damp forehead. There would be no point in talking to Banna just now. She would have to make time to do this later on in the day.

Soon the room was quite dark and warm. From behind the curtain came the first snore. Mara heard light footsteps pass the door and go up to the room above. So Frann was going back to her cold room, to sleep, to think about the future, to plan? That reminded her and she went to the curtains and beckoned.

'Go over to the kitchen and ask if someone can see to the fire in Frann's room,' she whispered to the maid.

Banna was now snoring continuously so, once the maid had left the room, Mara took the opportunity to look around. There was a large press for clothes, as well as a chest in this room and she decided to have a quick peep. A padded jerkin hung there – Mara recognized it; Mahon had worn it last night at supper. There was also a voluminous purple gown. Mara opened the press door a little wider; the gown was a very dark purple in shade, but she had the impression that the hem was even darker than the rest of the garment. She bent down and touched it. Yes, it was wet. Of course it was possible that it had trailed on the wet ground last night, but it had not been snowing, not even raining, when the guests had emerged from the refectory after supper and the path from the cloister to the guest house was paved. In any case, if it had got wet, then why not hang it near to the fire so that it dried overnight? Mara shut the door of the press quietly; there were footsteps on the stairs. By the time the maid entered the room she was seated quietly by the fire warming her hands and gazing thoughtfully into the blaze.

'They're bringing over some wood for the brazier now and some other comforts,' the servant whispered. She looked slightly embarrassed and ashamed. No doubt, it was by Banna's orders that no attention was paid to Frann so Mara gave her a reassuring smile and with a last peep through the curtains at the sleeping figure on the bed she got up and went quietly down the stairs. She looked into the parlour, but there was no sign of Ardal, but when she went to the window she saw him waiting outside. No doubt, he had not risked a second encounter with his hysterical cousin.

'She's fine, now, Ardal,' she said reassuringly. 'She's asleep and she'll feel better when she wakes up. Were they very close, she and Mahon?'

He stopped for a while to consider this and then shook his head. 'I don't think that I know the answer to that question, Brehon.'

He was a very enigmatic man, she thought with a certain amusement. She had known him for a long time; he had become *taoiseach* of the O'Lochlainn clan soon after she was made Brehon of the Burren, and yet she felt that there was a secret core to him that she did not know. She turned him over in her mind as they walked along the snowy path. It was only when they reached the lay dormitory that Mara remembered the last words that Frann had said.

The noise, of course, had been tremendous. Banna had screamed, thrown a stool at the window, and then exploded into fully blown hysterics. The maid had pleaded in a high-pitched voice. Turlough had yelled. Even Ardal had shouted. The situation had to be dealt with instantly; there had been no opportunity to ask Frann to repeat what she had said.

But now, underneath the memory of all that noise, the girl's quietly spoken sentence asserted itself in Mara's mind.

I said: '*So you will go back to your mother, won't you?*' thought Mara and Frann had replied:

'*No need for that now; my son and I will have a castle by the sea of our own.*'

Four

Bretha Nemed Déidenach
(The Final Laws Concerning Nobility)

The king's servants and attendants may carry out acts of violence during the course of their duties without liability.

Sayings of Fithail
'What are the exempt fists which are permitted in the attendances of kings?

Bodyguard, charioteer, champion, dispenser, cupbearer.'

Mara stopped for a moment on the path and then walked on. She would go back to Frann later on, and ask her what she meant, she thought. Now there were more important matters to see to. Ardal looked at her enquiringly and she said hastily:

'Ardal, I must just see Fergal for a moment.'

The two bodyguards were standing outside the abbot's house and Fergal came immediately at her call.

'Fergal, could I just ask you something?'

He still looked white and shaken, she thought, as he gave an uneasy glance around. That was natural, she supposed. Despite Brigid's words the chances were still very high that Turlough was the intended victim. Mara laid a comforting hand on his sleeve.

'Fergal,' she said gently. 'This must have been a terrible morning for you.'

He bowed. He did not look directly at her, she noticed. His eyes still scanned the high walls that surrounded the abbey site. She followed the direction of his eyes and looked all around appraisingly. There wasn't too much to worry about, she thought. The abbey buildings were inside about five acres of grounds. The walls were about twenty feet high and the only way in was through a huge iron gate on the western side. The gate was still locked, she noticed, pulling her hood over her hair. Already her dark mantle was spotted with white flakes of snow.

'I was wondering what happened this morning,' she said looking at him closely. 'I know that Cumhal woke the two of you,' she added. 'Just tell me everything that happened afterwards – every little thing that you can remember.'

Fergal's eyes returned to hers. 'Well, Cumhal shouted at us that it was dawn and that the king might be on his way to the church and we got up and Conall was saying . . .' he gave her an apologetic glance and she smiled.

'I suppose you didn't expect the king to get up so early. To be honest, neither did I. I thought he'd forget all about it and sleep through.'

He looked relieved at her words and a little colour crept back into his young face.

'Anyway we were getting dressed and Conall opened the shutters of the window and then he shouted out: "Oh, Jesus, Mary and Joseph, he's gone already!"'

'You saw him!' exclaimed Mara.

Fergal shook his head. 'No, it was the line of footsteps,' he explained. 'We could see them leading right across through the snow.'

'I see.' Mara looked around. The guest houses and the royal lodge lay at about fifty feet to the south of the main abbey buildings. The abbey was built on the four sides of the square cloister garden. The church was to the north, the chapter house, parlour and abbot's house to the east with the monks' dormitory above them. To the west were the cellars and storerooms with the lay dormitory above them and to the south were the kitchen and the refectory where they had all dined the night before, but the guest houses were outside this complex of monastic buildings.

Normally this garth was kept well cropped by some sheep, but now the whole ground was pitted and churned up with the numerous feet that had crisscrossed it during the last hour; at dawn the footprints would have showed up as clearly as a sparrow's trail across a churn of cream.

'And where did the footprints go? To the cloister?'

'To the west door of the church.'

'And they led from the lodge? Not from the guest house?'

'I'm not sure,' confessed Fergal. 'We were in such a rush and a bother and we just went flying out and over to the church.'

It would have been easy to be confused. The windows were set high up in the walls and they would only have seen the track at about ten feet from the lodge. The footsteps were undoubtedly those of Mahon O'Brien and perhaps another set also. Did the assassin follow Mahon out of the guest house?

'And when you got to the church?'

'Well, we walked up and down for a while and then we looked in to see that he was there all right and then we saw him slumped on the floor.'

'A bad moment for you,' said Mara sympathetically. The clouds had probably not been there then; they had just been gathering when she had come out, so the opening of the door of the small church would have been enough to flood the place with light.

'And I tried to lift him. I thought he might have passed out. And then I saw the blood.' He stared at the blood on his own sleeve as if he had only just noticed it.

'I see,' said Mara. 'Go and join the king, now, Fergal. And,' she paused for a moment and then continued, 'I don't need to tell you that you must keep a close eye on him.'

'You believe the king to be still in danger, Brehon?' asked Ardal as Fergal bowed his head silently and hastened back to his position outside the abbot's house.

Mara nodded. 'I do, Ardal. I think that everyone needs to be vigilant. As you said yourself, no one could have got in last night, but that means that no one could have fled, either. The man who committed this murder is still within the abbey grounds – man or woman,' she added with a quick memory of Brigid's suspicions. She didn't altogether believe that the enormously fat Banna would have exerted herself enough to get up at dawn and to hit her straying husband over the head with a mallet, but it amused her to see the look of horror on Ardal's face at the very idea of a woman committing murder. She was fond of Ardal and admired his handsome good looks, but she couldn't resist teasing him from time to time.

'I've told one of the brothers to keep all of the travellers in the dormitory until you had time to talk to them,' he said after a short silence when he had obviously reverted to the idea of the threat to the king. 'There are just five of them so it shouldn't take you long. The brothers can vouch for two of them and two of them are merchants travelling back from Thomond to Kinvarra who were forced to seek shelter from the storm.'

'And the fifth?' asked Mara as Ardal held open the door to the cellars.

'The fifth is a pilgrim,' said Ardal.

Mara had already begun to climb the stairs to the lay dormitory when something in his tone made her look back at him. There would be nothing unusual about finding a pilgrim in the abbey. These men often wandered right across Europe to Spain and to Rome, and as well, in the opposite direction, came to the west of Ireland in order to visit the sacred shrine of St Eanna on the Aran Islands.

'Yes?' she questioned.

'I'll leave you to make up your own mind, Brehon,' said Ardal firmly. 'You'll see him in a minute.'

There were six men inside the dormitory – Father Peter O'Lochlainn, Mara already knew. He was a small, thin, toothless man dwarfed by the grey Cistercian robes – a distant relation of Ardal. He was the prior of the abbey as well as the herbalist.

'God bless you, Brehon,' he said. His smile was engaging, just like a child's, but his eyes were sharp and intelligent.

Mara greeted him, looking around the dormitory. The two small, high-up windows faced west, out to the valley, and the light was very poor. The five men were sitting silently on their beds, obviously waiting for her.

'They haven't had their breakfast, yet, poor souls,' said Father Peter, 'so perhaps they could go down to the refectory, Brehon, as soon as you finish with each.'

'Possibly the two that you can vouch for first, Peter,' suggested Ardal.

'Well these two here have been working for us for the past three weeks repairing our beautiful church. Master Mason and Master Carpenter, will you come forward?'

The two men rose from their beds; the carpenter came quickly, but the mason slowly and reluctantly.

'This poor soul is worried about leaving his hammer there in the church,' said the Cistercian indicating the mason.

'Where do you come from?' asked Mara.

'We come from Galway, Brehon,' said the carpenter.

'Both of you?'

'Yes, Brehon,' said the carpenter. He had the ease of a man who is highly skilled and highly respected for his skill. 'We are brothers,' he added.

Mara looked at the mason. He was a broad-shouldered man, not tall like the carpenter, but immensely strong, she thought. He had white hair and a white beard and looked very much older than the other. There seemed little resemblance between them, but probably the carpenter did not mean blood brothers. Travelling masons and carpenters often worked as a pair, repairing churches and tower houses all over the country. Galway, with its fine stone-built houses and its many churches would give work to a couple like this for most of the months of the year.

'Did you leave your hammer in the church, Master Mason?' she asked.

He bowed nervously. He thrust his shaking hands beneath his mason's apron.

'I did, my lady,' he said in a deep husky voice. 'I'm very sorry for it. I was working late and I was tired and the light was going before I finished. I didn't make sure that I had all of my tools before I left the church.'

'Don't worry about it,' said Mara gently. 'Only the person whose hand struck the blow needs to worry. Now go and have your breakfast, both of you.'

As he passed her she smelled a strong odour of *brocóit*, that very intoxicating drink made from a mixture of beer and mead. It was unlikely that he had got that from the brothers, she thought. The ale that they were serving last night seemed to be very small beer, indeed. He was not as old as she had thought initially; the light from the opened door showed younger hands, smoother skin than she had expected. Perhaps he and the carpenter were blood brothers after all.

'I'll see the two merchants next, Father Peter,' she said aloud, resolving to interview the pilgrim in the abbot's parlour, or out of doors. Ardal was sharp and clever and if he had noticed something suspect about the pilgrim, then she would make sure that he was who he said he was.

The merchants were voluble in their account of their journey and their reasons for stopping off at the abbey. They had been to a fair at Coad in Corcomroe; Mara idly mentioned a few names and the descriptions came flowing back. She dismissed them quickly and then turned to Father Peter.

'Do you think that Father Abbot would mind if I used the parlour to talk to the last man, and of course, other people?' she asked. 'It's a bit chilly here. Perhaps you would be kind enough to ask him?'

'Lord love you, of course I will,' he said quickly. 'It's cold in here for a lady like yourself. I should have thought of that. I'm used to the cold; we're half-perished most of the time, but you'd be used to better. I'll go straight down and see about it. I'll make sure that there is a good fire there also. Give me two minutes and then I'll be back for you.'

After he had gone, Mara sat quietly and said nothing. Ardal, a man of great stillness, stood by her side and made no move. Mara kept her eyes fixed on the pilgrim. He had turned slightly away from her and sat with his head bowed, his brown hood well pulled over his face. He wore sandals, she saw, and also the regulation pilgrim's badge. She stood up and walked towards the window and looked out.

'It's snowing hard, now,' she announced to Ardal, and then came back and stood by the doorway. She had seen what she had gone to see. For a pilgrim, tramping over stony, rough roads in mid winter, his feet were surprisingly clean and well cared for.

'Bring the pilgrim down to the parlour in a few minutes,' she murmured to Ardal as she went out the door and followed Father Peter down the stairs and across the trampled snow of the cloister. She had little fear that the abbot would refuse her the use of the parlour; like every other inhabitant of the Burren he was under the jurisdiction of the Brehon and was bound to assist her in every way.

The parlour was a warm, comfortable room with windows facing east and a small fireplace filled with brightly burning ash logs. Mara refused all offers of hospitality in the form of mead and honey cakes from Father Peter, but begged him to stay. She was fond of the little man. He would not often get the chance to toast his feet in front of a fire and, in any case, he might be useful for cross-questioning this pilgrim on religious matters.

Ardal, to her satisfaction, allowed quite an interval to elapse before escorting the pilgrim into her presence. That was good, she thought. The man could be perfectly innocent, but if he were, then no harm would be done. However, if there was something wrong about him – and her own intuition, as well as Ardal's hesitancy, made her feel that there was – then this delay before questioning would make the pilgrim feel more on edge. Carefully she placed a chair in front of the fire. It would be kind to the pilgrim, but it would also mean that his face could be studied in good light from the east-facing window, by both herself and Father Peter.

The pilgrim came in quietly, politely ushered in by Ardal, head bowed, hood well pulled forward. Nevertheless, he was assured in his bearing. He bowed to Mara and then, uninvited, took a seat in a dark corner, leaving empty the chair in front of the fire.

'Sit here.' Mara's voice was quiet but it held a note of command. She got up and pulled the chair a little nearer to the fire so that it looked like a courtesy to the man. She stayed standing until he had obeyed and then she resumed her own seat.

'Please remove your hood,' she said.

For a moment he made no move, but then he bent his head even lower so that the hood completely covered his face and shook his head violently from side to side.

'What do you mean?' said Mara impatiently. 'Please do as I ask.'

The pilgrim lifted his left hand, drawing the loose folds of the hood even more completely over his face and with his right hand made a motion as if to mimic writing.

Mara turned to Father Peter, but he was already on his feet crossing the room to the abbot's desk. The pilgrim was as quick as he; he followed the priest over and took the quill from his hand and bent over the piece of vellum. She watched him narrowly; there was no doubt that he was a most unusual pilgrim. There seemed to be quite an air of arrogance in the way that he taken the quill and then selected the vellum. She rose to her feet and quietly walked across, looking over his shoulder. His hands, she noticed, like his feet, were clean and well cared-for, not the hands of a man who had spent months on the pilgrim path.

'Thank you,' she said, taking the piece of vellum from his hand and glancing through it. '"I have made a sacred vow not to reveal my face or to speak until I reach the shrine of the Eanna on Aran of the Saints,"' she read aloud. The words were in Latin but she read them out in Gaelic; she was unsure of how schooled Ardal had been. The handwriting was educated, she decided; though there was an elementary blunder in the words 'sacred vow' of the type that not even ten-year-old Shane, the youngest scholar at her law school, would make. Still that would not condemn a man. She passed the piece of vellum to Father Peter, and saw his eyes flicker over it rapidly. He, too, had spotted the error, she noticed. He lifted his head and looked across at the pilgrim.

'But no vow of temperance,' he said mildly, smiling his toothless smile.

The pilgrim's head jerked up and, for a moment, Mara thought that he would speak, or, at least, reveal his face. Quickly he lowered it again and preserved his silence.

'You see,' said Father Peter apologetically, 'I was keeping a bit of an eye on our Master Mason as he is inclined to indulge himself too much on occasion and I noticed that he was sharing a flask of *brocóit* with you and you did not refuse it.'

'Unusual for a pilgrim to drink anything other than small beer,' commented Mara. She watched the man carefully, but this time he was on his guard and made no move. It was unlikely that he would now reveal himself, unless force was used. Mara shot a quick glance at Father Peter. Though not a naturally pious person, still she always felt it was her duty to keep on good terms with the church. Perhaps this unwillingness to show a face or to allow a voice to be heard was the latest fashion for pilgrims. Perhaps she might be greatly offending religious sensitivities if she ordered the man to be forcibly unhooded.

However, Father Peter's eyes, like her own, were full of suspicion. He compressed his toothless mouth and shook his head slightly. It was impossible to mistake his meaning; he, like she, did not believe that this was a true pilgrim.

She would summon the king's bodyguards, she thought. This man was on her territory and therefore under her jurisdiction. It was indeed possible that he was one of the O'Kelly clan. The disguise of a pilgrim would be an easy way of ensuring a night's lodging at an abbey. The largest of the Aran Islands, just off the coast of the Burren, was a magnet for pilgrims, many of them making their way across Ireland from the east, and stopping at the cathedral of Kilfenora, then on to Kilinaboy with its relic of the true cross, then a night at the abbey and finally a perilous sea crossing the following morning.

At that moment, as if in answer to her thoughts, Fergal, the king's bodyguard, put his head around the door.

'Brehon, the king . . .' he began, but in mid-sentence, he was hastily plucked back and the tall figure of Turlough filled the doorway. He had to bend his head to fit under the low sill, but Mara could see enough of his face to register that he was in a flaming temper.

'Mara,' he said and his voice was choked with anger, 'you won't believe what that sanctimonious prig . . .'

Mara acted quickly. Turlough had no discretion. When angered he trumpeted forth his feelings to the world.

'Ardal,' she said quickly, 'would you take this man outside? Fergal and Conall will help you to guard him. Father Peter, will you excuse me for a moment. I need to confer with the king.'

The quick-witted Ardal had them all on their feet and was ushering them through the door almost before she had finished speaking. The pilgrim, she noticed, passed the king with his back towards him and his head bowed deeply upon his chest. Then she dismissed him from her mind as the door closed behind them all and she took Turlough by hand and led him over by the fire.

'What's the matter, my love,' she said, smoothing the snowflakes from his heavy *glib* and then parting the rough hair and pressing a kiss on his forehead. 'Who's a sanctimonious prig?'

'That cursed abbot, that . . .'

'Shh,' she said, placing her mouth over his for a moment. 'Walls have ears.'

'Do that again.' Now a grin was spreading over his face. Turlough was like a pinewood fire in his fits of anger: hot flames one minute and cool ashes the next.

'In a minute,' she said. 'First tell me what's wrong, but tell it quietly. Your voice can be heard for miles around. You're not on a battlefield now, you know.'

He took a deep breath. 'Well, the fact of the matter is that the abbot has come to me and that . . .'

'Shh,' she said again as his voice began to rise.

'He says he can't marry us on Christmas Day.'

'What? Oh, because of his brother's death, is that it?'

Turlough shook his head vigorously, dislodging a few more icy snowflakes from among the crisp curls of his greying hair.

'No, no, that at least would make some sort of sense, though there was not much love between them. Still a death can change that. No, he won't marry us because the Holy Mother Church of Rome,' here Turlough's voice took on a note of deep sarcasm, 'won't permit marriage with a divorced person and you, my love, are a divorced person.'

'But why didn't he say that before?' Mara was bewildered. She dodged his outstretched arms and stood up beside the fire.

'Well, apparently he has only just found out.'

'Really, I thought everyone in the three kingdoms knew about my divorce.'

Mara had been married at fourteen to a fellow student at her father's law school. Three years later, a year after the death of her father, she had divorced her husband. Memories of the divorce case, which she had conducted herself, still lingered in the minds of most people on the Burren.

'He even knew all the details of the divorce,' said Turlough with a grin beginning to spread across his face. 'He knew that the divorce was granted because your husband spoke about the details of your lovemaking in the alehouse. He found it all very shocking.' Turlough screwed up his face in a good imitation of the abbot's tight-lipped disapproving expression and then laughed heartily. He had begun to regain his good humour.

'But how did he suddenly come to hear about it? It must have been some time last night. He was very polite to me yesterday, almost friendly. I thought he was delighted to have the marriage take place here in the abbey.'

'He got a letter about it.' At the thought of it, Turlough was almost choking from rage again.

'A letter? From whom?'

'It wasn't signed. It was just written on a scrap of vellum.'

'You saw it then?'

'Saw it!' Turlough's voice rose in unison with his fury. 'I took it from him. Someone had placed it inside his door. He found it this morning after the first service.'

He felt in his pouch and produced the piece of vellum. Mara took it and began to read. There was an unexpected degree of knowledge about her divorce case in it, she thought. Most people would by now have forgotten the name of her husband. She seldom thought of Dualta, herself. She neither knew nor cared where he had gone when he left the Burren after the case was found against him. He had never qualified as a Brehon; she was sure of that. The Brehons in Ireland made a habit of visiting each other during the summer months; someone would have mentioned him.

Mara read the letter again. Even the date of her marriage was correct. Who had written it? Placed inside the abbot's door either last night or first thing this morning seemed to indicate that someone in the abbey had written it. Surely no one would have battled through the storm in order to acquaint the abbot with a piece of gossip that was fifteen years old. She took from the writing table the piece of vellum where the pilgrim had written about his vow and compared the two.

'What's the matter?' Turlough had noted her start of surprise.

Mara did not reply for a few moments. She had expected the pieces of vellum to look the same, and they had. Weight, texture, grain, all those things spoke of the same calfskin, but what she had not expected was that the script was identical. The careless, rushed letter *a*, the arrogant sweep of the letter *m* and the dashing tail of the letter *s* – all these things confirmed that the letter to the abbot had been written by the pilgrim. But why? And who was this false pilgrim? Mara's agile mind rushed through the possibilities. And suddenly a name occurred to her: a man who needed to keep his face hidden from both Brehon and king, a man whose voice must not be heard, a man who resented the marriage between the Brehon and the king, a man who feared rivalry from the possible offspring of this marriage; now she knew who this pilgrim really was. There had, after all, been something very familiar about the tall figure with its jaunty, self-possessed bearing. She went to the door and called:

'Please bring the pilgrim in.'

He came in reluctantly, pushed by Fergal and Conall and

guarded from the rear by Ardal. He stood there in the abbot's parlour, his head bowed and his face still hidden. But now Mara had no doubts. Now she recognized the form and the build of the man and knew what would be shown at his unveiling.

'My lord,' she said to Turlough. 'Here is your son, Murrough, come to greet you at this Christmas-tide.'

Five

Córus Béscnai
(The Regulation of Proper Behaviour)

The unworthy son is deprived of his share of the inheritance because a son should be subject to his father.

A proclaimed or outlawed son, a macc fóccrai, *is called a son of darkness.*

Murrough, King Turlough Donn's twenty-two-year-old younger son, had always been a man full of courage. Hardly a moment elapsed after Mara's words when, with a contemptuous laugh, he shrugged off the pilgrim hood and then stripped off the gown and stood facing them all. He had shaved off the great curved moustache, the proud mark of all Gaelic warriors, and he was now clean-shaven except for a small trim beard. He was dressed in Christmas colours of red velvet doublet and knee-length green breeches, all in the latest fashion from the Tudor court of London, surmised Mara. With an aching heart she watched Turlough; the look of fury that he had summoned up, with clenched fists and bristling moustache, was struggling with the sorrowful affection for this rebellious young son of his, which showed in his green eyes.

'What are you doing here?' he barked.

'It's Christmas time. I wanted to see you, Father. I wanted to express my repentance. And I wanted to see my brother Conor. He's not looking well.' Murrough's voice held just the right note of sorrow mingled with respectfulness. Soon, Turlough, a simple man who always expressed everything that was on his mind, and expected everyone else to do the same, would forgive this prodigal son and take him back to the bosom of his family.

Mara narrowed her eyes. She did not believe in this repentance. No doubt, the Earl of Kildare, Murrough's father-in-law, a man of great importance in the court of King Henry VIII and essential to the Tudor rule in eastern Ireland, had decided that Murrough would be of more use to him over here in the western kingdoms of Thomond, Corcomroe and Burren than he would be hanging around London and living at the expense of the Kildare properties. It was time for her to take part in this family discussion.

'And, of course, you wanted to wish your father well at the time of his marriage,' she said sweetly.

Murrough turned his gaze on her. 'My lady judge,' he said, sweeping her a courtly bow. 'You are looking very well.'

He was so like his father with the wide smile, the green eyes, brown hair and broad shoulders that Mara had to harden her heart. She allowed half a minute to elapse before holding out the piece of vellum to him.

'Or did you? This is your hand here, is it not?'

Mischievously he allowed his eyes to widen with horror as he read the scurrilous details of her divorce case. A smile puckered the corners of his lips and his eyes lit up with amusement.

'Certainly not, my lady judge; how very shocking!' The mockery was unmistakable.

Ardal was looking uncomfortable, and the two bodyguards bewildered. It was time to put a stop to this. Turlough and his son would have to be allowed some privacy. She knew how it would go. Turlough would shout. Murrough would feign repentance. Turlough would soften. Murrough would make some promises. And then Turlough would take him back into the bosom of the family. The king was a man of warm affections. His sorrow at the parting from his son had been huge. Despite his abhorrence of English ways and English customs, and his deep disgust at the deeds of his son, Murrough was still his dearest child.

'My lord, we will leave you,' she said, putting the piece of vellum back into her pouch. 'You and I will talk later. Fergal and Conall will stay on guard outside the parlour. Ardal, would you be kind enough to accompany me to the church?'

The snow was beginning to fall heavily when they got outside. The rounded bulk of the abbey hill protected them from the full force of the north wind, but the cold was intense. A family group of half-grown grey crows huddled in the leafless trees above the

church and even the insides of the twenty-foot walls were daubed
with patches of snow like clotted cream against the grey of the
limestone. The air was bitterly cold with that chill that seemed
to penetrate even fur and wool.

Ardal said nothing as they walked down the path from the
abbot's house to the church and Mara was grateful for that. Her
mind was busy. She brushed aside the cancellation of her marriage
by the abbot; all this pomp and ceremony mattered more to
Turlough than to her. She was only grateful that her daughter
Sorcha was expecting a baby at Christmas-tide and so could
not be there. Sorcha would have been upset and Oisín, Sorcha's
husband, would have been outraged. What concerned her now
was the possibility that Murrough, whom she knew from the
past to be unscrupulous, could be the murderer. Could he have
tried to kill his father? Conor, his elder brother, was very ill;
everyone knew that. Did Murrough hope that the clan, with
its great affection for his father, King Turlough Donn, would
immediately elect him as *tánaiste* and, after the death of Conor,
he would then be king of the three kingdoms of Thomond,
Corcomroe and Burren.

A few of the young monks were indulging in an illicit game
of snowballing on the north side of the church, she noticed with
a sympathetic grin. She pretended not to see them as they withdrew into the corner behind the north transept. Let them enjoy
themselves while the abbot was otherwise engaged, she thought.
Unlocking the great west door with the huge key, her mind
flitted through the sequence of events. Turlough had publicly
declared his intention of spending the first hour alone in front
of the shrine of his ancestor; Murrough had been present and
could have heard that, could have crept into the church once the
service of prime was over. In the church, kneeling facing the
shrine, one hooded figure could look like another, and Turlough
and his cousin, Mahon, bore quite a resemblance to each other.
She stood for a few moments looking around her and then turned
to her companion.

'Ardal, you are very good to help me like this. Could I ask
you to fetch the abbot? I really need to know which doors would
have been open here this morning when Mahon O'Brien came
to the church.'

'Yes, certainly, Brehon, would you like me to leave you alone with the abbot, then?'

Mara considered this for a moment and then shook her head. 'No, if you don't mind, Ardal. I would prefer you to stay.' She considered trying to account for this, but then didn't bother. Ardal would not feel that any explanation was due to him and she could hardly offer her real reason which was that she wanted to meet the abbot and discuss the murder with him without any of the feelings of awkwardness about his decision not to marry her which might occur if they were alone together.

The abbot looked ill at ease when he arrived. Mara watched him amusedly. She felt a certain satisfaction that he had obeyed her summons so promptly.

'Ah, my lord abbot, I would like to discuss the security arrangements about your church.' Her voice was cool and crisp and she could see him wince.

'We rely on the protection of the Almighty God, Brehon,' he said. He tried to make his voice sound as usual, but she was pleased to note an uncertain timbre to it.

'And yet a man was murdered here in the church of God,' she said mildly.

He bowed and did not reply and then she felt somewhat ashamed. After all, it was his own brother who had been killed and, although rumour said that there was not much love lost between them, nevertheless this must be a heavy blow. She hastened to put the meeting on a more amicable footing.

'I will be glad of your help and your knowledge, my lord abbot; we need to use all the wisdom that God has given us to find out about this sad affair,' she said portentously and he nodded.

'First of all can I give you my heartfelt condolences on the death of your brother,' she added politely.

This time he bowed and Mara thought that his face softened slightly. But still he said nothing and there was a wary alertness about the way that he looked at her.

'Just one thing puzzles me a little, Father Abbot,' she said carefully. 'I understand that you sent a note to Mahon O'Brien telling him that Teige had brought a message saying that King Turlough had changed his mind about the early morning vigil. Is that correct?'

He considered this for a moment and then said stiffly: 'That is correct.'

'So why did you think that it was the king's body that had been found?'

He was ready for this question. He had all the mental alertness of the O'Brien family. 'I presumed that his own bodyguards would know the king,' he said. 'It would not be unknown for him to change his mind,' he added triumphantly.

True enough, thought Mara. However, it was still strange. And there was no doubt that his eyes were uneasy. There was a tension within him as if he were a man under great strain. She glanced around. 'Are all of these doors locked at night?'

The abbot shook his head. 'Only the west door,' he said. 'The door to the night stairs that connects with the monks' dormitory is left open for the night services, as is the door to the lay dormitory.'

'What about the door to the cloister?' Ardal asked. The abbot turned to him in a startled and slightly affronted way.

'Of course,' he said firmly. 'That is the way that I would enter myself from my house.'

'And the west door,' queried Mara. 'Would Mahon O'Brien have found that open when he crossed over from the guest house, or would he have had to ask for the key?'

'I opened that myself, after the service of prime had finished.'

'Did any of the men in the lay dormitory attend the service of prime, other than the lay brothers, I mean?'

The abbot shrugged. 'I really could not tell you. My thoughts were on the service and my eyes were directed towards the altar.'

'And did you open the west door before the monks departed or after?'

'Before,' he said. 'The custom is that I leave the church first.'

So perhaps one man could have remained within the church, perhaps hidden behind one of the beautifully carved pillars, or perhaps have stolen in afterwards.

'Ardal,' she said aloud, 'would you be kind enough to kneel over there in front of the tomb and pull your hood over your head.' He did so without a word, neatly avoiding the body and

the large stain of blood on the tiled floor, and Mara walked over
to the cloisters' door and from there to the door that led to the
monks' night stairs and the lay night stairs and lastly to the west
door. From all doorways only a vague hooded shape could be
seen. Certainly there would be nothing to distinguish the king
from his cousin Mahon O'Brien in that dim light and from those
angles.

'Thank you, Ardal,' she said aloud. She turned to the abbot.
'Father Abbot, you may give orders for the body of your brother
to be prepared for burial. The church may now be cleaned and
purified. I have finished my business here. Will you come with
me, Ardal? We'll go across to the guest house now.'

Even though Mara had deliberately left the church by the west
door – as far away as possible from the abbot's parlour – the
thunderous sound of Turlough's voice came clearly to their ears
as they crossed the trampled snow, through the guest house garth,
on their way to the guest house.

'What's my marriage to do with you? How dare you . . .'

'So it looks as if anyone could have got into the church this
morning, Brehon,' said Ardal hurriedly. He was obviously trying
to cover up the king's voice by starting a conversation. He would
want to spare her the embarrassment of hearing herself discussed.

She smiled up at him, grateful for his sensitivity, though inwardly
amused. Dear Ardal, always the soul of nobility!

'That's right, Ardal, at least anyone from the abbey,' she said
and then, hunting around to continue the conversation as
Turlough's voice rose and swelled like the sound of a stormy sea,
she added, 'Father Abbot didn't get on that well with his brother
Mahon O'Brien, I seem to remember. Do you know anything
about that, Ardal?' Ardal O'Lochlainn bred horses on the rich
limestone land of the Burren and sold them in Galway. He had
many friends among the merchants in Galway city and among
the chieftains in the surrounding lands. He, if anyone, would know
all about Mahon O'Brien.

'Well, I think it was because of his son, the priest.' Ardal glanced
around nervously. He would be loath to offend the abbot, but
with Turlough roaring like a bull there was no point in low
voices.

'Mahon's son? I thought he had no children.'

'No, the abbot's son. It happened a long time ago when Father
Abbot was a young monk. He wasn't abbot, then, of course.'
Ardal's voice was apologetic.

'Of course,' agreed Mara solemnly.

Well, well, well, she thought. The old hypocrite! Her spirits
soared. Turlough will enjoy this, she thought. She herself did not
care that much about the abbot's decision not to marry them,
but one glance at Turlough's face had shown her the depth of
his hurt feelings.

'Come into the Royal Lodge, Ardal,' she said, tucking her
arm inside his. 'We'll go to the guest house in a minute, but
I feel frozen and I'm sure that you are also. Brigid,' she called
as she opened the door, 'could you bring some of your
wonderful spiced ale into the parlour for myself and the
O'Lochlainn.'

There was a gloriously warm fire blazing in the huge fireplace
in the parlour. Mara shook the snow from her mantle and hung
it up behind the door. Ardal did the same while she dragged two
stools near to the warmth.

'I've got a couple of my pies, too,' said Brigid, coming almost
instantly with the steaming cups and closely followed by her
husband Cumhal bearing a platter of small pies.

'I've been keeping these warm; I knew that you would be
cold,' she continued, putting the drinks on the stove and taking
the pies from her husband.

After they had gone, Mara busied herself giving Ardal the cup
and a pie. He was not a natural gossip, she knew, and she wondered
how to get all the information without it sounding as if she were
just curious.

'It's a very serious affair this, Ardal. I am very worried about
the king's safety. I need to know everything possible about the
other people who were at the abbey last. So unless it would break
any vow of silence I would like you to tell me all that you know
about the abbot, his son, the priest, and the abbot's relationship
with his brother Mahon O'Brien,' she said frankly, after a minute's
pause to pick the right words. If it had been anyone else, she
thought, she would just say: 'Oh, do tell,' and then they would
have a delicious gossip together.

Ardal swallowed a large gulp of the spiced ale, but when he spoke it was with no reluctance and his voice was calm and practical.

'Father Denis is a man in his early thirties,' he said. 'Someone pointed him out to me last night and that's what I would judge him to be. I hadn't seen him since he was a boy.'

'Last night!' exclaimed Mara.

Ardal nodded. His face was set into serious lines, but his eyes looked worried. She resolved not to interrupt him again.

'Yes, Father Denis is spending Christmas here at the abbey.'

With his holy father, the abbot, thought Mara, a bubble of laughter suppressed within her throat.

Ardal took a bite of his pie and then with a look of appreciation took another almost immediately. Mara sipped her ale and tried to look relaxed.

'Yes, I would say that he is about thirty,' continued Ardal. 'It would be a young age for promotion, but Father Denis had hoped to become the abbot of Knockmoy since the former abbot was removed by the head of the Cistercian Order at the beginning of this month.' He looked at her, inviting comment.

'I see,' said Mara thoughtfully. 'And why was the former abbot removed?'

Ardal coughed with a slight air of embarrassment. 'Apparently he was in the habit of having his hair washed by a woman.'

Mara nodded. She did not trust her voice to comment on this so she gazed steadily at the fire until the rising giggle had been stifled.

'Anyway, the abbey of Knockmoy is within the territory of Mahon O'Brien.'

'The uncle of Father Denis,' commented Mara, her voice now under control.

'Just so! However, Mahon O'Brien refused to back his application, in fact he declared his intention of reporting to Rome that Father Denis is the son of a professed priest and an unmarried woman and, as illegitimate, would be barred from such high office.'

'I see,' said Mara thoughtfully. Under Brehon law there was no such thing as illegitimacy; the only question was whether the father acknowledged the son. However, under Roman law and

English law, the position, she knew, was quite different. 'It does happen, though, doesn't it?' she queried. 'I thought that there was something like this with the Bishop of Killaloe and his son who is an archdeacon.'

'Oh, it happens,' agreed Ardal, 'as long as no one bothers Rome about it.'

'That's what I thought,' said Mara. 'A few sons here or there or a few wives for that matter, shouldn't condemn a priest. It would make him more human,' she added light-heartedly.

Ardal gave another one of his polite coughs and Mara returned to the subject. 'So this Father Denis would have little reason to be fond of his uncle Mahon O'Brien.'

'Little reason,' confirmed Ardal.

'And where did he stay last night, Ardal? Do you know?'

'I think,' said Ardal thoughtfully, 'that he would have stayed last night at the abbot's house.'

'And so would have gone to church with him at prime,' said Mara. But did he return to the abbot's house once the service was finished, she wondered? She looked over at Ardal and wished that he were different. What she needed now was someone to debate possibilities, even to make wild guesses. She missed her law scholars. She normally discussed all her cases with them. By now they would all have been speculating freely and her mind would have taken sparks from theirs.

'Ardal, you have been very good,' she said decisively. 'I wonder could I ask you to do two more things for me. Could you ask your cousin, Father Peter O'Lochlainn, to come and see me for a few minutes and then could you go over to the guest house and tell Banna that the abbot is having her husband's body coffined and that I will be with her as soon as possible. I'm sorry to give you so many errands, Ardal.'

'It's a pleasure to serve you, Brehon.' Ardal immediately rose to his feet and did not even give the platter of pies a second glance. As soon as the door closed behind him Mara went out to the kitchen.

'Could you make some more spiced ale, Brigid, and perhaps heat a few more pies? Father Peter O'Lochlainn will be coming over in a few minutes and I'd like to give him something. I think these poor monks here have a hard life. They all look very thin, except for the abbot, of course,' she added and Brigid rose to the bait immediately.

'Oh, he'd look after himself all right,' she sniffed. 'One of my cousins used to work as a herdsman here and he said that it was always the best for the abbot. And him so holy!'

Brigid didn't volunteer any information about Father Denis, noticed Mara. She would have if she had known. This was interesting. It meant that the news of the abbot's son had not reached her and that surely meant that not many people knew of it. Certainly Turlough had never mentioned it. Brigid prided herself on knowing everything that went on in the kingdom of the Burren. The abbot must have been very careful and very discreet, and of course it was all a very long time ago. Probably, he had little to do with his son until fairly recently and he would have been announced to the monks as a distant relation, perhaps even a friend.

'So you have twelve brothers here at the abbey and then with Father Abbot and you, the Prior, that makes fourteen monks that slept here last night,' said Mara innocently.

Father Peter's white thin face was flushed a rosy pink from the warm fire. He sipped slowly at his ale as if determined to make the exquisite pleasure last as long as possible and his toothless jaws chewed resolutely on the succulent pie. When he replied his voice was indistinct and he continued to mop up stray crumbs from his grey habit and slot them back into his mouth. Nevertheless the one-word answer was unmistakable.

'Fifteen,' he said.

'Really? So where did the extra monk come from?'

Father Peter hesitated, eyeing her. There was a glint of amusement in his faded grey eyes.

'Have some more ale,' said Mara, hospitably insistent. Luckily Brigid had placed a good-sized flagon on the hob of the fireplace.

This time Father Peter tossed back the cupful with the careless abandon of a man who had resolved to make the most of this unexpected foretaste of paradise. He leaned forward and stated solemnly: 'Brehon, I know I can rely on your discretion.'

'Of course,' said Mara. She also leaned forward so that their heads were almost touching. A single knotted piece of pine suddenly blazed up with a blue flame and then subsided into the red glow of the heart of the fire. Outside the window the snow continued to fall from a lead-heavy sky.

'And you wouldn't say a word about this to the man who is coming from Tintern Abbey?'

'Not a word,' said Mara solemnly. Who's the man from Tintern Abbey, she thought, but there was no point in breaking the conspiratorial mood which had been established between them; she could always question him afterwards about this.

'This Father Denis O'Brien, he's the abbot's son!' said Father Peter in a sibilant whisper.

'Really!' exclaimed Mara. Her tone was amazed, with an undercurrent of incredulity. She had perfected this note from years of gossip with Brigid.

Father Peter nodded. 'And that's the God's-honest-truth,' he said with emphasis.

'Strange that the abbot had him here for Christmas with the king himself present,' said Mara in shocked tones.

Father Peter nodded. This time he himself leaned over and tipped a little more of the spiced ale into his cup. 'God forgive me, but this is great stuff, Brehon,' he muttered. He tossed it back and then smiled broadly at her. 'The abbot brought him here because he knew that it was probably his last opportunity to try to persuade Mahon O'Brien to nominate the lad as abbot of Knockmoy.'

'And did it succeed?'

'Not a bit of it,' he said with emphasis. 'There was a big quarrel yesterday morning. I was in the chapter house writing up the big book and I heard every word of it.'

'I can't imagine the abbot quarrelling.' And this, thought Mara with surprise, was actually true. The abbot was always so icily cold, so remote, so sure of himself, that it was hard to imagine him condescending to quarrel. Still perhaps love for one's child can change natures. Her feelings warmed slightly towards him.

'And what did he say?' She took a companionable sip from her cup and Father Peter responded instantly.

'He yelled at him, really yelled at him. "You'll regret this, Mahon O'Brien," that's what he yelled.' Father Peter lowered his gaze for a moment and then looked at her. She could see that struggle between loyalty to his abbot and the desire to round off his tale struggling on his small pinched face, but then the love of a good story won almost instantly and he ended triumphantly: "'You'll regret this, Mahon O'Brien; you'll regret this at your dying moment." And that's what he said, Brehon.'

Mara considered this for a moment. It probably didn't mean too much, just the war-like O'Brien blood triumphing over the layer of Christianity, she thought dispassionately. However, there was no doubt that not much more than twenty-four hours later Mahon O'Brien was lying dead in the abbey church. It would probably have been about half an hour after the service of prime that he had been killed, she thought. She tried to picture the scene.

'Do you remember this morning, Father Peter, at the service of prime, do you remember the monks filing out of the church? It would have been very dark, I know, but you would have had candles, wouldn't you?'

Father Peter nodded emphatically. 'That's right, Brehon, every choir monk has a candle; even the abbot has his own candle.'

So each face would have been lit up, thought Mara.

'Just describe the scene for me, Peter,' she said slowly. Her concentration was so intense that she called him Peter, as did Ardal.

He was quick-witted and did not question her.

'Father Abbot went down to the back of the church and he unlocked the west door. Then he went to the cloisters' door, on the south side, as always – mostly he goes out first, but this morning he just stood there so we all stood up. I was the first, because I am by way of being second-in-command. We turned and went towards the back of the church. We go up the night stairs, you know, the stairs that lead to the monks' dormitory.'

'And you went up first?'

Father Peter shook his head. 'No, I stood there and allowed them all to go ahead of me. That's the custom; it's my responsibility to see them all safely into their beds.'

'And there was no one in the church for the service of prime, except the choir monks, the abbot and Father Denis O'Brien,' asserted Mara, expecting a ready agreement, but Father Peter hesitated.

'Well, that's what you would expect,' he said hesitantly, 'but it was strange, because as I walked down with my candle, I half-thought I saw a movement at the back of the church.'

'But you didn't recognize anyone?'

Father Peter shook his head. 'Far from it; I wouldn't even be sure that there was a person there, just a movement or a shadow, a bat perhaps.'

She did not pursue it. She would allow him to turn it over in his mind. He was sharp and clever and would come back to her if anything awakened his memory to a more certainty. 'And then?' she asked.

'Well, we all went down the church and turned to the left once we reached the night stairs.'

'And the abbot had already gone?'

'No,' said Father Peter, and his voice sounded startled. 'No, and I've only just realized that. No, he didn't go first. He always does, normally. No, he stayed there, standing beside the door to the cloister.'

'Alone?'

Father Peter shook his head. 'Father Denis was with him. He seemed like he was waiting. They both seemed like they were waiting; waiting for the rest of us to go, perhaps. They were just . . .' He broke off and got to his feet. The door of the nearby guest house had been flung open and the confused sound of voices filled the air. Mara jumped up also, her heart pounding. Let it not be Turlough, she prayed soundlessly. I'll never forgive myself if something has happened to him. She was at the door as soon as the knock came.

'Is Father Peter there?' The scared young monk was white with apprehension. 'We need Father Peter. The king's son is unconscious.'

Mara's heart slowed down. It was nothing to be surprised at that Conor had fainted; he had looked almost bloodless the last time that she had seen him. She turned to her companion.

'You go ahead, Father Peter,' she said urgently. 'I'm sure that your skills, with the help of God, will save him.'

They were fetching Turlough, she noticed. She would wait for him and be by his side, if his son's last hour had come. All else could wait.

Six

Cáin Íarraich
(The Law of Fosterage)

The father of a child to be fostered pays a fee to the foster father. This fee corresponds to the honour price of the father. Thus, the fee for the son of a king of three kingdoms is thirty séts *or fifteen ounces of silver, or fifteen cows. The fee for the son of an* ocaire *(small farmer) would be three* séts, *one-and-a-half ounces of silver, or two cows.*

When the child leaves fosterage, then the foster father gives the child a sét gertha *(a treasure of affection).*

Conor was stretched on the bed, his face whiter than the sheepskin bedcovering and dark blue shadows etched under his closed eyes. Turlough dropped to his knees beside the bed and took one of the transparently thin hands within his own. All the humour and fun was gone from his face and his green eyes were large with tears. Murrough, the sick man's brother, was there also, standing in the shadows. Ellice, the young wife, stood gazing out of the window. She turned as Mara came in, gave her one scornful glance and then turned back again, gazing on the snowflakes that still drifted down from the dark grey sky. There was such a look of angry bitterness on her face that Mara was appalled. She hesitated for a moment. Father Peter was giving quietly spoken orders to the three young monks. One was sent for herbal medicines, one for more charcoal for the brazier and one for some heated stones for the fire. If anyone could save Conor now, it would be Peter. There was nothing for her to do. She crossed the room and stood beside Ellice.

'What happened?' she asked in a low voice, scanning the young woman's face.

Ellice shrugged. 'The monks brought him over after he got that fright. He thought his father had been killed. He sat by the fire for a while. Then he said that he felt a bit better.' She shrugged her narrow shoulders again. Her dark eyes were hooded, but her compressed mouth spoke of anger and resentment.

Mara said nothing, just continued to look out at the snow while keeping her attention fixed on the girl beside her. How old would she be? Mara remembered the year of the wedding. About five years ago, she thought. Shane, her youngest scholar, had just come to the law school. Ellice had been fourteen then. She must be about nineteen now and the mother of three children. The children were all placed in foster homes, as was the custom, and Ellice, herself, was probably bored. A permanently ill husband and nothing to do was probably a bad combination for a lively, intelligent girl of her age.

'I went out,' muttered Ellice suddenly and explosively. 'I couldn't stand hanging around. Then I came back and found him on the floor.' She cast a quick glance over her shoulder and so did Mara. Turlough was talking in loud anguished tones into Conor's ear, trying desperately to rouse him, Father Peter was patiently feeding drops of a cordial from a flagon into the sick boy's mouth and Murrough was lounging at the bed head, looking appraisingly down on his brother's corpselike face. No one was paying any attention to the two women at the window.

'It must have been a terrible shock for you.' Mara's comment was perfunctory, just a means to keep the conversation going while she studied the young wife.

'I'm used to it.' Ellice's shrug would have once been a very pretty gesture in the blooming raven-haired beauty that she was a few years ago, but now, even at the age of nineteen, discontent and unhappiness had soured her face, turned her slim body into an angular thinness and her well-cut features into sharpness. 'I thought that he was getting a bit better, though. We've been staying here at the abbey for the past month and Father Peter has been doctoring him. He's even been taking him for walks by the sea.'

'And you?' queried Mara.

Again the shrug. 'What does it matter about me?' she said sullenly. 'I hung around. Nothing for me to do. He was getting better, though. I thought that at least he would last . . .'

And then Ellice stopped. Perhaps she felt that she had said too much. *Last?* Mara studied the girl thoughtfully as she rubbed the frost patterns from the diamond-shaped half-frozen panes of glass and leaned forward to peer out at the snowy scene. *Last* until when? Did Ellice mean last until Christmas was over, or was there perhaps a more sinister meaning behind her words. Last for long enough to be declared king? If that was her meaning, then had she any hand in the killing of the man in the church, the man she had every reason to believe was Conor's father, the king? She was a tall girl, strong and well-made, a great horsewoman. The sheer weight of that mason's hammer would be enough to kill if one had the strength to lift and swing it – no extra strength would be needed for the blow. She examined the girl appraisingly, noting the width of her shoulder, the strong neck, the broad muscular hands.

And then Ellice gave an exclamation of annoyance. Quickly she unlatched the windowpane and pushed it open, dislodging great white cakes of snow that clung to the outside of the thick green glass.

'What's he doing, the old grey crow?' she muttered. Mara craned her neck over Ellice's shoulder. The abbot was coming through the snow of the garth between the cloister and the guest house. A young monk, with a candle that wavered dangerously in the cold air, preceded him. That was not all, however. The abbot had a black stole around his neck and in his hands was obviously the box bearing the sacred oils. The abbot was coming to give the last rites to Conor.

'No!' Ellice's startled exclamation roused Turlough and he turned an annoyed expression towards his daughter-in-law. Ellice did not hesitate. She was out of the room in one bound and clattered down the stairs. Mara followed her quickly. Nothing should be allowed to disturb Conor, now. She was down the stairs almost as quickly as the girl and caught her arm before the knock came to the door.

'Wait and see what Father Peter says,' she whispered. The door above had opened so noiselessly that she knew who was following them. It could only be Peter. Turlough had never opened or closed a door quietly in his whole life.

'Lord love you, there's nothing to be upset about.' He was down the stairs and beside them in a second. His toothless jaws were bared in an appealing smile and he patted Ellice's shoulder as if she were only four years old. 'He's doing fine, your husband, the blood beats strongly in his wrist and he is breathing well. With the help of God he has many years of long life ahead of him.'

Mara went to the door and opened it quickly before there was any loud hammering to disturb the sick man above. The abbot looked slightly taken aback to see her, but quickly rearranged his face in lines of lofty piety. Mara looked an appeal at Father Peter. She could understand Ellice's indignation. The sight of the abbot and all of the paraphernalia associated with death might be enough to make the boy give up the struggle to live.

'He'll sleep through it. I've given him a dose of poppy syrup. He won't wake for an hour or so.' The voice was soothing and he continued to pat the girl's shoulder. 'We'll do it all very quietly, Father Abbot,' he said looking directly into his superior's icy face.

It was odd, thought Mara, how the distinctive O'Brien face, with its high-bridged nose and tall forehead, could look so warm and full of humour on Turlough; quite different to the abbot's face that appeared chiselled from stone. She went quietly back up the stairs, opened the door of the sickroom, and crossed over to kneel beside Turlough and to be ready to cut off any exclamation of annoyance or distress. She made a quick decisive gesture to Murrough to move away from the right-hand side of the bed and he obeyed her instantly with a mocking inclination of his head. He was her enemy; she knew that. But was he also an enemy to his father and to his sick brother? How far would ambition take him, she wondered as automatically she murmured the prayers for the dying and allowed her eyes to wander from Murrough's face to the sullen face of Conor's wife. What would happen to Ellice if Conor died? She would be sent back to her father, probably and then he would barter her to the highest bidder. Her prospects would not be good. Under Brehon law she would get very little of her husband's goods. All would go back to the *derbhfine*, the family group, and to the clan.

The ceremony did not last long. The abbot heeded Father Peter's warning and everything was conducted in a low murmur. Conor slept peacefully and did not move even when the oil touched his eyes, nostrils and mouth. When he had finished the abbot looked uncertainly at Ellice. This was the moment when he would administer some consoling remarks to the relatives of the dying man, but she turned her face away from him. She rose from her knees, went across the room and continued to gaze intently at the window. There was little that she could see from there. The north wind had strengthened and penetrated the abbey enclosure; now spume from the driven snow had completely blocked the small diamond-shaped panes of glass.

Father Peter left Ellice and went to the door, holding it open. Turlough stood up stiffly. His glance avoided the abbot; despite his sorrow for his son, there was no doubt that the king was still furiously angry at the abbot's refusal to marry them. The abbot went out with his head lowered piously and his young monks followed him.

'I think it would be best if everyone left him, now,' whispered Father Peter. 'I'll stay with him, but I think that he will sleep peacefully and when he wakes up, if God is merciful, he will feel a lot stronger.'

At his words, softly spoken though they were, Ellice reacted instantly, almost as if she were a prisoner waiting for release. She plucked her mantle from the nail behind the door and was first down the stairs. Mara, Turlough and Murrough followed her. She did not turn at the parlour but, without hesitation, pulled open the front door and strode out into the snow. Mara followed her quickly. Where was Ellice going? Two of the monks were shovelling snow into a large bank on either side of the path leading from the guest house and the Royal Lodge across to the cloisters' gate. Ellice walked firmly down the path, keeping her balance well on the frozen snow. Mara watched her with interest. A girl who was at home in the out-of-doors, an athletic girl. She opened the cloister gate and a minute later they could see her pacing around the covered walk which framed the four sides of the cloisters.

'Odd weather for a stroll! These cloisters must be freezing. Why doesn't she stay indoors by the fire? She could keep me company,' commented Murrough from behind his father's shoulder. Murrough was irrepressible. There was no trace of embarrassment or even penitence in his voice. It was as if the events of two months ago and the added offence of the letter to the abbot this very morning were wiped clean in his mind.

'She spends most of her days out-of-doors; she's always either riding or practising with her bow. She's even had a target set up just outside the main gate to the abbey and her horse is stabled here. She's happiest on her own; she has no interest in company,' said Turlough, his voice easy and friendly. Like his son, he too seemed to have forgotten the past. 'Not normal for a girl of her age, but I suppose everyone is different,' he added.

As far as Mara could see Ellice was no longer alone. A tall thin figure in a snow-besmirched grey cloak had joined her. It was obviously a monk, but which monk could it be? Who would risk the abbot's wrath by strolling with a young woman, alone and without the protection of her husband, on a freezing day in December? She narrowed her eyes. Could this be Father Denis, the illegitimate son of the abbot? Certainly she did not recognize him and she knew most of the monks there at the abbey. She turned to the king.

'My lord,' she said, 'I need to visit the church once more. Will you wait here for me, or will you return to the lodge?'

'I think I will return to the lodge and wait for you there,' said Turlough. There was an undertone to his words that made her cheeks sting with colour.

'Fergal and Conall will keep good guard on you there. I'm sure that I don't need to remind anyone,' here her eyes went to the two bodyguards, 'the danger to your life may still exist until I can uncover the truth of this murder.'

They both straightened their backs. They were devoted to Turlough; she knew that. Any enemy could only get to Turlough over their dead bodies, she thought and felt comforted by their presence. She would insist that they slept within Turlough's bedchamber tonight. Pleasant and all as the previous night had been, no risks could be taken until the murderer had been caught.

Without waiting for a reply, she briskly threw her mantle over her shoulders, tucking her hands into the fur-lined sleeves. She did not follow Ellice towards the cloisters and its square of snow-blanketed grass, but took the well-trampled route to the west door of the church.

The door was widely opened and the noise of hammering echoed off the tall stone ceilings and walls. The carpenter was hammering the lid on to the coffin. Mara stopped in surprise.

This was very hasty, she thought. The custom was to hold a wake where the body of the deceased was exposed so that friends and relatives could come to pay their last respects. The only usual reason for such a rushed sealing of the coffin a few hours after death would be if the weather were terribly hot or the person had died of some terrible decease such as plague.

What had made the abbot give instructions to have his brother's body sealed into the coffin so quickly? And what about his wife, Banna? And his new wife, Frann? Had they time to make their last farewells?

The mason was there also. Both men stopped their work to look at her for a moment, but then resumed it again. Mara stood watching them for a moment. It would be best not to be too obviously following Ellice. Better allow a few minutes to elapse before she emerged innocently from the cloisters' door, she thought, as she moved over to examine the mason's work.

One of the twelfth-century floral pillar top decorations had crumbled and he was chiselling out an exact copy of a harebell. There was still that smell of strong drink from him, she noticed, but it did not affect the sureness of the hand which chipped out the delicate curve and allowed the frilled end of the flower to stand proud of the inner circle.

'You have great skill, Master Mason,' she observed.

He bowed gravely in acknowledgement of the compliment, but continued to work away busily. She did not linger; he would not welcome to be delayed. Tomorrow was Christmas Eve and the abbot would want to have the pillar repaired and the church cleared of all signs of work before the ceremonies began at midnight. The funeral of Mahon would probably take place tomorrow for the same reason. A funeral would sadden Christmas Day and even if postponed to the feast of St Stephen, the presence of the coffin within the church would cloud the day for all. There was no grave to dig in the frozen ground; the body would be placed in the O'Brien vault and he would be mourned by his two wives, his brother and cousins. Probably there were no other close relatives whose presence at the burial was essential.

It took just a matter of moments for Mara to cross the floor and gently and softly to pull open the door to the cloisters.

Quickly she closed it behind her. By luck the couple, strolling
under the shelter of the cloister-walk roof, had their backs turned
to her and would not have noticed the momentary gleam of
candlelight from the church.

Mara waited quietly for a few minutes, watching them as they
paced the tiled ground of the walk in front of the chapter house,
the parlour and the abbot's house. The walk had been swept clear
of snow and the ground was easy to walk on. Nevertheless, the
air was bitterly cold and it was a surprising moment to choose
for a midday stroll. She examined the pair carefully. He was a
fine, broad-shouldered specimen of a man, this monk, she thought,
and he and Ellice were a well-matched couple. Mara had visited
the abbey at least four or five times during the year and she was
almost certain that she had never seen this monk before. When
they reached the end of the eastern side of the cloisters' square
they turned to go along the south side, in front of the refectory
and the kitchens. Now she could see the profile of the man and
she knew instantly who it was. His paternity was stamped on his
face: that high-bridged nose and lofty forehead. This was an
O'Brien and there was no doubt in her mind that it was Father
Denis, the illegitimate son of the abbot.

But what was he doing walking here with the wife of the
king's son? How had they got to know each other? Was their
meeting fortuitous? Or arranged? Mara raised the latch of the
door behind her quietly, and pushed it back, opening it widely
to allow the light to flood out on to the snow. Both turned
hastily. She stood for a moment looking across at them. The monk
murmured something to the girl by his side and then bowed
ceremoniously to her and hastened along the east side of the
cloister walk and disappeared into the abbot's house. Without
hesitation, Mara followed him, giving Ellice a wide smile as she
passed. She felt no anger against the girl. She was young, she was
healthy; she had been tied to a dying husband for the last year.
Let her have some fun with this handsome, fine-looking monk.
As long as murder was not involved, Mara did not care. Gaelic
society, and even the Gaelic church, unlike the Roman church,
was very tolerant about sexual matters. Brehon law merely stated
that the wife of a priest should have her head covered in church.

The door had been closed behind the young monk and Mara

lifted her hand to knock and then paused. The abbot's voice was not raised; unlike Turlough, he would be careful and circumspect in scolding his son, but there was no doubt about his anger.

'I told you to keep away from that young woman.'

'She sought me; I did not seek her.'

'Don't lie to me. I've been watching you. You could have bowed and moved away . . . gone into the church . . . said your prayers . . . asked pardon for your sins. God knows that you need to do that.'

Which sins? wondered Mara. The sin of lingering overlong with a young married woman, or was it a greater sin that the abbot spoke of? And how long had Father Denis being staying at the abbey? She had understood from Father Peter that he had arrived just to spend Christmas. Perhaps he had been here before, though. Conor and Ellice had arrived here two months previously. There must have been enough time for a certain dangerous intimacy to arise between the wife of the king's son and this monk, illegitimate son of the abbot.

Father Denis had said something which Mara had not quite caught. However, the words 'Tintern Abbey' were clear and distinct. She had moved a little closer when suddenly the abbot spoke.

'Hush!' In the quiet stillness of the enclosed cloister the sibilant whisper bounced off the stone-carved roof.

Instantly Mara rapped sharply on the door. The abbot opened it immediately and Mara had the satisfaction of seeing his marble-like face redden.

'Ah, my lord abbot,' she said, 'I am sorry to trouble you when you are occupied with one of your . . . brothers.' Deliberately she allowed a pause before the word 'brothers' and watched his face carefully. There was no doubt that he was flustered and angry. Father Denis, however, gave her a courteous bow and stepped back into the shadows.

'I wondered when the burial of your brother, Mahon O'Brien, will take place,' said Mara, gazing curiously at the young man.

'We've decided to bury him tomorrow morning.' The abbot was still flustered. He made a quick, impatient gesture with his left hand, but Father Denis did not move.

'And this is . . . ?' queried Mara with a lift of her dark brows towards the young man.

'This is Father Denis,' said the abbot briefly.

'A new brother?'

'I'm from Galway, my lady,' said Father Denis coming forward and sweeping a low bow.

'I see.' Mara allowed a puzzled note to enter her voice. She still kept her eyes on the abbot.

'He is a relative of mine.' The abbot's voice was curt.

'The family of Mahon are happy with the burial tomorrow?' asked Mara, still eyeing him closely. The abbot looked like a man who has received a grave shock, she thought. She had been talking to him at supper last night and he had looked his normal self. Undoubtedly he was gravely shaken by the events of this morning.

'Yes,' he said curtly, and then with an effort, 'I have spoken with Banna, the *ban tighernae,* and she is quite happy. The weather is too bad for other members of the family to travel for some time and then his immediate family are all here, present at the abbey.'

And what about Frann? thought Mara, but she decided not to press the matter. There were more important questions to be asked.

'I also wanted to ask you about this morning, after the service of prime, I thought I understood you to say that you left the church first before the other monks.'

The abbot hesitated. A wary look came into his pale grey eyes. He nodded. 'That is the normal procedure.' His voice was cautious.

'But you didn't this morning,' asserted Mara. 'You and Father Denis remained in the church after the other monks had left it.'

'Father Abbot was showing me the work that had been done on the church,' explained Father Denis smoothly. He came forward and smiled down at Mara with the air of one who is accustomed to charm ladies.

'Indeed.' Mara allowed a minute to elapse. She did not look at him but she kept her eyes fixed on the uneasy face of the abbot. 'What I wanted to ask you,' she explained then, 'was whether either of you saw anyone in the church that morning, any member of the laity, who might have stayed behind after the monks had gone back up the night stairs towards their dormitory?'

'No,' said the abbot, at the very same moment as Father Denis said, 'Yes, I think there was.'

Mara turned her eyes towards the young monk. 'You saw someone?' she queried.

'Yes, my lady.'

'Call me "Brehon",' she said curtly. Ellice could do better for herself than this false young man, she thought. If she has to have some male company there must be more decent suitors around.

'I thought I saw a figure behind the pillar, m— Brehon,' he said, still smiling in a self-assured way.

'Oh, and who was it?'

He hesitated for a minute. The abbot gave him an angry glance and opened his lips as if to say something, and then closed them firmly. In the distance, from the refectory, a hand bell rang vigorously. This would be the dinner bell and both men moved as though to answer its summons.

'Yes?' Mara stood directly in the middle of the doorway and did not move. She looked enquiringly at Father Denis's smooth face. And after a moment's hesitation he spoke.

'I thought it might have been the mason,' he said. 'But possibly I was mistaken.'

It was interesting, thought Mara, to watch the expressions of both men. Neither said much, but the two pairs of grey eyes seemed to speak volumes. The look that the abbot shot his son was not in any way paternal, but seemed to be full of suspicion and even perhaps dislike. Father Denis slightly lifted his eyebrows and stared back blandly. There was a hint of a smile lifting the corners of his lips.

'So the church may not have been empty when you left it, is that correct?' Neither spoke but left her question hanging in the air, so she added: 'Which of you left first?'

There was a long silence after this and Mara thought this question, also, was going to be unanswered. The abbot had opened his mouth as if about to speak, but then he shut it firmly. Father Denis stared at him triumphantly for a few moments before saying firmly: 'We both left the church together, Brehon.'

Seven

Canones Hibernenses
(Irish Canon Law)

Neither a priest nor a bishop may marry or have a relationship with a woman. The stumbling bishop loses his nemed (noble or professional) status, as purity is required of a bishop.

Crích Gablach
(Ranks in Society)

The wife of a priest shall be removed from the church if she comes there with her head uncovered.

'I don't want to go into dinner,' grumbled Turlough when she joined him at the door of the guest house. 'Let's go into the lodge. Brigid will fix us something to eat. You told me that she and Cumhal brought a cartload of food with them. I'd much prefer one of her pies to that pigswill Donogh serves up for his monks. I bet he keeps supplies of his own in the abbot's house. I notice he eats very little in the refectory.'

'No, I think we had better go. You can't offend the abbot by spurning his food while accepting his hospitality,' said Mara with an indulgent smile. It would give grave offence, she knew, if the king did not turn up for a meal. In any case, she wanted an opportunity to observe faces and hear conversations. It was interesting, she thought, how sometimes a lie can be as revealing as the truth.

Murrough was at the table when they came into the room and he rose ceremoniously with the others as the king walked through the room. Turlough sat down in the seat of honour in the centre of the top table and she seated herself beside him. Murrough had been placed on her left-hand side, and the abbot, she noticed, had taken Conor's seat and was speaking in a low tone to Ellice as they entered. He stopped abruptly as they took their places. Mara wondered what he had been saying to her. Was he reproving her? Or, possibly, just enquiring after Conor? She looked around the table. There was no sign of Banna, but Frann was sitting at the very end of the table and beside her was Ardal O'Lochlainn. They appeared to be deep in conversation. Frann was wrapped closely in a splendidly furred mantle and had drawn the hood over her head. Nevertheless there was a glow from the half-seen face and an allure from the half-revealed curves of her young body that drew the glances of all the monks as they filed in and took their places at the lower table. Could the girl be pregnant? wondered Mara. And if she were, what would her position be? Resolving to talk to Frann again once dinner was over, she turned towards Murrough.

'So, what are you proposing to do now that the piece of play-acting is over?' she asked briskly.

'Do?' he queried, putting a piece of salted cod into his mouth. His green eyes were alight with mischief. Turlough, as she had guessed, had undoubtedly simmered down and now all was well between father and son.

'Are you planning to live in Thomond, or in Kildare near to your father-in-law? I trust that you will not think of showing your face in the kingdom of the Burren after what happened,' said Mara bluntly.

He looked amused. 'My lady judge,' he murmured. 'Always so trusting.'

'Not trusting . . . not trusting at all. In fact, so far untrusting that I want to know, as Brehon, what you were doing at dawn this morning when Mahon O'Brien was murdered in the chapel here. I hope that you can prove to me that you had nothing to do with this crime.'

'Why should I wish to murder Mahon O'Brien?'

'He was one of the *derbhfine*,' said Mara. 'As such he could put himself forward for the office of *tánaiste*. That may interfere with your plans if anything happens to Conor.' The *derbhfine* was the family group descended from the same great-grandfather. Anyone within the *derbhfine* could become *taoiseach* or king of the clan. 'And, of course,' she added, 'only the assassin knows whether Mahon O'Brien was the intended victim, or whether, indeed, it was the king, your father.'

Murrough chewed thoughtfully. He did not trouble to cry out a protest. He knew her, as she knew him. His eyes wandered down the length of the refectory. Mara followed his gaze and then was suddenly distracted by the intent look on Father Denis's face. He was seated with the other monks at a lower table, but he seemed to be making no effort to eat and was staring hungrily at Ellice. That had been no chance meeting this morning; Mara was sure of that. These two must have known each other for some time now. It looked to her as if their feelings might be deep for each other. She resolved to speak to Father Peter about the matter and then turned back to Murrough.

'You were considering how to convince me that you had nothing to do with this murder?' She raised her dark eyebrows at him and her hazel eyes held a challenge.

He turned a blandly smiling face towards her. 'There's a man down there who could tell you that I was in my bed in the lay dormitory at daybreak,' he indicated with a well-manicured fingernail.

'Who?' Her voice was sharp with disbelief.

'Master Mason, see him sitting down there at the end table . . . we shared a drop of liquor from his flask of *brocóit* in order to keep the cold out this morning at daybreak. Which reminds me, now that my fortunes have risen in the world and I am a king's son, not a poor pilgrim, I must give that man a piece of silver. Only his strong drink kept the life in me this morning when I woke and found even the water in the ewer frozen solid and the snow blowing in through the shutters and piling up on the floor and over the man's boots.' Before she could say anything, he replaced his knife on his platter and sauntered down to the end table.

Mara allowed him to go. She could not get to the mason before him and in any case, the man would undoubtedly say whatever the king's son wanted him to say. She had been out-witted, for once. Slowly she drank half a cupful of sour Spanish wine. Better than nothing, she thought, as she turned to the king.

'I think, my lord,' she whispered to him, 'it would be best to make an announcement now of the postponement of our wedding.'

'What?' Turlough turned to her, his face colouring angrily. 'Do you think that I am going to allow that to happen without a fight?'

'It's a fight that you can't win,' she reminded him quietly. 'The abbot will rely on Rome to back him. Do it now, and we will all get through this matter with grace and dignity.'

'He'll not get another piece of silver out of me for his precious abbey,' snorted Turlough in her ear. 'Do you know that I gave a communion cup last year that was worth a hundred marks? And who do you think is paying for all these repairs? He's had that carpenter and that mason working here for months. I saw them when I came to see Conor in early November.' He rose to his feet and banged angrily for silence with a pewter flagon on the table. A spurt of wine splashed out and marked the abbot's grey robe. Turlough eyed it with satisfaction and then said abruptly, 'The Brehon has asked me to make an announcement that the wedding between us has been postponed due to the murder of my cousin, Mahon O'Brien.' Then he sat down heavily, with one shoulder turned towards the abbot, and helped himself to the remaining wine.

There was a brief murmur while some of the guests commented on this announcement. Mara looked down the room and saw Brigid's eyes wide with astonishment, but no one else seemed to show much surprise. It was, after all, a very respectable reason for the postponement of a marriage, she thought. In fact, many people may have been expecting that announcement before it was made. Murrough finished his whispered conversation with the mason and then returned to her side, smiling mockingly at her.

Mara ignored him, but patted Turlough's hand as he sat back on his chair. He had done what she asked him and now he would have his reward. She leaned across in front of him and then spoke to the abbot in clear, carrying tones.

'That young man, Father Denis, what relation exactly is he to you, Father Abbot? One can see that he is an O'Brien.'

The sudden quietness from the nearby monks' table after that remark made Mara realize that Father Peter O'Lochlainn was not the only one of them who had surmised about the abbot's relationship to the young man. She looked around. Ardal O'Lochlainn tugged his red-blond moustache with an air of embarrassment, but Teige O'Brien was visibly chuckling as he bent down to whisper into the ear of the O'Connor. The monks all fixed their eyes upon their platters, though Father Peter shot Mara a brief, mischievous look. The abbot swallowed a few times and then took a sip of small beer to ease his dry throat.

'Distant,' he said shortly. 'Very distant.'

'I see,' said Mara. She would not pursue the matter in public, she thought. She had had her revenge for the insult and the pain that this sanctimonious man had caused to Turlough. In private, though, she promised herself, she would not let him get away with this. If he and Father Denis were really the last to leave the church after prime then there was a cloud of suspicion over both heads. She would have to solve this murder quickly. She had noticed, as they had walked across the cloister garth towards the refectory, the wind from the north seemed already to have swung around to the north-west. Once it went to the west, this snow would cease and the roads would thaw. She would have to solve this murder quickly before the guests rode away from the abbey. Whoever was guilty would have to be accused and brought to justice at the dolmen of Poulnabrone, that ancient stone monument which was the place of judgement for the people of the Burren.

'So who's this Father Denis, then?' queried Turlough in her ear.

'Tell you later,' she murmured. 'Let's go back to the lodge straight after dinner.'

'Now, if possible,' returned Turlough. With an effort, he was keeping his voice low, though the abbot was now deep in conversation again with Ellice. He began to rise to his feet, but then stopped as the door swung open and in came a maidservant followed by Banna, swathed in an enormous piece of white linen. She stood in dramatic silence and stillness just inside the doorway, while the icy wind blew through the room setting the oil lamps smoking and the candles flickering. In a moment the abbot was on his feet, looking from her to the king. With a muttered curse Turlough sat down again. Ardal got up from his place beside Frann and moved up the table to squeeze in between Finn O'Connor and Teige O'Brien.

Banna was tired of being immured, thought Mara unchritably, as she got to her feet and went towards the door. The new widow wanted an audience for her mourning and some food sent to her room on a platter would not have suited her. Now there was a startled silence in the refectory and every eye turned towards her.

The abbot left the company of Ellice and went down towards his dead brother's wife with his hands outstretched.

'My dear Banna,' he said solicitously. 'Are you able for this?'

Banna gave a loud convulsive sob and moved towards his brotherly arms. Mara reached around her bulk and managed to get the door shut against the icy wind.

'Come and sit by me,' she said soothingly, taking the cushion-like wrist in one hand and leading Banna across the floor and up the steps to the high table. Turlough, she noticed, was looking apprehensive; undoubtedly he had had enough of Banna during his interview in the morning, but Mara steered a steady course towards them followed by the abbot.

'I'm sure you won't mind giving up your seat so that Banna can sit by me,' she said to Murrough and he responded with his usual charm and grace, carefully holding the chair until Banna had lowered her weight on to it and then sending a lay brother for a clean platter and a cup of wine.

'I just couldn't stay in that room any longer,' sobbed Banna. 'It holds too many memories.'

You were only there for one night, thought Mara, but aloud she said: 'I suppose you keep picturing him going out this morning and then not returning.'

Banna answered only with a sob, so Mara added: 'Or perhaps you didn't expect him to go out. Perhaps he went while you were still asleep, was that it?'

Banna nodded her head vigorously and the yards of linen, which she had wound around her head, came loose. Impatiently she pulled the covering off and eyed the platter of hot food placed before her. She gulped down some wine and then attacked the cod with small, rapid, ladylike mouthfuls, her full cheeks creasing as she chewed on the rubbery fibre.

'Perhaps Father Peter would be good enough to come up here and recommend something for the Lady Banna,' suggested Mara to the lay brother. It was cold enough up here with a large brazier of charcoal to their backs. It must be almost unbearable further down in the room. Peter would appreciate the thought and he might have some poppy syrup or something which would quieten the lady if she started to become hysterical again.

'So your husband, Mahon, left this morning while you were still sleeping,' she continued. 'Were you surprised when you woke up and found him gone?'

Banna took another gulp of the wine.

'No,' she said in an almost normal voice. 'I knew where he had gone.'

'You knew?'

'He told me that he had arranged it with the abbot?'

'With the abbot?' Mara still felt puzzled about this matter. Of course the abbot had said that he thought the king had changed his mind and that his bodyguards should have known their own king, but didn't it occur to him at least to check the body? He of all people should have known that the two men, Turlough and his cousin Mahon, were very alike. It did seem quite odd that the abbot, the man in charge of all matters to do with the establishment had not verified the first hasty guess of the bodyguards. And should he not have administered the holy rites instantly? Was that not canon law?

Banna nodded. 'Yes, he told me that Father Abbot had asked him to do it and he had told him to keep his hood up so that if one of the brothers entered the church, it would look as though the king were there.'

'I see,' said Mara soothingly. 'So you felt no surprise when you woke and found that he was gone.'

There was a short silence as Father Peter, carrying a stool, inserted himself like a small sparrow just behind Mara. Soothingly he took Banna's wrist in small frozen hands and felt the pulse.

'I've sent a young brother for some poppy syrup,' he said, looking at her moon-like face, 'but the best medicine for you now would be to talk about everything that is on your mind. Free yourself from the heavy weight of sorrow and of worries.'

'Well, I am a bit worried.' Thus encouraged, Banna began to reveal her concerns. 'I know so little about these things. What happens now? God did not bestow the gift of children upon us, so I don't know what my position is now. Will that last piece of madness, and I don't think my dear husband was in his senses

when he did it . . . What could he have seen in that girl . . . ?'
She gulped and drank some more wine.

'Perhaps he just wanted to ensure an heir for his property,'
murmured Father Peter tactfully.

Banna ignored him. She shuddered hugely, the mound of flesh
on the chair moving like an upturned bowl of jelly, before continuing bravely, 'that girl, whatever her name is, that girl young
enough to be his daughter . . .' She closed her eyes with the air
of one turning faint and then opened them and fixed them
intently on Mara. 'I just wonder whether that girl can take what
is rightfully mine.'

'I don't think that you need to worry,' said Mara gently. Was
this also in Frann's mind, she wondered? If it were, then she
would be disappointed. 'Yours was a marriage of the first degree,'
she continued. 'It is called a union of equality. Most of Mahon's
possessions and wealth will go to you and although the land goes
back to the clan, you will have about twenty acres for your lifetime. After your death this, also, reverts to the O'Brien clan.
However, your own Brehon will tell you more about all of these
matters.'

Banna was listening intently, even suppressing her sobs in order
to hear correctly. However, as soon as Mara finished speaking the
small, sharp brown eyes welled up with tears again.

'I'll never forget this morning,' she wailed. 'He went out and
he did not come back.'

'It was a terrible shock for you, poor soul,' said Father Peter
solicitously. 'Did you hear him going out at all?'

Banna paused for a moment. She looked around her. Turlough
was engaged in a loud conversation across the table with his
cousin Teige O'Brien, the abbot and Ellice still had their heads
close together, one of the brothers, a heavy burly young man, at
a tall desk was reading in a strong rough Galway accent from the
Life of St Columba and the sound of busy knives on wooden
platters created a barrier of sound which made it almost impossible to be overheard.

'I did see him go,' she confessed hesitantly. She swallowed some
more wine and Mara hastened to refill her cup from the flagon,
eyeing the woman with interest. Did Banna really see her husband
go out? And, if so, why did she lie about it earlier? Perhaps, though,

she was just extracting the last ounce of drama from her sad situation. That was possible from the way Banna looked all around at the interested faces before turning her attention back to the table, gulping down some more wine and mopping her eyes with the corner of the flowing linen that now swathed her shoulders.

'I didn't know where he was going, then. I thought that he was leaving my bed for that harlot, that Frann,' she muttered.

'Not something you could accept easily,' murmured Mara.

'I quarrelled with him.' Banna looked as if she were about to burst into tears again, but fortunately took another sip of wine. 'I told him that he was dishonouring me, that it was barbaric to take another wife when he had one living, I told him that I would speak to my cousin, the O'Lochlainn, and get him to write to Rome.'

So Banna thought that her relations would take her part in this affair. That was interesting. Could Ardal O'Lochlainn have taken this late and hasty marriage to a young girl as an insult to his family and to his clan? And, if so, would he have been inclined to avenge it? She dismissed the idea. He had seemed to be very friendly with Frann ten minutes ago.

'What did Mahon say?' she asked.

'He told me then that he was going to the church, that he was going to take the king's place for the first hour of the vigil. He was furious with me. He said Father Donogh would be angry that he had told me and that there was enough bad feeling between them as it was.' Banna's tears flowed again. She began to gulp noiselessly and every eye turned towards the top table.

It was time to put a stop to this, thought Mara. Banna had given her the information that she needed; it was likely that no one else, apart from Frann and the abbot, did know that Mahon O'Brien, not King Turlough Donn, would be in the church – even the abbot may have been unsure as to whether Mahon would answer his summons. This was a perhaps an explanation, though an unsatisfactory one, of his behaviour that morning when he had appeared to be certain that it was the king who had been killed.

Mara glanced around the refectory. The young monk had ceased reading, the book was closed, the knives were replaced and the abbot had risen to his feet.

'Father Peter will take you back to the guest house,' said Mara soothingly. 'Please do not worry about your future. Your own Brehon will explain everything to you once you return home.'

The abbot waited while his brother's wife stumbled out of the refectory, leaning heavily on Father Peter's arm, and then he turned to his monks.

'There will be recreation and exercise for one hour,' he announced. 'Then one hour's work for everyone. Vespers will be a special service in honour of my brother Mahon. The passing bell, which was omitted because of the formal legal procedures this morning,' here he shot a quick sour look at Mara before continuing, 'the passing bell will be rung at the end of the service. After vespers, the fire will be lit in the warming room until compline. I hope that our guests will join us in the church too as we lead up to the celebration of the birth of our saviour.'

'Let's go back to the lodge,' said Turlough in her ear. 'It's going to be a short night; I feel like a rest now.'

'Just a minute,' she said with a small private smile for him. 'Let the others go out first.'

There was a moment's hesitation while the brothers looked up to the top table, but when no one there moved, the monks all got to their feet and filed out decorously, followed by the abbot. Murrough moved from his position by the fire as the lay guests went out also and he came up to the top table.

'Ellice, are you coming too?' he asked with a charming smile and a brotherly hand under her elbow to assist her to rise. 'I feel like some fresh air and some exercise and I'm sure you do also. Dear old Conor had best be left undisturbed for some time; sleep is what he needs now.'

She went with him readily, her bright smile illuminating the olive-skinned face with a flash of white teeth and a softening of the black eyes. A girl who liked men, thought Mara, perhaps there was nothing other than boredom in her friendship with Father Denis. The abbot gave Mara a quick nervous glance and then hurried after them. Frann followed, with her head bent modestly and her eyes on the floor.

'What's all this about that Father Denis, then?' asked Turlough. Only the king, his four *taoiseach*s and Mara were left in the refectory.

'Didn't you know, Turlough?' Teige's ruddy face was sparkling with mischief. His wife giggled and took some more wine and so did the O'Connor's wife. 'Father Denis is Father Donogh's son.'

'What, the abbot's son?' Turlough roared. 'Well, the old dog! Who would have expected it?'

'And they say, "like father, like son"', confided Ciara O'Brien. 'There was talk of a girl in Galway; this Father Denis set her up in a house near the abbey of Knockmoy and I did hear tell that the girl's parents insisted on a marriage. That's right, isn't it, Ardal?'

Ardal looked embarrassed. 'I think it was just a marriage of the fourth degree.'

'Still a marriage, nevertheless! I wonder what the Holy Father in Rome would say about this,' chortled Turlough.

'What did Mahon O'Brien feel about the matter?' Mara addressed them all, but after a moment's silence when the O'Briens and the O'Connors looked blank, her eyes turned to Ardal.

'I think he was not happy for Father Denis to become abbot of Knockmoy,' said Ardal reluctantly.

'Of course, his mother, the mother of Father Denis, God be good to her, she was an O'Brien from the Arra branch,' said Teige after a minute's pause.

'Was she indeed?' said Turlough. 'I never heard that.'

'The family don't speak of it,' said Teige. 'She made a good match afterwards and this boy Denis was fostered somewhere in the midlands with some relations of hers – they would be on her mother's side, of course. Let me see, what was their names – not related to the O'Briens of Ara – they'd have been the O'Briens of Carrigunnell – now what was that man's name?'

Mara looked on amused. This tracing of relations could go on for hours. However her interest sharpened when Teige said musingly: 'Of course this death of Mahon has worked out well for young Denis. It's his uncle, the mother's brother, the O'Brien of Arra, who was the *tánaiste* to Mahon O'Brien. Now that Mahon is dead, the lands and all the property will go to the O'Briens of Arra and, of course, the abbey of Knockmoy will be in his gift, then – that's if Rome approves, of course.'

'So you're saying,' said Turlough eagerly, 'that Mahon's death will mean that Denis can be abbot of Knockmoy after all.'

'That's exactly it,' said Teige. His eyes turned towards Mara and so did Turlough's. Mara busied herself with the remains of the cod on her platter.

'So Denis might have murdered Mahon,' said Turlough, in the jolly tones of one who was enjoying a good day's hunting.

'Or the abbot, his father . . . his holy father,' put in Finn O'Connor, while his wife made a few scandalized noises with her tongue against her upper gums.

'So could one of our dear cousins have murdered the other, Teige?' enquired Turlough eagerly.

Teige chuckled mischievously, but did not answer. His wife looked shocked. 'Surely not,' she said. 'His own brother!'

'It was a particularly brutal killing,' said Ardal quietly. 'I noticed that. The head was quite beaten in. The man must have been dead after the first blow, but the assassin kept on striking again and again.'

Mara looked at him with interest. Ardal spoke little unless a question was directed at him; it was unusual to hear him give his views unasked.

'Could it have been that the murderer was unsure?' she asked him tentatively. 'Perhaps someone who had never inflicted death before; someone who had never been on a battlefield, had perhaps never seen violent death? Someone who had to make certain that the man was really and truly dead?'

He took his time about that, stirring a piece of cod around the centre of the platter and separating out the coarse fibres with the precision of a surgeon.

'To me it looked more like a furious and hate-filled onslaught,' he said finally and she knew he would say no more.

There was a moment's uncomfortable silence and then Turlough and his cousin, Teige, started swapping stories about their child-hood – both had been fostered in the same household – and the others listened, smiling. No one wanted to consider this murder too closely, thought Mara. She looked at the man beside her, a man whom she loved, and then for comfort looked behind him where the two solid figures of his bodyguards stood. Her eyes met Fergal's. Fergal was particularly devoted to Turlough. His own father had been a bodyguard and the young man had been brought up with a strong sense of fealty. He was looking troubled and she understood this. If Turlough had been the expected victim, then a murderer, full of hate, would try and try again until the deed was done and the hated man lay dead. She heard the door open while she was looking back and immediately both body-guards had their hands to their knives; they were certainly alert and ready for any attack.

'Father Peter,' said Turlough happily. 'Come in and join us. Have a cup of wine.'

'No, my lord, wine is not for me,' said Father Peter demurely. 'I came to say that your son, the *tánaiste*, is awake and asking to see you.'

'How is Conor?' asked Turlough, the cheerful look fading from his face.

'He has some fever,' said Father Peter compassionately, 'but, lord, don't trouble yourself too much about that. The fever will help the body to fight the sickness. Will I tell him that you will come when you have finished your meal?'

'We have finished now,' said Turlough rising to his feet. Mara instantly rose also and slipped an arm through his. How long could Conor's frail body last while those constant fevers racked it, she wondered as they went through the door and out into the cloister.

Eight

Bretha Forma
(Judgements of Trapping)

If a person traps a bird, or shoots one, on Church land he must surrender to the Church two-thirds of the bird's flesh and all of its feathers. However, a heron or a hawk may be trapped with no penalty.

Outside, the air was still cold but the wind had died down and there was a hint of softness in the air. A pale watery gleam of sunshine streaked across the snow-covered heights of Gleninagh, casting blue shadows that deepened the divisions between the terraces so that the whole hill looked like the rampart-girded *dún* of some ancient legend. The buildings that walled the cloister had lost their patches of snow and now showed smoothly and severely grey against the white carpet of the enclosure. There was no one there, but as they passed under the archway beneath the lay dormitories, they saw an animated scene.

A large target of alderwood, covered with coils of twisted straw rope, had been set up at the north side on the garth, the ground between the guest houses and the church. One by one the monks were running up, snatching up a bow from the pile on the ground, fitting an arrow and aiming at the target. Then each would run to retrieve his arrow and another would take up the bow. It was a busy and cheerful sight with the young monks flushed with excitement and pleasure and even the abbot was indulgently smiling in the background.

'Donogh was a great man with the bow when we were young,' said Turlough in Mara's ear. 'Just you watch now. Abbot or no abbot, he'll find an opportunity to show off his skill.'

'Let's see if he's passed it on,' said Mara quietly, watching Father Denis as he came to the top of the queue. He picked up the bow but then turned and bowed towards Ellice who was standing beside Murrough.

'You'll honour us, my lady,' he said. His voice was smooth and respectful, but nevertheless it held a hint of intimacy.

A shadow passed over the abbot's face but Ellice came forward eagerly, almost pushing Murrough aside. Father Denis handed the bow to her, standing very close to her shoulder as she lifted it and stretched back the bowstring.

'I'll tighten it,' he said. 'You like a taut bow.'

He was unnecessarily near to her, thought Mara, wondering at the effrontery of the man. After a minute's hesitation the abbot stepped forward and stood beside her also, but she impatiently took a step away from him and turned back to Father Denis.

'That's just right,' she said. 'Give me the arrow.'

He picked it up and handed it to her with a smile. She laid the bow to her shoulder, fitted the arrow and then, almost carelessly, let fly. The arrow shot through the air and with a soft thud, landed almost directly in the centre of the target.

'Now see if you can beat that, Denis,' she said triumphantly, gazing teasingly at Father Denis.

There was a look of distaste on Turlough's face and Mara acted swiftly. This girl, the king's daughter-in-law, was flirting openly with a priest while her husband lay dying within the guest house. It was time to put a stop to this.

'Father Abbot,' she called. 'I hear you are a great shot. Let's see if you can get nearer to the centre.'

The abbot took the bow from Ellice's hand with a deprecating look and spent a long time adjusting the string to his taste. Father Denis submissively stepped back into the line of monks and Ellice's eyes followed him. A young monk handed the abbot an arrow and he fitted it to the notch and raised the bow. The arrow flew with deadly accuracy and hit the target in the exact centre.

'A lucky shot,' said the abbot modestly. He held out the bow towards Turlough.

'My lord?' he queried. Turlough shook his head.

'Conor is unwell,' he said quietly, with a glance at Ellice, who averted her gaze. 'I must go to him.'

There was a cold damp feeling even in this sheltered place, thought Mara as they turned away. The air was no longer crisp and clear and dimpled slabs of snow, like fat white pancakes, slid

down the stone slates of the church roof and collapsed into heaps
of slush in the brimming lead gutters.

Mara had felt the west wind in her face as they came through
the archway into the garth in front of the guest houses. The thaw
had begun. Soon the snowfall, which had blocked roads and
mountain passes, would be just a memory to be discussed over
and over again, but possibly not to be repeated in the lifetime of
many.

'Should Ellice come with us?' she asked tentatively.

'No, no, let her enjoy herself.' Turlough's momentary irritation
had vanished. 'She's a great shot,' he said indulgently. 'She amuses
herself shooting birds around the abbey grounds.'

'And what does the abbot think of that?' asked Mara with
interest. Even from the king's daughter-in-law this seemed to be
rather presumptuous behaviour.

'Oh, he's probably quite pleased as she always brings it to the
kitchen and then he has it for his supper; one bird would not
go far among fifty monks, but it does very nicely for one man.
He's a man who likes to feed well, in private, I'd say.' Turlough
dropped his voice slightly but from the amused glance that Father
Peter threw over his shoulder the king was obviously clearly
audible to him.

At the door to the guest house, Mara stopped for an instant.
There was a loud hammering coming from the church. Everyone
else stopped also. The monk running back with an arrow froze
for a moment, his head turned towards the church, and even
Murrough lowered the bow that he had just lifted and Teige
O'Brien made the sign of the cross.

'They're opening the vault,' said Turlough in her ear. 'They seal
it up after each burial and then hammer the mortar out when a
new one has to take place. The last person to be buried there
was Teige's brother.'

Mara nodded. Soon Mahon O'Brien's body would be placed
there, but the killer was still at large and she had not yet even
made up her mind as to who was the intended victim. Something
nagged at the back of her mind. Some sentence uttered carelessly
but bearing some significance. What was it?

'What's the matter?' asked Turlough.

'Nothing,' she said and tucked her hand inside his arm with

a quick glance behind to see that the two bodyguards were still in attendance. Until she could solve this case, then Turlough's life might be in danger.

Conor's room smelled of sweat. Conor himself was obviously in a high fever, his face flushed and his blue eyes large and empty of expression. He should never have gone out this morning into the icy snow. Ellice ought to have prevented him, thought Mara. Unless, of course, she was tired of this sick husband and wanted it all to be over as soon as possible.

'Where is he, where is he?' he was muttering. Father Peter came to the bedside and placed a cold hand on his forehead. It seemed to quieten Conor for a moment, but then the feverish mutterings broke out again. 'I must see him, I must tell him.'

'This is terrible,' said Turlough, his voice broken. 'I can't bear to see him suffer like this. Can't you give him something?'

'There's something worrying him, fretting him,' said Father Peter. 'He won't rest until he gets it off his mind; he wanders, but then he comes back to himself and he knows what he is saying. He asked for you a few minutes ago.'

Turlough lowered his bulk to kneel beside his son. He reached out and took the emaciated hand within his large brown fist. Mara could see how he squeezed it as if he tried by this means to force some of his own life and energy into Conor's veins. Conor shifted uncomfortably. The grip was too tight and Mara was about to whisper to the king when she noticed that the delirious sounds had ceased and that Conor's large blue eyes, fixed on his father's face, were now lucid.

'I didn't want anything to happen to you . . .' he said and his voice was so weak that the words were barely audible.

'No, no, no,' said Turlough distressed. 'Of course you didn't.'

'Ellice . . .' Here Conor was interrupted by a bout of coughing. Father Peter slipped around to the other side of the bed and lifted him slightly, massaging his back. Mara came around and plumped up the pillows, keeping them in place while Father Peter lowered Conor back on to them. He coughed strongly once again and then looked back at the face so close to his own. His eyes were still clear. It was obvious that he knew his father.

'She wants me to be king, and young Donough after me,' he said.

'Of course she does,' said Turlough soothingly. 'Yes, of course she does. That's only natural. And so you will, too, please God.'

'She says . . .' the young voice was faint, just a frail sighing sound but it was perfectly audible. 'She says . . . I won't live to be king, she says, unless you die soon . . .' His voice strengthened a little and the words came out quite clearly: 'I don't want to have anything to do with . . .'

And then, quite suddenly, his eyes shut and his head slumped on the pillow. Mara bent over him. For a moment she feared that he had died, but he was breathing softly but naturally. She placed her hand on his forehead. He seemed a little cooler.

'Poor lad, poor lad,' growled Turlough. His eyes were brimming with tears. He strode over to the window, opening the curtains and slipping inside them.

Mara got to her feet. Her gaze met Father Peter's shrewd grey eyes and she found her own apprehensions mirrored in his.

'Have a care to the king,' he murmured.

Mara nodded and looked across to the two bodyguards. Conall was lost in thought, but Fergal was wide-eyed and startled. He had obviously heard Father Peter's words and perhaps the words of the king's son also. Hesitantly he moved across and joined the king at the window. Mara followed him.

Turlough had opened the shutters a little and was leaning out taking great gulps of the icy air. Conor and Ellice's room was in a quiet place for the invalid at the back of the building and the view stretched for miles over the valley right as far as the Aillwee Mountain. Mara had little fear for Turlough's safety at that window. The threat was from within the abbey, not from outside. Conor had relieved his mind, but now the weight was on her shoulders. Conor, himself, she ruled out instantly. He was as weak as a newborn kitten and had always been an amiable, if rather colourless, boy. His wife was a different matter, though. She was strong and healthy. She had pulled that bow as well as any of the men. A great horsewoman, too, according to the king; her muscles would have been toned by hours of riding; there was no doubt that she had the ability to swing a mason's hammer. But would she have done it?

'Come, my lord,' said Mara, tucking her arm inside the king's. She closed the shutters again and led him gently away. 'Let us leave your son to Father Peter's care. He is sleeping soundly now and that will help to break the fever.'

Although the snow on the ground and the roofs was melting fast, the white light from the heaped-up piles to the side of the paths dazzled them for a moment as they came out from the darkness of the guest house. Mara put up her hand to shield her eyes. The monks had gone; their hour of fun and recreation must be over. Only Murrough and Ellice were left shooting at the target. Through the archway to the cloister, Mara could see the abbot, with Father Denis, pacing up and down, deep in conversation. Mara focussed her eyes on the face of Father Denis. How did he feel to watch Ellice laughing uproariously with another man? And then suddenly she felt herself thrust violently aside.

'*Dá n-ó pill fort!*' swore Fergal, throwing himself across the body of his king.

Ellice, still laughing, had swung her bow around and was pointing the arrow directly at the king's heart.

'Take care!' shouted Mara angrily.

'All right, Fergal,' grunted Turlough, disentangling himself with an uncertain glance at his daughter-in-law.

'Only a joke,' she said merrily. Without hesitation she loosed the arrow from her bow and it landed directly in the very centre of the target.

She's a superb shot and as fast as lightning, thought Mara. I hardly saw her turn; certainly she took no time to aim, and yet the arrow was as placed as precisely as possible.

'Not a good joke, Ellice,' she said loudly and clearly and saw the abbot stop at the sound of her voice and then come hastening through the stone archway followed by the young priest.

'Who taught you to shoot, Ellice?' continued Mara in the tone of voice which would warn her scholars that the matter was serious.

'The abbot,' said Ellice sulkily. Murrough looked from one to the other, his mouth curved in an amused smile.

'I'm sure, Father Abbot,' Mara turned sharply towards the grey-cloaked figure, 'I'm sure that you told your pupil never to aim an arrow at a living person. Now, I suggest that the target, the bows and the arrows be put away; the brothers have finished their recreation.'

'I must go and see to my horse,' said Father Denis smoothly. 'I need to get back to Galway and I think I will find the roads easy to travel by tomorrow now that the thaw has come. My lord, you will excuse me,' he bowed politely in Turlough's direction. 'My lady,' another bow in Mara's direction and then he was gone, striding across the slush towards the stables on the south side of the enclosure.'

'I must go to the stables, too,' said Ellice defiantly. 'I might be able to walk my mare around for a while. She's like me; she hates to be kept locked up indoors.'

She did not look in Turlough's direction, but gave Mara a glance of bitter dislike as she ran after Father Denis, her bright red, fur-lined mantle blowing back behind her in the strong south-westerly wind.

'She's tired of being cooped up; she's very young,' said Turlough indulgently.

'Hmm,' said Mara, her eyes following the pair. Ellice had now caught up with Father Denis. They seemed to be talking earnestly. For a moment Father Denis stood very still, looking down at her, and then he strode on again. Once more, Ellice quickened her steps to a run and was by his elbow, still talking earnestly, and then they were around the corner and out of sight.

'We keep them in the press at the end of the church,' the abbot was saying to Murrough, who had gathered up the bows and arrows. 'Yes, the target goes there also.' He seemed to think that some explanation was needed so he said hastily, 'Our sister house at Islandlough was attacked while the monks were at prayer and the communion cup and plate was stolen. Now all my monks are trained to use a bow and they can be found quickly and easily if the need arises.' He bustled ahead of Murrough who made little of the weight of the target in addition to the bows and arrows. Turlough looked proudly after his son. He was indeed a son to be proud of, charming manners, handsome face and a well-built body. Mara's eyes followed his. This was another problem and it had to be addressed.

'Turlough,' said Mara urgently. 'Where is Murrough going after this?'

An uncertain look came into Turlough's face. His green eyes clouded over, even his war-like moustache seemed to droop.

'I don't know,' he said shortly. 'Perhaps he'll go to Kildare. He seems to be great friends with his father-in-law, the earl.'

'Let's come inside,' said Mara, holding his elbow and urging him gently into the Royal Lodge.

'Brigid,' she called as soon as she had shut the door behind them. 'Brigid, bring some spiced pies and some hot wine to the parlour. The king and I are still hungry.'

Brigid popped out from the kitchen. 'I'm not surprised after that dinner,' she said. 'I'll just be one minute, my lord. You go upstairs, there is a good fire burning in the brazier,' she said to her mistress before disappearing back into the kitchen.

'Salted cod!' Her voice came faintly back to them as she shut the door.

Turlough and Mara looked at each other and both laughed.

Thank God for Brigid, thought Mara. Suddenly the tension between both dissolved and they went, hand in hand, up the stairs and into the parlour.

The room was dimly lit with one candle, but it was warm and snug with heavy curtains pulled across the wooden shutters and a hot, smokeless fire of bright red charcoal burning in the iron brazier. Mara went around lighting more candles while Turlough stretched himself on the cushioned settle before the fire.

'Salted cod!' repeated Turlough with deep enjoyment as she came to sit beside him.

'The abbot was probably just trying to show how holy he is,' said Mara. 'I suppose it is a fast day, today.' She would say no more about Murrough, for the moment, she thought. She would enjoy a half hour of Turlough's company but then she would have to continue with her enquiries. The snow on the roads and on the mountain passes would definitely have thawed by tomorrow. Father Denis would leave, Murrough would probably ride east; it made sense for him to join his father-in-law and his wife on their lands near Dublin. Others, too, would want to leave. The travellers in the lay dormitories, the workers in the church, they would all want to be home by Christmas.

'Is there any possibility that Ellice would want to kill you,' she asked abruptly.

He turned an amazed face on her. 'Why on earth would the girl want to do that?' he asked.

'If you died this morning,' she said flatly, 'Conor would be declared king; he is the *tánaiste*, and Ellice would be queen. Even if Conor died soon after, her honour price would always be that of a queen, and she might be the mother of a future king.'

'A little girl like that!'

'Not so little,' said Mara. 'She's strong, healthy and she aimed that arrow directly at you.'

He laughed uncomfortably. 'That was just a joke,' he said.

'She could have swung that mallet this morning,' said Mara mercilessly. 'She chose one of the heaviest bows today and she handled it like a man.'

'Here is your wine,' said Brigid, coming in with a quick knock and bearing a tray with two silver wine cups and a flagon of steaming wine on it.

'I'll just go back and get some pies,' she continued. She paused, looking at her mistress.

'I'll come and help you,' said Mara rising to her feet. Brigid could perfectly well have fitted a platter of pies on the same tray. The signal was obvious. Brigid had something that she wanted to say to her.

The kitchen was warm and dark and filled with the aromatic smell of Brigid's famous spiced pies warming on a stone beside the fire. Mara took one in her hand and nibbled at it absent-mindedly. Certainly the abbot's dinner had not been very satisfying, she thought.

'Brehon,' said Brigid. She had taken a wooden platter from the shelf, but made no move to transfer the hot pies to it.

'Yes, Brigid,' said Mara looking at her attentively. There was a shape and a form, like a dance, to these conversations with Brigid; skip one stage and the whole pattern was lost.

'I'm not one to gossip, as you know, Brehon.'

'No, of course not, Brigid.' Mara's voice sounded the right note of reassurance, backed by eagerness to hear the latest news.

'It's just that some of the lay brothers were talking about something in the kitchen and I felt you should know.'

Mara took another bite of the spiced pie and waited.

'I was just getting some butter from the pantry and I heard them. They were talking about Ellice, the wife of the *tánaiste*. And they were saying that she would be lonely when Father Denis went back to Galway.'

'She hasn't known him long, though, has she?' queried Mara in a casual fashion. 'Just a few days, isn't it?'

'That's where you're wrong, Brehon, he's been here at the abbey off and on for a few months. He's always riding over and staying for a few days and the word is that he comes to see her. He's some sort of relation to the abbot,' added Brigid, showing that the abbot's secret was not known to the lay brothers among the monks.

'Surely he just comes to see the abbot.' Mara's voice was causal and beautifully calculated to get the last ounce of gossip from Brigid who gave a hasty glance over her shoulder towards the shuttered window and then lowered her voice.

'That's where you're wrong, Brehon. One of the lay brothers, a young fellow, who sees to the horses, saw them kissing and cuddling in the stable. And when she was shooting at that target one day he was standing behind her, and him a priest, no less, and he was pretending to help her to hold the bow right, but his hands were . . . well, you can guess, Brehon!'

'I can indeed, Brigid,' said Mara with enormous enjoyment. 'And you think that I should tell the king about this?'

'Wouldn't do any harm to drop a bit of a hint,' said Brigid cautiously. 'She should be in looking after her sick husband, poor lad. He doesn't seem as if he is too long for this world, God bless him and save him. Cumhal was saying to me this morning what a blessing it was that nothing happened to the king. Conor is *tánaiste,* but would the clan want to name him? No, mark my words, there would be trouble.'

Mara nodded, watching Brigid load the platter with the hot pies. Of course, no man could be king, or *taoiseach* until he had been 'named' by the clan. The ceremonial circling sunwise around a mound or a cairn, the handing over of the peeled rod, all these things would be just the preliminaries to the moment when the clan named him as *the* O'Brien. Unlike the laws of inheritance in England, where the eldest son automatically became king at the moment of the death of his father, under Brehon law, the clan had to ratify the appointment. It would be unusual, but not unheard of, for the clan to refuse to nominate the *tánaiste*.

'I'd better get back,' she said thoughtfully, taking the platter from Brigid. 'The king will be starving.' She did not thank Brigid; it was understood between them that once the piece of gossip was imparted, no further mention would be made of it. There was some more information that she needed, though, and Brigid would be the best person to get it from.

'I suppose no one from the lay dormitory heard Mahon O'Brien go out this morning,' she said casually as she turned to go out of the kitchen. 'Or anyone else, either, from the guest house, perhaps?' she added over her shoulder. Her eyes met Brigid's and then Brigid rifled through the stores in one of her baskets and then gave an artistic jump.

'Would you believe it,' she said. 'I've come without enough ginger. I'll see if Mahon O'Brien's servants have any. If not, I'll try the abbey kitchens.'

'I'll see you in a while, then,' said Mara with a satisfied nod. She had just reached the top of the stairs when she heard the front door of the Royal Lodge slam behind Brigid.

'You've been a long time,' grumbled Turlough as she came in. Greedily he snatched two spiced pies from the platter and crammed them into his mouth.

'I've been talking to Brigid,' she said quietly, as they both sat down again on the cushioned bench by the fire. 'She's been telling me some kitchen gossip about Ellice.'

'Don't want to hear it,' mumbled Turlough. He chewed for a moment, looked at her defiantly and took a large bite from a third pie.

'That's not like you,' she said gently, but she did not press him. He was frightened; she knew that. He was as brave as a lion and was famous for his prowess in the battlefield where he was always to be found at the front of his clansmen; what he could not endure was any hurt to the warmth of feeling that he possessed for his family. Ellice was one of his family; he would hear nothing against her.

I will have to think over this case in my own mind, thought Mara. She wished she knew for sure whether Mahon had been the intended victim, or was it, as seemed likely, Turlough? If Ardal were right, someone hated the victim badly enough, not just to kill, but to lash out again and again in a frenzy of hatred. Who could that person be? If it had been Ellice, then the killing would be a matter of ambition: a killing to achieve an end rather than through any feelings of dislike for Turlough. He always seemed fond of her and sympathetic towards her position.

What about Murrough, though? What did Murrough feel about Turlough, the father who had publicly cast him off? She cast a quick look at Turlough; his face was drawn and unhappy. He looked tired, an elderly man over-burdened with problems that gnawed at his affectionate nature. Quietly she put some more charcoal on the brazier and slipped her hand into his. It would do him good and do her good just to sit peacefully and silently for a while in the warm, candle-lit room.

'Have some more wine while it is still hot,' she said softly and filled his cup.

He drank quickly with an abrupt nervous tilting of the cup and then his head sank down on his chest. His eyelids drooped. She got up quietly and took some cushions from the seat by the window and placed them at the end of the bench. Gently she pressed his head until it lay on the cushions.

'Lie down for a few minutes, my love,' she said and seated herself on the stool opposite to him. She had never loved him so much, she thought, as she looked at him stretched out there deep in an exhausted slumber. She envied him for a moment. It would be good to be able to forget everything in a heavy doze. However, that was something that she could not do. Her mind was busy and active sorting through possibilities, but she had an inner conviction that somewhere, in something that was said, she had the clue to the early morning murder. If only she too could sleep, perhaps suddenly a name would spring to her mind when she woke. She sighed. It was unlikely, she thought. From the age of five, her life had been a hardworking one; the answer to her problem would, as usual, be found in a tireless commitment to hear every possible piece of evidence and then the careful sifting of the statements.

She stood up and moved across to the window. The king's bodyguard, Conall, was marching up and down outside the lodge;

Fergal must be indoors, perhaps in the guards' room downstairs. As she watched she saw Brigid appear and with a quick over-the-shoulder glance at Turlough, she took her fur-lined mantle from the back of the door, opened it cautiously and ran lightly down the stairs.

She thought she made almost no sound, but Fergal immediately appeared from the guards' room. She smiled at him.

'The king sleeps,' she said in a low voice. 'I'll leave him in your care.' She hesitated for a moment and then added, 'Let no one come to him, unless you are present yourself. Those blows this morning may have been meant for him, and yet most of those present here at the abbey are friends, relations or members of his clan. Remember this, Fergal.'

He paled a little at her words, but nodded silently. He had understood what she meant. He had been as shaken as she this morning when Ellice had turned her deadly bow and aimed it at the king.

'And tell Conall, also,' she said as she slipped through the heavy oaken door. She left it slightly open; Brigid would be coming in and she did not want the king's sleep to be interrupted.

The thaw was coming fast; the air was softer and the wind had turned to the south-west. The snow's reign would soon be over. The subtle silver-grey of Gleninagh Mountain showed its curved terraces, clear and sharp, as the rain washed away the whiteness that had blurred and clogged its sculpted outline. Water dripped from the black branches of the nearby ash trees and a blackbird sang melodiously.

'You wouldn't believe it, but there is not an ounce of ginger in the whole place,' announced Brigid. She did not sound particularly upset and Mara guessed that Brigid had plenty of spices in those baskets that she had insisted on bringing in the cart.

'I even saw the brother who does the buying from the Galway merchants,' continued Brigid. 'He said they had a barrel of wine, but no spices, brought the day before we arrived.' She lowered her voice and added: 'He said that same cart brought the pilgrim.' She eyed her mistress carefully and Mara nodded.

'Did he know who the pilgrim was?'

'He knows now. The story is all over the place. No one can understand it. Why should the king's son come dressed as a pilgrim?

A joke, they say, but if it was a joke, why did he not show himself on that first night?'

There have been too many jokes during these two days, thought Mara. Yes, indeed, why did Murrough not show himself on the first night? Was he perhaps going to do this until the king had announced that he would be alone in the church for the first hour after dawn on the following morning? And why come dressed as a pilgrim and riding in a cart? This seemed to show that it was not just the impulse of a moment; that the deception had been carefully prepared. Murrough was a young man who had a great regard for appearance and for his dignity. It was not the sort of thing that he would do for a joke.

'Brother Melduin said that the pilgrim spoke to no one except to the mason,' continued Brigid. 'He couldn't understand it, could Brother Melduin. Why would a man want to eat with the servants and passers-by, when he could dine at the king's table? And why would a man want to be lodged in the cold of the lay dormitories when he could have slept on sheets of linen in warm rooms? That's what Brother Melduin said.'

'He sounds like a man who thinks about things, this Brother Melduin,' said Mara thoughtfully.

'Of course, he is an O'Brien, not like that Brother Francis – you know, that tall dark fellow that was reading in the refectory last night. He's an O'Kelly, Brother Melduin said to be sure to tell you that.'

'I see,' said Mara. It was true that the O'Kellys of Galway and the O'Briens were enemies. On the other hand, she thought it was unlikely that Brother Francis would suddenly attack the king. Unless, of course, instructions had come from his *taoiseach*; family bonds were very strong and family loyalties did not cease on initiation into holy orders.

'He wouldn't want anything to happen to his king, would Brother Melduin,' added Brigid.

'And he didn't observe anyone in the cloisters or in the garth around the hour of dawn?'

Brigid shook her head. 'I asked him that very question,' she said, 'but he said he was busy pumping water at that time. He didn't hear a thing. He said that the mason might have heard something because he might have been up early to do some extra work in the church. The carpenter's work is finished, but the mason has still work to do before Christmas comes upon us.'

Mara sighed. It was unlikely that the mason would have anything to contribute. After all, Murrough had talked about them sharing some *brocóit*, in the icy cold of the lay dormitory around the hour of dawn. Still it wouldn't hurt to check.

'And the servants in the guest house?' she asked.

Brigid shook her head. 'They heard some shouting between Mahon O'Brien and his wife, Banna, but then the door slammed and they went to sleep again.'

'Thank you, Brigid.' Mara hesitated for a moment, but Brigid and Brigid's husband, Cumhal, had been with her since the time of her birth and had been her father's servants for years before that. She could trust no one if she could not trust them. 'Brigid,' she said in a low voice, 'I do believe that the king is in grave danger. No one should see him, not even . . . not even a member of his family, unless his bodyguards are there. Tell Cumhal this.'

Brigid nodded. 'I know, Brehon, you can trust us. You take care of yourself, too. Who knows, someone who wanted to kill the king might want to kill you too.'

Nine

Di Astud Choir
(On the Binding of Contracts)

Inherited property must be kept within the fine *(kin group) and it is normally inherited by a man's sons. The man's wife only has a life interest in a small share of the property: she is not entitled to more than the house in which she lives and land fit to graze seven cows.*

However, a man who has increased the value of his property may bestow that increase on whomsoever he pleases: the Church, a relation, a friend or a wife.

Once outside, Mara hesitated for a moment. She had to decide between seeing the abbot and going back to question Frann. In the end she decided to do the second; she would have to make sure that her orders were followed and that Frann's icy room had been warmed. Also, she acknowledged to herself, she was curious. It seemed, perhaps, that she had only heard half the story.

There was no one around on the garth when Mara crossed it. For a moment she thought she saw a movement from an upper window in the guest house where Conor, Ellice and now Murrough were lodged, but when she looked up sharply the window showed back the reflected bulk of Moneen Hill. The clouds were scudding across the sky and the seagulls were boisterously riding the wind, so either of these could have caused the movement, but somehow Mara did not think so. She had a strong impression that she was being watched from above. She passed the small guest house where Finn O'Connor and his wife had been lodged and then paused outside the door of the large guest house which housed Ardal, Garrett, Teige and his wife and, of course, Mahon and his two wives.

The door was just latched so Mara opened it quietly and tiptoed up the stairs. There was only the sound of snores from

Banna's room; hopefully Father Peter's poppy medicine would continue to work for a few hours more.

She tapped lightly on Frann's door and a young fresh voice said: 'Yes?' on a note of enquiry. There was a sudden creak and Mara quickly opened the door.

Frann was standing by the hastily opened chest at the end of her bed. In her arms was an untidy bundle of parchments which she seemed to be stuffing into the chest. She stopped when she saw Mara and a lovely smile spread over her beautiful face.

'Oh, good,' she said with the wholehearted openness of a child. 'I was just eating these hazelnuts and hoping that they would give me the wisdom to read and now here you are, Brehon, and you can read for me.'

Mara shut the door and laughed. 'I remember that old story, too,' she said good-humouredly. 'I think I could do with some hazelnuts myself. I need some wisdom.'

She sat down on the bed beside Frann, helped herself to a nut from the platter and looked around. The room was transformed since the last time she had been in it. One of the abbey servants, or perhaps it was Banna's maid, had taken pity on the friendless girl. Now a glowing fire warmed the air, there was a richly embroidered cover on the bare-looking bed and a flask of wine stood warming beside the brazier. A platter of oatcakes, as well as the hazelnuts, was placed beside the bed.

'What do you want to read?' Mara asked, though she guessed the answer to that. The scrolls were obvious. One was half-unrolled and she could see the neat legal hand. She waited, smiling, but now Frann seemed reluctant to let it out of her hand.

'You see we were married in November,' she said hesitantly.

Mara nodded encouragingly. 'But you had known him for a while before, though.'

'About two months,' said Frann and once again the smile appeared. 'I had known him since September, but by the beginning of October, I knew . . .'

'Knew?' Mara asked, though once again she knew the answer to her own question.

'I knew that I was pregnant and that I would have a baby in May.' Frann hugged herself with an expression of delighted glee.

'That's lovely,' said Mara warmly. 'And all is going well?'

'Yes, of course.' The girl had all the assurance of youth and good health. 'And it's a boy,' she added. 'My mother is a wise woman and she told me that it would be a boy. We were in my bedchamber, my beautiful bedchamber hung with silken cloths, in the house that Mahon had got for me. It was in the evening and we had finished our supper and I was sitting in front of the fire in my purple nightgown and I was talking about the baby and wondering what the future would hold for us both and then my mother asked Mahon for his ring of gold and she held it on a thread suspended over my stomach.'

'And how did it show that the baby was going to be a boy?' asked Mara with amusement.

'Don't you know? The ring turned sunwise and that means the baby is going to be a boy.'

Fairly easy to manipulate a ring to do that, thought Mara cynically, but in the face of such simple joy and happiness she could do no more than smile warmly.

'So Mahon then promised to marry you?'

Frann nodded. 'Yes, we were married. He gave the house to my mother and he took me to his castle at Dunguaire and we were very happy together. And then one night, a few weeks ago, after we had made love, he felt the baby kick; he couldn't believe it. He had been married for thirty years and had never had a child and now he was going to have a son.'

'I see,' said Mara.

'And then he got worried,' confided Frann. 'He was afraid that something might happen to him before the baby was born. One of his cousins, a man who was five years younger than he, had just died. The next day his Brehon came, he rode on a big white horse and he spent a long time with Mahon while I went walking in the hills. When I came back Mahon was waiting for me with these scrolls in his hand. He told me to keep them safe. When I asked what they were, he would only say that he was going to make sure that this little baby boy was going to have all that a heart could desire.' Once again the girl's voice took on a sing-song, storyteller's rhythm.

'Shall I read this now?' Mara asked, stretching out her hand towards the scroll of parchment. She did not want to rush the girl and it was lovely to watch such happiness. However, she had to see the abbot, and it would be better for Frann if she were to know the exact truth of the provision that Mahon had made for her and for the unborn baby, whether girl or boy.

'There are three of them,' said Frann, handing them over while a smile tugged at the corners of the perfectly moulded poppy-red lips.

Mara scanned the first document rapidly. Her eyes widened in amazement. Yes, it was true that Mahon O'Brien had left the castle of Dunguaire, newly purchased from Mael the silversmith, to Frann, his 'beloved wife of the second degree'. Mara knew Dunguaire. She had often passed it on her way from the Burren to Galway. It was a large tower house, or castle, perched on a small knoll by the edge of the sea, just past Kinvarra. How would the girl be able to live there, though? A castle of that size would need a considerable income to maintain it, even to heat and light it and servants, workmen would be needed.

Mara put down the first scroll without speaking and then picked up the second one. She cast a quick glance at Frann, but the girl was just staring into the orange flames of the fire, her lips parted in a slight smile, her green-blue eyes full of dreams. Mara read on rapidly. Mahon had been a rich man; his lands were only a small part of his revenues. He had also owned a limekiln and had obviously drawn a large income in silver, or in cows from the sale of the lime. Much of it was shipped abroad from Galway – used for mortar, guessed Mara – and more was sold as a fertilizer to the owners of the rich grassland in Thomond and in Ossory. This, of course, would be his own property and would be for him to leave where he wished. The law was quite clear on that. He had left that limekiln to Frann, and unlike the castle, this would just be in her hands until the son of their union – obviously Mahon, also, had believed in this gold ring spinning in a sunwise direction – had attained the age of eighteen. The third document came as no surprise. Mahon, like Mara, had known how much it would cost his young wife to keep up the castle at Dunguaire and he had left her the revenues from his three fishing boats for this purpose and for the whole of her lifetime. At her death these also would be the possessions of the unborn child.

'Well, Frann,' Mara said, carefully rolling up the three parchments into one scroll and taking a piece of pink linen tape from her pouch. She waited until Frann had turned around to face her and then said slowly and meaningfully, 'Mahon has left you a castle and the silver from his fishing fleet for the whole of your life and the silver from his limekiln until your son is eighteen. This then becomes his property and both the castle and the fishing fleet become his when you die. You will be rich and he will be a rich young man.'

'I know; Mahon promised me,' Frann smiled as a child smiles with the present of a kitten.

'You must look after these very carefully, Frann,' said Mara solemnly. 'After the feast of Christmas you must go and see Mahon's Brehon and talk to him about this. Say nothing to anyone else. Let him make the announcement.'

Carefully she handed the scroll into the girl's hands and watched her stow it away in the leather satchel that lay on top of the chest at the end of the bed before asking:

'Frann, did you see Mahon go to the church this morning, before he was killed?'

'No.' Frann shook her head carelessly. She made no pretence of shuddering or showing any signs of sorrow, though Mara had deliberately mentioned the word 'killed'. Her thoughts now were all for the future, were all absorbed by her unborn child and the splendour of her new prospects.

'So the last you saw of him was when he left your bed to go to Banna in the middle of the night.'

'Yes,' said Frann cheerfully, popping another hazelnut into her mouth, 'that was the last that I saw of him.'

When Mara left the room, she closed the door very quietly so as to run no risk of disturbing Banna. For a moment she stood on top of the dark stairs, deep in thought. This disclosure of Frann's changed matters. Now the girl had a strong motive to kill the elderly man to whom she was married. The will left her goods and riches beyond any fantasy fairytale. Why have the bother of an elderly, if rich husband if the riches have already been given to you? Frann obviously had, probably never had, no affection for Mahon. And yet, why show the scrolls? If I had not seen these, thought Mara, I would have taken no interest in Frann.

Perhaps the girl was what she appeared to be: childlike, but with that strong streak of practicality that most children possessed.

The outer door was unlatched and then shut with great caution. Someone had come in and was stealing past the parlour, up the steps towards Banna's room. Mara waited quietly. She was curious. At first she presumed that it was Banna's maid, but those footsteps, quiet though they were, sounded far too heavy for the girl.

The footsteps passed Banna's door, stepping gingerly, and then proceeded to steal up the next set of steps. Mara stayed very still, confident that the dark grey of her cloak kept her hidden against Frann's door. It was a man, and a tall man; she could just see his shape outlined against the dim light. But which man was visiting Frann with such secret care? He came on, right up to the second storey landing, and paused. In the darkness, Mara could hear his breathing.

And then the outer door was pushed wide open and Murrough entered, shut it behind him and, without a glance upwards, noisily tramped his way into the parlour. That one minute of light had been enough, though. Mara had identified the figure.

'I'm sorry, Ardal,' she said courteously. 'You've been waiting for me, probably. I just wanted to see Frann for a minute. Shall we go down together?'

'No need to apologise, Brehon; no arrangement had been made. I merely came over to see whether I could assist you in any way.' Ardal's voice, after the first few seconds of silence, sounded unperturbed.

'It's dark, isn't it. I was just thinking of going back to borrow a candle from Frann.' Without waiting for an answer, Mara pushed open the door. Frann was now on her knees before the chest, taking out a gown and spreading it on the bed. Her hand was lovingly stroking the blue-green velvet and she looked up in a startled way. Mara stood slightly to one side to allow the girl to see the figure of Ardal O'Lochlainn.

'Could I just borrow a candle, Frann?'

Mara's voice was easy, but her eyes went quickly from the girl's face to Ardal. There was no doubt in her mind. Frann looked at Ardal in the way that a woman looks at a lover. Ardal had quickly averted his eyes and looked at the floor while Frann, with pretty grace, bent down and lit a spare candle from the brazier and politely turned the handle of the holder towards Mara.

'Thank you, Frann; we'll leave it on the window ledge by the door.'

And, yes, indeed, my dear, you will look very sweet in that green gown, she thought, as she went down the stairs, following Ardal who politely held the candle high.

And there is no doubt that he is a very handsome and desirable man, her thoughts continued as she waited while he opened the door for her. Tall, lean and athletic with those intensely blue eyes and his red-gold crown of hair, Ardal would be attractive to anyone. Lovemaking with him would be rather more fun than with the solid, boring Mahon. *You can do what you like, my pretty little Frann, as long as no murder is involved*, she thought, waiting while Ardal carefully blew out the candle and placed it on the window ledge.

'You've known Frann before, then.' Mara often found it best to make a quick statement rather than asking a question and it worked this time. Ardal turned a startled face at her, shut the outer door with less care than he had opened it and then after a few seconds for reflection, said guardedly, 'Well, yes, I met her some months ago, in the summer.'

'Oh!' She allowed the exclamation to stand. He could take it as a question or a comment. Again she had to wait for a few seconds before he said any more.

'I went to see Mahon's limekiln. I was thinking of setting up something like that, myself, at Lissylisheen. We have a quarry there and we could easily do it. He was telling me that he made lots of silver from it. He said it was the best thing that he had done, it was far less risky than fishing.'

'I see.' Mara knew that Ardal's energy was always seeking new outlets. 'What did you think of it?' He obviously had not gone ahead with setting up a limekiln business. Brigid, or Cumhal, would undoubtedly have told her if there had been any talk of that.

'I decided against it.' His tone was firm now and quite assured. 'I didn't want any of my people to work in those conditions. I saw a girl's hands; they were in a terrible state.'

'Frann's?' queried Mara, and then when he hesitated, she added, 'She told me that she worked there. That was how Mahon got to know her.'

Ardal nodded. 'This was before Mahon got to know her.'

Got to know her in the biblical sense, thought Mara wickedly. Ardal was a man of high honour, he would not have dallied with Frann if she were another man's property, but before, yes, well, he might have spent a pleasant evening or two. Mara could just imagine how Frann's strange beauty would have beguiled him. She would have told her sad story, shown her damaged hands, roused his pity and then probably his desires. He would have seemed a very good prospect before the master of the limekiln himself came on the scene.

'So you haven't seen her since then,' she said pleasantly.

He looked uncomfortable and her interest sharpened. 'Well, yes, I have, as a matter of fact.'

She waited and then he blurted out. 'Mahon wanted a horse for her a couple of months ago. I had a nice, quiet chestnut mare so I took it over there.'

'I see,' nodded Mara, suppressing a smile. Ardal O'Lochlainn had many horsemen working for him. It was astonishing that a *taoiseach* would trouble himself to go all that way just to sell one mare. Obviously Frann had made a memorable impression on him when he saw her the first time.

'She was a horsewoman, then?' Mara hoped that her question sounded innocent and was pleased to see a frank smile play around his well-moulded lips.

'Why no, she had never even sat upon a horse before; she began to pick it up well, though, after a few days.'

No doubt the tuition was pleasurable to both, thought Mara. But how far had the relationship progressed? Would it have gone far enough for Ardal to think of getting rid of Mahon? Would he have known about the deeds giving Frann those rich pieces of property? Mara looked at the bright blue eyes and then dismissed the thought. No, Ardal was rich enough; the property would not have been a motive — but the girl herself, now that was a different matter. In any case, there was no need for Frann to have shown the Brehon these scrolls if Ardal had already read them to her. What was Mahon thinking while these riding lessons were going on? She suddenly realized that she knew very little about the dead man. Turlough had disliked him and dismissed him as a sanctimonious bore, but somehow Frann's account of him had shown a different picture.

'Ardal,' she said suddenly and impulsively, 'could you tell me something about Mahon O'Brien?'

'A good businessman,' said Ardal judiciously. 'He seemed to be successful in anything that he undertook and of course he had extensive properties; he had the whole of one of the *Triocha Céts* and, of course, the *baile biataigh*. You may remember that those were the lands where there was a dispute with Teige O'Brien and then there was . . .'

'Yes, yes,' said Mara. This recital of lands could go on for a long time, she knew from experience. 'Yes, thank you, Ardal, but what I really meant was what was he like? What sort of man was Mahon?'

His eyes suddenly grew cold. 'I'm afraid that I couldn't tell you about that, Brehon. I hardly knew the man.'

'I see,' said Mara. 'Well, I must leave you now, Ardal. I see Father Peter coming from the guest house and I want a quick word with him.' Purposely she did not look to see where Ardal was going, but from the sound of his firm footsteps he appeared to be tramping in the direction of the church. She smiled to herself: as soon as she moved away, she guessed that he would go back to Frann.

'How is the *tánaiste*?' Father Peter was looking cheerful, so her question was casual. She guessed that there was no great problem with Conor. It seemed to be part of this condition of the wasting sickness that the sufferer appeared well at one time of the day and almost at the point of death at another.

'Sleeping peacefully and the blood beats strongly, thank God.' Father Peter's answer was brief and from the enquiring look he turned upon her, Mara knew that he guessed she had something else upon her mind.

'You mentioned something about the man from Tintern Abbey,' said Mara coming directly to the point. There was no point in dissimulating with this clever priest. 'I wondered was that the important guest that the abbot was talking about last night?'

'It was, indeed.' Father Peter's eyes sparkled with pleasure as one who was pleased at an inquiry from a clever scholar.

'And,' said Mara, feeling her way carefully, 'this would be a Cistercian monk, would it not?'

'Abbot,' said Father Peter tersely. 'Head of the whole *meitheal*, God forgive me for using an expression like that about our holy brothers in England.'

'So, very important.'

'Very, very important.' Father Peter gave a quick glance around and lowered his voice. 'This holy abbot has been appointed by Rome to give a report on all of the Cistercian abbeys in Ireland.'

'So Father Donogh wants a good report for *Sancta Maria Petris Fertilis*, well that's only natural, I suppose.' Mara's voice was mild and only faintly interested; there would be more to come, she knew.

'Not just that.' Father Peter gave another hasty glance around. 'You don't keep up with the news from other parts of the country, Brehon. God love you, why should you? You have enough to do in your kingdom, but you've heard of the abbey of Mellifont?'

Mara nodded. This was the biggest Cistercian abbey in the whole of Ireland.

Father Peter gave her a gentle, toothless smile. 'Well, the abbot there died a few weeks ago. A messenger came last week to tell the news and to say that no successor had been appointed. Then, three days later, a messenger to announce the visit of Father Abbot from Tintern Abbey. We've all been kept busy since. Everything has been scrubbed and repaired; every piece of silver in the house has been polished, lists made, all ready to show when the great man arrives.'

'I see,' said Mara. And she did see. A lot of what had puzzled her was now clear. Father Donogh O'Brien, like all the O'Briens, was ambitious. This abbey here in the Burren was too small, too unimportant for a man of his ability and high lineage; now he had the golden opportunity of attaining an important position which would match his talents. No wonder he wanted the burial of his brother out of the way before the abbot from Tintern Abbey arrived. The surprising thing was that he hadn't also moved this embarrassing, illegitimate son of his out of the way before the arrival. Rome would not be impressed by such an episode in his past history.

Or did the abbot have a plan about this?

Ten

Di Astud Chirt & Oligid
(On the Confirmation of Right & Law)

A cleric, without family to pay his fine, who commits murder, must go into exile for ten years. He undertakes seven years of penance and during that time must abstain from all food, beyond the minimum to ensure life. After another three years of exile he must return, make what compensation that he can and offer himself as son to the bereaved person.

The abbot was coming out of his house when Mara came out of the guest house and she walked resolutely towards him. He only saw her as she came through the archway and on to the cloisters. For a moment, it looked as if he was going to disappear inside again, but Mara called out a quick greeting and he stood very still, watching her come. Funny how like his face, with that high-bridged nose and wide forehead, is to Turlough's, she thought and yet there was a world of a difference: the one heavily mous-tached with a high colour, the other clean-shaven, pale-faced. But the greatest difference was in the eyes. Turlough had light green eyes, sparkling with fun and affection, while the abbot's eyes were as grey and as cold as the stone around them.

'Could you spare me a few minutes, Father Abbot?' said Mara briskly. 'We'll go inside, shall we?'

The sky was very dark and a heavy drizzle of thick, soft rain, more wetting than any showers, was beginning to fall. The surrounding mountains were veiled and the birds silent.

'I was just on my way to the church. I have to give instruc-tions to Master Mason about the vault. He will need to prepare the space for the body of my brother,' said the abbot.

'It will only take a few minutes,' said Mara resolutely. From the church she could hear the sound of the heavy mallet crashing against stone and guessed that the mason would already have had his instructions. The coffins of the dead members of the O'Brien *derbhfine* were always placed inside stone chests, made from slabs of the limestone that paved the fields and then the lids sealed with mortar before the vault was closed up again.

The abbot compressed his thin, bloodless lips, but he bowed slightly and stood aside to allow her to enter the house. Confidently she opened the door to the parlour and went within. The room was warm with a good fire of turf burning in the chimney. Clearly the abbot did not feel that the austerity he imposed on his brother monks applied to him. No wonder that Father Denis preferred to stay in these comfortable surroundings rather than in the monks' dormitory, even at the risk of arousing comment. Mara seated herself by the fire and looked up at the abbot. He remained standing for a long minute, an expression of impatience on his face, but she did not speak so eventually he had to seat himself opposite to her.

'And, of course, you knew that your brother, Mahon O'Brien, was to take the king's place at dawn this morning in the church.' She said the words quietly.

He looked at her in an annoyed fashion, but then as she raised one eyebrow, he nodded reluctantly. 'Yes, I did.' His voice was as impatient as his expression. He glanced over his shoulder towards the door, clearly indicating that he wanted to go about his business.

'And did your son, Father Denis, know?'

'No,' he said briefly. Obviously he had decided that it wasn't worth denying the relationship.

'How do you know?'

He said nothing so she continued. 'Did he tell you that he didn't know?'

'We didn't discuss the matter,' he said stiffly.

'And yet you spent a long time talking after the service of prime and on other occasions today. Don't deny it; I observed you.'

'We had other matters to consider,' he said after a long pause during which he managed to convey a sense of outraged displeasure.

'Such as the abbey of Knockmoy.' Mara heard with pleasure how crisp and authoritative her voice sounded. How dare this hypocrite give such pain to Turlough? She would love to cry his sin aloud to the people of the Burren.

He said nothing so she pressed on. 'I understand that there will be no problem now about Father Denis's appointment as abbot to Knockmoy. Is that true?' she added sharply when he did not answer.

'It's not a matter for me,' he said after a while.

'But there is now no obstacle,' she persisted.

He looked at her. By the light of the fire, she could see his grey eyes glitter. She could read their expression well. There was fear there, and hatred also. Was the fear for himself or for his son, she wondered? The hatred was undoubtedly directed at her. Suddenly she remembered Brigid's words. Was she in danger from this man?

'*Qui tacet, consentire videtur,*' she said to him in Latin, but still he didn't answer. She waited for a moment and then translated into Gaelic: '"He who remains silent is seen to consent", is that true of you?' He shot her an angry glance – whether for assuming that he needed a translation, or because he resented the in-sinuation, she did not know. Still he did not reply. She didn't care. Sometimes no answer was as revealing as a flow of words.

'So the death of Mahon O'Brien smoothed the road to promo-tion for your son,' she stated, looking intently at him, then leaning over and carelessly tossing another few sods of turf on the fire.

He had himself under control by the time she looked back, but for a moment the smooth face had been marred by a fury that could not have been surpassed by his famous ancestor, Teige, the Bone-splitter. Why should he look so angry about this? This time the anger did not seem to be directed at her, but had erupted at the word 'son'.

'So you see,' she continued, still pretending to occupy herself with the fire, but at the same time covertly studying his narrow face. This man puzzled her. 'I must ask questions of all who may have had an interest in causing the death of either King Turlough Donn, or his cousin, Mahon O'Brien, your brother.'

He did not respond and she had not expected him to do so. It was time for some plain questions to which she would expect plain answers.

'I understand that the custom here is for you to be the first to leave the church after a service. Why did you and your son stay behind in the church this morning after the service of prime?'

'I wished to see how far Master Mason had got with the

reparation of the carvings. I wanted to make sure that all was ready for Christmas.' He answered more readily than she had expected. Obviously he had been prepared for this question.

'And did you?' Her reply was purposefully fast. She would have to throw him off balance to get at the truth.

'Did I?' He tried to make his tone sound puzzled. She looked full into his face now and he evaded her eyes.

'Did you talk to the mason?'

Now he was in a quandary. She could see him wondering whether perhaps the mason had been in the church, wondering whether he might be caught out in a lie.

'No,' he said after a moment. 'I was feeling tired and I thought I would go back and have an hour's rest before breakfast, as I had advised the brothers to do. Tomorrow night will be a long night for us all. The tradition is that we stay awake from matins to dawn. Of course, the days are very short at this time of the year so it is customary to give the brothers extra sleeping time when the weather is bad and the light is poor. No, I decided that I would see the mason later on.'

'It wouldn't have taken long to stroll across the church floor and look at the carvings?' she said sharply and when he didn't reply she got to her feet.

'Let us go and look at them now. You were on your way when I delayed you.'

Without waiting for an answer she swept through his parlour door, passing a lay brother in the small dark hallway. He went to the door and opened it and then she saw that this was the young brother who had read during their dinner of salted cod.

'Thank you, Brother Francis,' she said politely and then, as she and the abbot walked side by side along the eastern side of the cloister, she said in a low voice to him, 'I understand that young brother is an O'Kelly from Galway?'

'That is correct.' Again there was that sideways look as if he endeavoured to read her mind. She stopped, then turned and faced him fully and the abbot's eyes slid away from hers.

'Surprising that he did not attach himself to one of the Galway abbeys, Knockmoy, for instance.'

He gave her a sidelong glance and then said after a slight pause for reflection, 'Actually he was at Knockmoy.'

'And why did he transfer?'

'There was some sort of trouble,' said the abbot, picking his way carefully through the words like a man would tread over sharp stones. He began to move forward again towards the church.

'What sort of trouble?' asked Mara impatiently. No wonder this abbot annoyed Turlough so much!

'Well,' said the abbot reluctantly, 'there was an enquiry into the former abbot's behaviour and Brother Francis O'Kelly gave evidence.'

He shut his mouth tightly and Mara did not press him further. In any case she was not sure that she could trust her voice as an unholy glee was bubbling up inside her. So it was Brother O'Kelly who gave witness to the shocking affair of the hair-washing by a woman, she thought. It must have been a wonderful scene in front of some sour-faced prelate from Rome. She fell back a little and allowed the abbot to precede her through the cloisters' door to the church while she arranged her face into a suitably grave expression.

'One minute, Brehon, I'll just light a few candles.' His voice came back to her and almost instantaneously a sudden light shot into her own mind. Could Father Abbot have engineered the whole affair? Bribed this Brother Francis? The young monk looked dull and self-satisfied. Offered him a new position, and perhaps a promise of promotion and at the same time he would do a great service to his own clan. With the war-experienced Turlough dead, and Conor as king, the O'Kellys could probably easily defeat the O'Brien clan. This would give Brother Francis a motive, but would the abbot have any reason to wish death on his cousin, Turlough, who had always been so generous in his gifts to the abbey? On the other hand, it seemed too much of a coincidence that Brother Francis's evidence had been instrumental in removing the former abbot from Knockmoy; it was very likely that the abbot had engineered that.

The church was now quite dark so the light of the candle threw the stone carvings into startling relief. On the top of one of the fluted pillars, there was a circle of twelve carved harebells and beneath them had stood twelve stiff, upright poppy heads. Five of these poppy heads had broken off during the three centuries since and the gaps had been filled in with almost perfect replicas. The stems were so finely carved and the rounded sides, each capped with a brittle circle, were carefully scored. The poppy heads looked as if they could be crushed between finger and thumb; only the gleaming white of the limestone showed that these had not just been plucked from the herb garden.

The abbot moved the candle up and down inspecting the work and then nodded with satisfaction.

'Well done, Master Mason,' he called down the steps where the blows from the mallet had ceased for a moment. 'After a few years no one will know your work from the work of the mason who carved these stone flowers five hundred years ago.'

'So the chancel was decorated when the abbey was originally built.' Mara knew that, but it occurred to her that it would be well to end her interview with the abbot on a fairly friendly note.

Father Abbot seemed relieved and began talking animatedly, showing her the carvings and the repairs that had been done over the centuries.

'See here,' he said, holding up the candle and showing her a faintly incised cross just below the fluted crown of an arch, 'this is the mark of the original mason; his mark can be found all over the church. And here, look there where the curve of scallop shells outlines that arch, if you look closely you can see that some of these have been repaired: that was about a hundred years ago. I have a note about it in the abbey documents. Look, you can see that this time the mason signs his work with a pattern from the bible book.'

Mara stood on her toes and found the mark, a small spiral ending in a loosely trailing curve. The illuminated copies of the Holy Book were all decorated with these spirals; even a few of her own law books showed the same ornamental drawings.

'And now,' continued the abbot triumphantly, 'here we are fifteen hundred years after the birth of Christ and the mason now makes his mark with the Roman numeral for five hundred.'

Mara looked. The abbot was right. It was not the Gaelic letter ꝺ with its curved sides and scrolled top, but a square-cut straight-edged *D*. She understood the abbot's point; the use of this *D* probably showed a man who was literate.

'Why five hundred?' Mara spoke almost to herself, but the

abbot went straight to the open doorway leading down to the vault and called out:

'Master Mason, why do you use the Roman numeral five hundred for your mark?'

The answer was a while in coming, but then slow heavy steps could be heard coming up. The man was coated in the grey dust of the plaster, even the seams of his face seemed to hold the fine powder, and when he spoke his voice was even huskier than before.

'I am the five-hundredth mason in this part of Ireland, my lord,' he said. 'Or so my father used to tell me,' he added.

How does he know, thought Mara, but the abbot nodded with satisfaction. He was a man who liked everything to be neatly sorted. Mara could imagine how he would show this new work to visiting prelates and inform them that it was done by the five-hundredth mason in the west of Ireland.

'Could you spare me a moment, Master Mason?' she asked politely. 'The king's son, Murrough, said that . . .'

The man gave a sudden start and she thought that, even under the coating of grey dust, his face turned a little paler. She hastened to reassure him.

'The king knows of the merry prank that his son played,' she said reassuringly. 'No blame attaches to you. But Murrough reported that you were up and dressed when he woke and I wondered whether you had already been to the chapel.'

The mason cleared his throat noisily, but when he spoke his voice was huskier than ever.

'No, my lady,' he said. 'The king's son is mistaken. I had slept in my clothes as it was so cold.'

Understandable given the icy chill of that lay dormitory, but nevertheless Mara pursued her questions. 'And you were standing at the shutters, were you not?'

Murrough had not said that, but it was most likely that a man, rising from his bed, and finding everything frozen, would go to the shutters to see what the weather was like.

The mason bowed his head and muttered something.

'And did you see anything? See anyone?'

He thought about this quite carefully and then shook his head. He looked over at the abbot and the abbot intervened.

'If that is all, Brehon,' he said hurriedly, 'I think Master Mason had better be getting back to his work. The stone sarcophagus for my brother's body will need to be finished soon.'

'That is all, Father Abbot,' said Mara courteously. Why had the abbot been so quick to cut short her questioning? And why did the mason look towards the abbot in such a marked manner? Normally he seemed to hang his head. She watched the man carefully as he shuffled away, his heavy boots bound with strips of linen so that his feet made no noise as he went down the steps to the vault beneath. She heard him pick up his mallet, but there was no sound of a blow. It seemed as if he were waiting for something, perhaps for the abbot to join him, to give him more instructions, or was there some other significance in the wait? Had he perhaps seen something when he looked out of the shutters in that early dawn? Had he seen the abbot visit the church that morning?

The west door at the bottom of the church was pushed open allowing a stream of light to illuminate the darkness of the nave. Mara glanced around; no one had entered, but someone was there at the door, slowly pulling it shut again. The stealth of the action attracted her; someone was obviously trying to make as little noise as possible.

Swiftly she marched down the centre of the nave and seized the handle of the door, pulling it wide open.

'Ah, come in Father Denis,' she said suavely. 'Father Abbot and I were just speaking of you.'

Father and son were very uneasy in each other's presence, she thought, as she watched them stealing covert glances at each other. Did they share a guilty secret or was this just a lifetime habit where concealment was essential to allow this ambitious O'Brien priest to gain the approval of Rome? There had been a big change, during the last ten years, in these Cistercian abbeys. The easy-going lax behaviour of the Celtic church was no longer permissible; all had to be done according to the laws from Rome. Abbey after abbey in the whole of Ireland had been visited by abbots from England and from France and had been roundly condemned. The days had gone by when a powerful family, like the O'Briens, could automatically appoint a member of their own family to the position of abbot.

'How old are you, Father Denis?' she asked abruptly.

'I am thirty, my lady . . . Brehon,' he answered.

'And where did you spend your early life?'

Father Denis glanced quickly at the abbot, but that stony face gave him no assistance so after a moment, he replied.

'At Arra.'

No 'my lady' – not even a 'Brehon' this time, she noticed. His voice was curt and almost aggressive.

That's not what Teige said, thought Mara.

'From the time of your birth?' she questioned.

'I came to Arra when I was eight years old and stayed until I was eighteen,' he said stiffly.

'I see,' said Mara thoughtfully. This meant that Denis had been fostered by his mother's brother from that age. The relationship would be quite strong – what was it that Fithail, the judge, had said: 'A man's son is precious to him, but dearer to his heart is his foster child'? The O'Brien Arra, as he was known, would want to advance his foster-son in his chosen profession. Now, with Mahon O'Brien out of the way, the possibility of promotion to abbot was very strong – so long, of course, as no hint of scandal touched his name.

'When did you find out that your father was Father Donogh, here?' she asked bluntly.

They both stiffened at that; there was an expression of outrage on the abbot's face, but she ignored him, turning towards Denis. He was debating whether to tell the truth, or not, and she gave him a quick frown and impatiently tapped her foot on the stone floor.

'About a year ago,' he said after a pause. His eyes slid towards the face of his father and then looked away quickly.

'His mother asked to see him on her deathbed and told him.' The abbot's tone was bitter.

'Had you known she was your mother prior to that?'

'No,' said Father Denis. After a minute, he added, 'But I think I guessed. She often came to see me and once she gave me a chessboard.'

Despite her dislike of this young priest, Mara felt a slight softening of the heart. It was not the right way to bring up a boy; he would always be wondering, always trying to guess, always insecure and unhappy. However, there was one more question that she had to ask.

'I hear that you have contracted a marriage of the fourth degree,' she said. 'Is that true?'

'What!' Obviously that piece of gossip had not come to the abbot's ears. He rounded on his son with fury and then glanced at Mara and shut his mouth firmly. Father Denis looked back at him with equal dislike. There was a sneer in his voice when he answered.

'It is certainly true, but I don't think that it is anyone's business but mine.'

'But perhaps something that should not be allowed to come to the ears of Rome if you wish for promotion,' suggested Mara mildly.

He didn't answer this so she pressed home with her next question.

'Did Mahon O'Brien know of this marriage of the fourth degree?'

'No,' he replied promptly.

And yet Teige knew of it, thought Mara. Teige had nothing to do with that part of Galway, so his most likely source of information would be Mahon. She studied the young priest carefully. His high-bridged O'Brien nose was raised defiantly as if sniffing something evil-smelling, but his eyes were troubled and unhappy. No wonder that he looks so much of an O'Brien, thought Mara. His mother and father were first cousins – in fact, generation after generation of O'Briens married cousins; Turlough was one of the first to marry a MacNamara. The bone structure was bred into them and so was the ambition.

'I put it to you that Mahon O'Brien did know of this marriage of the fourth degree and also did know that that you were, in fact, illegitimate, in the eyes of Rome, and of English law, of course. This means that the death of Mahon O'Brien has been providential for you.' Mara watched the young priest's face as closely as she could, but he had his features well under control.

'I bore no ill-feeling towards Mahon O'Brien,' he said stiffly. 'If anything, like many others of our clan, I considered him more suitable than Teige O'Brien to be the *tánaiste* in the case of anything happening to the king's son, Conor O'Brien.'

'I see,' said Mara, 'and what would be your objection to Teige O'Brien?'

'It was the general view of the Arra *fine* that Teige O'Brien was a false flatterer who had gained a position near to the king by slandering other members of the family.' His reply was prompt and unexpected; Mara concealed her surprise, but she wondered at his words. Teige O'Brien had always seemed to her to be a harmless, jovial man, fond of his wife and his family and of his cousin King Turlough.

And then into the stillness came the sound of horse hoofs clattering over paved ground and then the startlingly loud summons of the gatehouse bell.

'Guests?' said the abbot with a puzzled air. 'I expect no one.'

Eleven

Coic Conara Fugill
(The Five Paths of Judgement)

There are eight stages of a law case.
1. *Fixing a date for the hearing*
2. *Choosing the proper path of judgement*
3. *The giving of security*
4. *The pleading*
5. *The rejoinder or counter pleading*
6. *The judgement*
7. *The forus (explanation of the basis for the judgement)*
8. *The conclusion*

By the time that Mara and the abbot had emerged from the church they heard the creak of the gate being opened and the sound of voices. Mara frowned in puzzlement; one of the voices was a light treble, a boy's voice, and then another, very familiar, young voice replying. Leaving the abbot who was proceeding at his usual stately pace she hurried down the path.

The younger of the boys had dismounted from his pony. His back was turned to her, but there was no mistaking the trim, neat head, capped with the fine black hair, the slim, upright figure, even the way that he was excitedly pointing to a golden eagle swooping overhead, all of these things were as well known to Mara as the skin on her own hands. The ten-year-old boy had been at her law school since he was five years old.

'Shane!' she called and he turned around instantly, his white teeth flashing in a huge grin.

'Brehon!' exclaimed his companion, a tall boy with a head of bushy curls. Fachtnan had also been with her since his fifth year and now, as a nineteen-year-old, he acted as her assistant as well as studying for his final legal examinations.

'We got stuck in Galway by the snowstorm,' said Shane.

'But where is your father?' asked Mara. Shane's father was Brehon to the O'Neill family in the north of Ireland and had come to escort his son home for the Christmas break. Fachtnan's home at Ossory had lain on their route and all three had left Cahermacnaghten two days ago.

'I'm here, Mara.' Patrick McBrethany emerged from the porter's lodge to engulf her in a huge hug. He was a man well past middle age; Shane was the youngest of his six clever sons and Mara had felt very honoured that he had entrusted the five-year-old to her after they had met at a summer conference.

'What happened?' she gasped, disentangling herself.

'Well, it's as the wee lad says; we had just gone a few miles beyond Galway when the snowstorm hit us. We turned and went back to Galway and spent a couple of nights in an inn. We heard this morning that the road to the north was still blocked so we took passage in a boat across the bay and landed at Bealnaclugga. We didn't know whether you would be here, or whether you would be still at Cahermacnaghten, so I was enquiring from the porter.'

'Did he tell you our news, Patrick?' asked Mara, eyeing him affectionately. He was a bear-like man, she always thought, not tall, but immensely broad in shoulder and with long arms. It was his head that impressed most people when they met him first. He had the head of a marble saint with the hairless ivory skin curving around the domed cranium. A full-lipped mouth and large parchment-coloured eyelids completed the impression of a head carved from stone. It was only when those eyelids snapped wide open, unveiling the intense intelligence of his sharp grey eyes, that the whole face suddenly came alive and the saint-like impression was lost.

'No,' said Patrick, his eyes hooded and his expression thoughtful.

'I'll tell you later,' said Mara. Suddenly she felt cheerful. Here was someone to whet her brain against, someone to share the burden. 'My lord abbot,' she said, turning around to introduce the newcomers to him, 'here is the O'Neill Brehon with his son, Shane, and my assistant, Fachtnan. Can we manage to find shelter for them within the abbey?'

The abbot greeted Patrick warmly – King Conn O'Neill was

powerful even in this part of the world and the abbot was never one to miss impressing a man of power or his representative.

'I think, Brehon, if you would honour my poor house, that will shelter you more worthily than our guest house,' he said with false humility.

Mara concealed a smile. The four *taoiseach*s of the Burren would not be pleased to know that the abbot considered them of lower status than a Brehon from the north of the country.

'That will be splendid,' said Patrick heartily. 'The wee lad and his friend can bed down with me.'

'No, no,' said the abbot quickly. Mara guessed that he didn't want any rambunctious schoolboys to disturb the hallowed quiet of the abbot's house. 'Father Peter,' he called as the prior emerged from the guest house and came hurrying up to greet the new arrivals, 'have we got a spare room for these two young scholars?'

'I was thinking,' said Father Peter slowly after Mara had introduced him, 'that it might be a good idea for the king's bodyguards to sleep outside his doorway, or, even better, one inside the chamber and one outside the door. God forbid, but it would be a terrible thing if the murderer was to make another attempt on King Turlough's life tonight.'

Oh dear, thought Mara, I'm not sure that Turlough will be too pleased about that. That arrangement would leave little chance for the king to slip into her bedroom that night. However, there was no doubt but that it was a good idea. As the minutes and the hours slid away she was very conscious of the terrible danger of a second attack.

'And then, of course, the two lads could have the bodyguards' room,' concluded Father Peter as she nodded her agreement.

'Where is the king?' asked the abbot, looking around.

'He's asleep in the parlour of the Royal Lodge,' Mara said. 'Fergal and Conall are on guard.'

'It will soon be vespers,' said the abbot reprovingly. 'King Turlough will not want to miss that. The service tonight is especially to commemorate the anniversary of his great ancestor, Conor O'Brien.'

'Lord bless us and save us,' said Father Peter. 'We've forgotten about the day of vigil!'

'How could we find the time for . . .' began the abbot furiously and then stopped abruptly and said with dignity to Patrick, 'My brother has been murdered as he knelt in the church this morning.'

'I am very sorry to hear that,' said Patrick. He bowed to the abbot and then glanced quickly at Mara. She did not respond. Time for explanations later on when the two were alone. Now she must see to the needs of the travellers; Shane looked cold and his father looked tired.

'I'll go and fetch the king myself,' said the abbot fussily as the monks began to move towards the church for the service of vespers. He set off towards the Royal Lodge and Mara did not attempt to stop him. It suited her to have Patrick to herself for the next hour; in front of Turlough it would be difficult to discuss the possibility of the king's son or one of his near relatives being involved in the murder. She even withdrew to stand concealed below the eaves of the porter's lodge when she saw the abbot come out, followed by Turlough and the two bodyguards.

'The wee lad is as excited at being present at the wedding of his Brehon as he was to be going home,' said Patrick, indicating Shane.

'Ah,' said Mara quietly, 'well, I'm afraid that the wedding has been postponed due to the murder of the king's cousin.'

Patrick's white brows rose slightly at this, though he said nothing and his eyes remained thoughtfully bent on the ground. She knew that he was surprised; violent death happened in these war-like societies; it seldom interfered with any planned merriment. She turned to Shane and Fachtnan.

'So you stayed the night in Galway,' she said in a low voice. 'That must have been fun. Did you have a look around the city?'

'We went to see Malachy. We stayed in an inn overnight and then, in the morning, we went around and looked at the shops,' said Shane. 'Fachtnan told me that it is against the law for anyone with an O or a Mac in their name to strut or swagger in the streets of Galway so we had to go very quietly and keep our hoods up and our mantles well wrapped around us.'

'If you can imagine Shane being quiet,' said Fachtnan affectionately. He was always very good with the younger boys. He had been assistant at the law school for three months now and, though not as gifted academically as Mara's former assistant, he was more successful at managing to combine friendliness with firmness.

'Well, just try to keep very quiet now for a moment,' said Mara, 'or the king will insist on you going to church as well.' She watched for a moment, but Turlough did not glance around and as soon as he disappeared into the church, she said hospitably, 'Let's go and see what Brigid can do in the way of food and hot drinks.'

'Lord bless us and save us,' said Brigid when they went into the small kitchen in the Royal Lodge. 'Well, look at the two of you. I was worrying about you two. Cumhal was saying that the snow came down from the north so that you would have a hard journey of it.'

'Could you feed and warm them, Brigid?' said Mara. 'The Brehon and I are going into the parlour and perhaps you could bring us something there. Join us when you are ready, boys.'

'So, you see, I was fairly sure that the intended victim was King Turlough and not his cousin, Mahon O'Brien, but then there was something suspicious about that young priest, the illegitimate son of the abbot . . .' finished Mara, dusting a few crumbs of cake from her fingers. The two boys were sitting quietly by the fire listening intently.

'And the abbot himself?' queried Patrick.

'Yes, he, also.' Mara nodded firmly, thinking of the stony face and then the sudden flare of anger. 'The strange thing is,' she went on, 'although there appears little love between the abbot and this son of his, Father Donogh is obviously trying to get him appointed as abbot of Knockmoy.'

'Even to the extent of murdering his own brother?' queried Fachtnan.

'I don't know,' said Mara doubtfully, 'but somehow, yes, it does seems possible. After all why did he make such a fuss about having someone in the church for the first hour of the vigil? He could easily have got one of the brothers to do it, or else do it himself. It's almost as if he wanted Mahon there in place of the king.'

'But if he, your abbot here, were intent on having everything in good order when the abbot from Tintern Abbey arrived, then he would hardly be likely to murder his brother two days before the arrival.'

'That's true,' said Mara slowly, 'but, you know, something came into my mind, just a while ago, just before you arrived. I was talking to the abbot and his son, this Father Denis, in the church and it struck me that their relationship was not one of love or even of friendliness.'

Fachtnan looked up sharply, his dark eyes alert and curious. He was an intuitive boy, she thought, he knew her well and could read the tone of her voice. She nodded at him, but turned towards Patrick before speaking:

'It struck me,' she repeated, 'that there was a measure of fear in the abbot's eyes and of mastery in Father Denis's.'

'What do you mean?' Patrick looked puzzled, but Fachtnan sat up very straight.

'Blackmail!' he exclaimed. 'Is that what you are thinking, Brehon?'

Mara smiled. 'That's exactly what I was thinking,' she said with satisfaction. 'You see the last thing that Father Donogh wants is to have the abbot from Tintern Abbey discover his guilty secret; if that got to the ears of Rome he would certainly not be promoted; on the contrary, he would be reprimanded, and perhaps even removed from his present position. He could not stand that.'

'So Father Denis was refusing to budge until the abbot got his brother to nominate him to the abbacy of Knockmoy,' said Patrick thoughtfully.

'Or, there could be another possibility. A darker one. Would you like to put the case, Fachtnan?'

Fachtnan sat up very straight, looking pleased. 'Let me put the case,' he said with dignity, 'the abbot appeals to his brother to use his influence, is turned down, according to this Father Peter, and then murders his brother so as to ensure that Father Denis's path to promotion is smooth.'

'Or, let me put the case,' said Shane, his black eyes sparkling with excitement. 'Let me put the case, may I, Brehon, that Father Denis murdered Mahon O'Brien, the abbot knows it but he doesn't dare say anything because Father Denis is threatening him.'

Mara exchanged a quick glance with Patrick who beamed

parental pride for a moment before lowering his eyes again. 'They could have come to some agreement,' she said thoughtfully. 'The price of silence could be that Father Denis will take the first opportunity to leave this abbey and return to Knockmoy and wait there for the O'Brien of Arra to ratify the appointment.'

'Let's shelve this for the moment and take the suspects one at a time,' said Patrick. 'If the king was murdered then your suspicions would include his son, Murrough, his daughter-in-law, Ellice, possibly with complicity from the *tánaiste*, Conor. And this Brother Francis, a member of the O'Kelly clan, do you suspect him also?'

'I think it might have been hard for him to get out of the brothers' dormitory without anyone seeing,' acknowledged Mara. 'I must have a word with Father Peter. He is in charge of the dormitory and he is very shrewd. I think it would be difficult for anyone to steal past him.'

'And what was the church like? You still had the snow then, didn't you? There would have been footprints. Did you see any?'

'Only from the bodyguards. They rushed into the church when they saw the body slumped over on the floor. I'll show you the church afterwards, but there are just two doors that lead outside: the west door that leads to the guest houses' garth and the door on the south that leads to the cloister garth. The abbot and Father Denis would have come in that way – unless the one or other had stayed behind after the service of prime, of course.'

'And was there any snow by that door?'

'No,' said Mara slowly, 'but you know that cloisters are sheltered from the north wind and roofed over. Even later in the day there was very little snow on that passageway between the abbot's house and the church. It would certainly be possible for a man to pick his way, dry-footed, and to arrive at the church with clean boots.'

'And how do the monks get into the church?' asked Shane.

'There is a third door. This just leads to the night stairs and divides at the top. One way leads to the lay dormitory, where Murrough . . .'

'The king's son?' queried Patrick.

Mara nodded, 'Yes, in his disguise as pilgrim, Murrough was sleeping in the lay dormitory.'

'And where's the monks' dormitory?' asked Fachtnan, helping himself to another piece of cake.

'That leads off the night staircase, also. The monks' dormitory is on the east side of the cloisters, above the chapter house and the abbot's house.'

'Let's turn to the man who was actually killed. You say that his wife, Banna, is a possible, though unlikely, suspect.'

'I don't really suspect her,' said Mara with a small smile. 'She is immensely fat, and quite lethargic. I think she would moan about her hard lot, but she would not have taken such a drastic step. There is, also, the wife of the second degree. I'm not sure what to think about her.'

Briefly she told the story of Frann and of Mahon's very generous provision for this late marriage and for a possible son.

'If it were Frann, she would have had to tramp through the snow so afterwards her gown would have been soaked. You might see if you can find something out from the maidservant if that is the case.'

'It's so good to be able to talk things through with you, Patrick,' said Mara gratefully. 'You see Ellice, Conor the *tánaiste*'s wife, is on my mind.' She told him about the episode where the girl aimed the arrow straight at Turlough's heart and finished: 'but, of course, anyone going from the guest house to the church would be much more noticeable than someone who just had to come down the night stairs.'

'Ay,' Patrick nodded.

'So if the king were the intended victim, then Murrough could have entered dry-shod, and then stolen away again up the night stairs – he may not even have put on his boots.'

'Ay,' Patrick nodded again. The Brehon MacEgan had told her that Patrick's nickname was 'the man of short judgements' and Mara could see why. It was funny, though, but talking with him, or perhaps explaining things to Fachtnan and Shane, seemed to be clearing her mind.

'What about the blood?' asked Shane suddenly. 'Wouldn't there be blood all over the clothes of someone who did that?'

'I thought about that,' said Mara, 'but the mallet that dealt the blow had a very long handle on it. I think that it would be quite likely that the murderer would not have got blood on him, or her.'

'Any way of doing a discreet search?' asked Patrick.

'Perhaps we could do it now while they are all in the church.' Shane jumped to his feet, full of the burning energy of a ten-year-old for whom nothing is as tiring as sitting still.

'I think we are too late,' said Mara regretfully. 'Listen; there's the bell. That is the passing bell.'

The clang of the bell came very clearly, borne towards them by the north-westerly wind. They sat very quietly counting the years of the man who had died that morning.

'Ten, eleven . . .' Shane began to count aloud and then stopped. They all listened intently. The bell had stopped tolling. There was a silence for a few minutes and then voices. For the second time that day there was a great clamour of voices. Mara moved quickly to the window and flung open the casement.

Monks, lay brothers and guests, they were all pouring out of the church from the west door. All were shouting the same words. They were calling her; she could hear her name, but there other words, also, that rose high above the strong westerly wind.

'The assassin again!'

Twelve

Berrad Oireachta
(Synopsis of Court Procedure)
Heptad Forty-Nine

Some persons are excluded from giving evidence in court. These are:
- *A slave*
- *A castaway*
- *A landless man*
- *An alien, an insane or senile person*
- *A prostitute*
- *A robber*
- *And a man who ingratiates himself with everyone*

In a second Mara was out of the parlour and tugging at the heavy oak door to the Royal Lodge. She was vaguely conscious of someone, Fachtnan perhaps, draping her mantle around her shoulders and then she was outside. The rain was pouring down and light was fading fast, but her eyes were fixed on Teige O'Brien who was running across the slushy grass of the garth.

'Brehon!' he was shouting. 'The murderer has tried again.'

And then, from behind him, Ardal O'Lochlainn: 'The king is safe, Brehon, but he only escaped by a few inches.'

Mara stopped, breathing slowly and deeply and trying to concentrate. 'What happened, Ardal?' she asked.

He looked white and shaken, she noticed, and Teige O'Brien's high colour had deepened to purple.

'Come and see for yourself, Brehon.' He turned and walked beside her as she began to move forward. Patrick walked on the other side, a restraining hand on his son's shoulder. 'We were all standing there saying the prayer for the dead and the bell began to toll, the passing bell, and then suddenly a huge chunk of limestone came crashing down and just missed the king by inches. In fact,' here Ardal hesitated for a moment, and then continued quietly, 'it's by the blessing of Our Lord that you yourself were not killed.'

Mara hardly noticed his last words. 'Please go back into the church, everyone!' she called loudly and then, as they all turned meekly to do her bidding, she said quietly: 'Ardal, will you go instantly to the abbot and get him to lock the door to the cloisters and then as soon as everyone is back inside the church he is to lock the west door. Will you, yourself, stand by the cloisters' door until this is done?'

'I'll stand by the west door,' said Patrick, and quickly he strode ahead of her, still keeping Shane with him and keenly looking at the faces as one by one they obeyed the Brehon's orders and filed back into the church.

Mara turned around. 'Fachtnan, go around the buildings and the gates and make sure that no one is lurking.' She hesitated for a moment, wondering if it were safe for him to do that, and then breathed a sigh of relief as a stocky figure pushed his way towards her. 'Ah, Cumhal, there you are, will you go with Fachtnan?' The boy would be safe with Cumhal. She noticed that her farm manager had already slid his knife from his pouch and held it purposefully in his hand.

Mara waited a couple of moments to make sure that everyone had gone back into the church and then glanced all around. There seemed to be no sign of anyone other than Fachtnan and Cumhal and she knew that she could rely on them to make a thorough search of the buildings around the cloister.

When she entered the church, the noise of conversation immediately ceased. Turlough came towards her but she did not look at him. He was safe; that was all that she needed to know, but the next few minutes could be vital if the killer was to be caught. The church was well lit by candlelight and she could see around clearly.

Two chairs had been placed for herself and Turlough at the top of the nave, quite close to the crossing screen. The chairs were placed a distance of about three feet from each other. When he had first seen the arrangement, Turlough had joked about the abbot fearing that they might hold hands during the church services. The king's chair was large and ornate with carved arms and a well-cushioned seat. Mara's chair, though also ornately carved, was smaller and without arms. A linen kneeler, well stuffed with springy wool, lay on the floor in front of each chair.

The king's chair was untouched, but little remained of the Brehon's chair. A large rounded block of limestone lay smashed on the floor, with the splintered chair beneath it. There was no doubt that if Mara had been in her usual place she would have been killed. However, her eyes did not linger on the floor. She glanced quickly upwards and the jagged, torn hole in the thin timber overhead confirmed that the block had fallen from the bell loft. By some extraordinary mercy it had not fallen on the king.

Ardal, Mara was glad to see, had taken up his position by the door to the cloisters on the south side of the church and the abbot was just locking it. No one else was near by. She glanced back. Patrick was standing like a limestone saint squarely in the middle of the closed west door and again no one was near to him. She waited until the abbot had locked that door also and then spoke:

'My lord abbot, with your permission, I would request everyone to go to the exact spot of the church where they were standing before the block fell.'

In a few minutes the untidy clumps of terrified people were ranged in orderly rows. Even the abbot himself went to the stone chair by the altar and lowered himself gracefully on to its seat. Ardal waited until all were in place before moving quietly to his position next to Teige O'Brien. Mara looked around. The choir monks were in the benches on either side of the chancel, seven seated beside the prior, Father Peter, and eight on the bench behind the abbot's chair. The lay brothers and servants, including the two travellers, the carpenter and the mason all stood modestly in four rows at the back of the nave, near to the west door. Chairs had been placed at the top of the nave for the guests. In the centre were the two elaborately carved and cushioned chairs for King Turlough Donn and his intended bride, Mara, Brehon of the Burren, placed at a discreet yard or so apart. Behind them ranged simple *sugán* chairs for the other guests, their straw-rope seats and backs softened by some linen-covered, down-filled cushions.

They are all there, thought Mara, all except for Conor and his wife Ellice. Murrough was next to the empty chairs for Conor and his wife. Just behind were Teige O'Brien and Finn O'Connor with their wives, Ardal O'Lochlainn and Garrett MacNamara – Garrett's wife had chosen to spend Christmas with her own people in Galway, so he, like the unmarried Ardal, was alone. And then there was another empty chair where Mahon O'Brien had sat, Banna in the chair beside his, then a gap and there was Frann wrapped in her furred mantle.

'My lord abbot and you, Father Peter, could you confirm that all brothers, servants and guests of the abbey are here?'

They both rose and each came solemnly down the church, holding a candle. They hardly glanced at the chairs at the top of the nave, but carefully scrutinize the rows in the dim light of the back of the church.

'All are present, Brehon,' said the abbot after a few minutes.

'Thank you,' said Mara. 'Now I know that my servant, Cumhal, is missing as I sent him on an errand, but could the guests turn around and check that their servants are all present.'

All turned around. Neither Ardal nor Garrett had brought a servant, she guessed, by their perfunctory glances, but Banna left her chair and walked down and then came back.

'My servants are here, Brehon,' she said.

'Of course, the king's son and his wife are not here,' said Mara. 'Did they also have servants?' She looked at Turlough who shrugged and looked at his bodyguards.

'We are both here, Brehon,' said an elderly woman from the back of the church. 'My lady told us to go to church and she would look after the *tánaiste*.'

So Ellice had stayed with her sick husband. That was not like her, thought Mara.

'Father Peter, could you go and make sure that the *tánaiste* and his wife are well and have not been alarmed by any noise,' she said aloud. She wished that she could go herself, but there was more that she had to do here. Strange that the noise and the abrupt cessation of the bell had not brought Ellice to the window; Conor, of course, was probably sunken into a poppy syrup-induced sleep.

Mara waited until the abbot had ceremoniously escorted Father Peter to the door leading to the cloisters. He unlocked it, then relocked it but did not resume his seat. No doubt he expected

Father Peter to return within a few minutes. Mara noticed how he and Father Denis seemed to exchange a quick glance. She beckoned to the rows at the back of the church.

'Please come forward everyone and stand here behind the chairs. Everyone keep in the same order.'

That was better: the candlelight illuminated all faces.

'Now I would like everyone to think carefully and tell me if anyone in the church arrived late or if anyone left their place for any reason?' She looked carefully around. As far as she could see, there was no uneasiness on any face. Patrick had left his position by the west door and had walked up quietly following the others. He also was scanning faces, she noticed.

'I saw no one arrive late, or move once the service had begun,' said Ardal solemnly and the other guests murmured an agreement.

'And no one moved at this end of the church, Brehon,' said Brigid with a quick toss of her head meant to emphasize her superior position to the other servants.

That was evidence worth having, thought Mara. There would be more chance for a rat, crossing a moonlit yard, to evade a watching owl than for anything to escape Brigid's eye. So that meant that everyone, except Ellice, was accounted for.

'So who tolled the passing bell?' she asked. No sooner was the question uttered than suddenly she realized how this attempt at murder could have taken place.

'I did, Brehon,' said a voice and a very young monk stepped forward. He looked white and shaken and Mara gave him a quick smile and a nod.

'Show me where you stood,' she said encouragingly and when he obediently took up his position with his hand on the bell rope she exclaimed quickly: 'Don't pull the rope!'

They all looked at her with puzzled faces. She glanced over at Turlough and saw him nod his head. He at least understood her meaning. He was standing with his back to the wall, with the two bodyguards flanking either side. She wished he were back in Thomond, or even within the walls of Cahermacnaghten Law School. Certainly there was no safety for him here until the assassin was caught.

There was a tap at the cloisters' door and the abbot opened

it to admit the small, thin figure of Father Peter. He came straight across to Mara.

'The *tánaiste* is sleeping peacefully and his lady wife is with him,' he said to her and gave a brief bow in the direction of the king.

'Father Abbot, will you permit Father Peter to show me the bell loft?' she said. Without waiting for an answer, she took a large candle from a side altar and walked across to the stairs where she stood waiting for the little monk as he came scurrying across the tiles with a deprecating glance at his superior.

'This way, Brehon,' he said aloud as he led the way up the wooden staircase. He stopped for an instant at the top of the stairs. To their left was a passage. Mara moved along it and saw that it connected to the night stairs leading to the dormitories. She grimaced. This was going to make her work more difficult. She had hoped that the mason or the carpenter might be able to tell her if anyone had mounted the stairs from the church to the bell loft at some time during the afternoon, but now it looked possible for anyone to get there in secrecy. However, it also showed how someone could have got into the church during the service. Once again the picture of Ellice came into her mind. She returned to Father Peter.

'Were they both there?' she whispered.

He didn't pretend to misunderstand her. 'They were both there, Brehon. There were no signs that she had been out. I had a good look at her gown and there were no wet marks on the hem of it.'

Mara smiled in the darkness. There was no reason to regret that she could not go herself; Father Peter made a worthy deputy.

'It must have been something to do with the bell,' she said quietly and he nodded.

'You think the rope dislodged the stone?'

Mara shook her head. 'I don't think so. Otherwise the stone would have fallen immediately. I wondered about the vibrations.'

The monk nodded thoughtfully. 'I'd say that you have the right of it. Sometimes the whole tower seems to sway with the sound of the bell. Anyway, you can see for yourself.'

It was obvious once Mara lifted her candle. A crude slope had been built with a plank propped up on a piece of wood. The rounded lump of limestone had been placed on it, probably carried up from the church, and once the tolling of the bell had begun then, sooner or later, the piece of limestone would start to roll.

'Carefully done,' said Father Peter thoughtfully. 'It's strange, though . . .'

Mara looked at him. 'What's strange?' She knew what he was going to say – it had immediately struck her.

'I would say,' the monk's eyes were hooded and his thin lips were pulled in over the toothless gums as if he sucked on the words before delivering them, 'I would say that the stone was intended to fall on your chair rather than the king's.' He let a silence elapse before adding, 'And, of course, that is exactly where it did land.'

'Why should anyone want to kill me?'

The monk smiled, a toothless smile full of ancient wisdom which only very young babies and very old men seemed to possess.

'Perhaps someone is afraid that you know the truth,' he suggested.

Mara said nothing, but her answering smile was rueful and it betrayed the confusion in her mind. Father Peter tilted his head to one side observing her with small bright eyes.

'The truth will come to you,' he said softly. 'Trust to God; He will open your eyes.' He looked at her keenly and then added: 'Your mind may already hold the key and some word, some sign, will reveal all to you. But in the meantime, keep yourself safe. The enemy is within the fold; the killing will not stop until all is uncovered.' He led the way down the staircase, saying aloud over his shoulder: 'The church has been open all day and people have been coming and going saying prayers at the shrine of the king's ancestor. No bells were rung all day so it will be impossible to find who could have placed that stone ready for the first vibration of the bell to set it rolling.'

Mara smiled to herself. The words would have been clearly audible to everyone in the church. Father Peter was sending a clear message that no single person could be suspected of this latest deed. However, she would have to go through the motions. Her experience had taught her that the more questions that are asked the more chance there was of uncovering the truth. Her father, Brehon of the Burren for over twenty years, had a favourite saying quoted from the wise old judge, Fíthail: 'Without knowing the truth a Brehon stands on water'. Her own safety was of small consequence; the essential was to uphold the law and keep the peace of the kingdom.

Rapidly she crossed the floor and went to stand beside Turlough. He was safe where he was, flanked by his two devoted body-guards, with his back to the wall and she had no wish for him to move.

'Thank you, Conall,' she murmured as he moved to make room for her and then in her clear, carrying voice, she said: 'Move forward, everyone. Please stand here around me.'

There were about fifty people present, she decided, doing a few rapid sums in her head: sixteen choir monks, about twenty lay brothers and servants, and then there were the guests and their servants as well as the two workmen.

'Anyone who has not entered the church between the end of dinner and the beginning of vespers, please move back,' she said.

There was a certain amount of shuffling and then the lay brothers under the eye of their abbot stepped back in one solid body. No doubt they were kept busy about their work and would have no time for odd visits to the church. These were followed by about half of the choir monks and then Finn O'Connor and his wife moved back, accompanied by Garrett MacNamara. Ardal stayed firmly in his position, as did Teige O'Brien and his wife. Banna visibly wavered. No doubt she was weighing up the consequences between appearing cold-hearted and neglectful of her husband's remains and the dangers of being implicated in a murder attempt. Mara could see her cast a suspicious eye at the blooming face of Frann, peeping out from her fur-lined hood, but Frann just smiled cheerfully and stayed where she was. Banna gave her a scornful glance and then, with a heavy sigh, moved away and sat down on the nearest chair. Frann promptly took another chair and placed her hand ostentatiously on her belly. The abbot turned away distastefully and Mara smothered a smile.

'So neither Banna nor Frann visited the church,' she remarked aloud.

Frann nodded and Banna stared at her rival with dislike. 'That girl did go out, though. I saw her from the window.'

'Did you go out, Frann?' asked Mara.

Frann nodded. 'In my condition I have to take a short walk twice a day; the physician advises it.' She smiled maliciously, observing Banna from the corner of her eye.

'But you did not go into the church?'

Frann shook her head so vigorously that the hood tumbled back and her black shining hair fell in loose curls over her face.

'She walked around the cloisters with me, Brehon,' said Ardal. His fair, slightly freckled skin flushed with embarrassment and his eyes slid away from her enquiring glance and rested for a moment on Frann.

Well, well, thought Mara, that is interesting. I wonder is Ardal smitten at last after all those years when every father with a marriageable daughter, in the three kingdoms, has been angling for his attention?

'And you saw Frann go back indoors without visiting the church, Ardal?' she asked.

He bowed. 'That is correct, Brehon. I visited the church myself afterwards to say a prayer for the husband of my cousin.'

'I see. And was there anyone else in the church, while you were there?'

'No one, Brehon,' said Ardal. 'The church was quite empty,' he added with his usual precision.

Mara nodded. 'Father Abbot?'

'I went in twice,' said the abbot briefly. 'Once to talk with the mason and once to say a prayer.'

'And was there anyone there the second time?'

'No,' he said with emphasis. 'The church was empty and I went to find Master Mason. I found him in the lay dormitory.'

Probably taking a quick drink from his *brocóit* flagon, thought Mara, but she wasn't interested in a wandering mason's drink habit. If the abbot had gone up the night stairs, it would only have taken him an extra minute to go into the bell loft and set up the deadly trap. He had spent all of his life, from the time he was not much more than a boy, in this abbey. He, of all people, would know the effect of the vibrations of the bell once it had begun to toll.

'Did you visit the bell tower?' she enquired innocently.

He frowned heavily and tried the effect of an icy stare on her. A silence ensued. Mara raised her eyebrows slightly.

'No, I did not,' he said eventually.

Mara glanced over at the mason and the carpenter, who were waiting patiently beside one of the pillars to her left. The carpenter was looking bored, obviously waiting for this to finish so that he could get on with his work; the mason, however, was looking at the abbot. Again, like earlier in the day, there was that strange, slightly appraising look of a man who knew more than he was saying. She addressed them both.

'You would both have been working here throughout the day,' she said, watching their faces carefully. 'You would have seen if anyone came into the church. Could you turn around now and tell me if any of those who have withdrawn entered the church at any time between dinner and vespers.'

The mason shook his head, but the carpenter roused himself to scan the faces of the lay brothers.

'That young brother, there,' he said, pointing, 'he came over to tell us that the cook had a warm drink waiting for us in the kitchen. You see, Brehon, our hands get very cold working here hour after hour so we take five minutes in the warmth and get the feeling back into our fingers. The abbot permits that.' He was fluent and confident and the finger he pointed unwaveringly indicated Brother Francis.

'Could you step forward, please, brother,' said Mara. She waited until he had done so before proceeding. 'You are Brother Francis from the abbey of Knockmoy, are you not?' She decided not to mention that he was an O'Kelly, one of a clan that was at war with King Turlough Donn O'Brien.

He gave a half-nod and a quick glance at the abbot. Mara slid her eyes in the direction also. The abbot was looking annoyed, but that was a fairly permanent expression with him. He did not look ill at ease, she decided. She turned back to the carpenter.

'Master Carpenter, can you remember whether the young brother accompanied you back to the kitchen?'

'No, he didn't, Brehon. I remember that when he delivered his message that he knelt down in front of the altar and crossed himself.'

'A perfectly proper action for a brother.' The abbot's intervention was delivered in dry, measured tones but his glance at

Brother Francis was curiously intent, almost, thought Mara, as if some message was delivered.

'And did you go up to the bell tower?' she continued, looking hard at the young face.

He shook his head. 'No, Brehon, I just said a quick prayer and then left. I'm sorry that it escaped my memory.'

'I see,' said Mara continuing to study him. 'Ah,' she said as a knock sounded on the door to the cloisters, 'that will be Fachtnan and Cumhal. Any sign?' she asked as the two slid past the abbot and entered.

Fachtnan shook his head, 'No, Brehon,' he replied. 'Only the *tánaiste* and his wife are in the guest house; the rest of the buildings are empty.'

Mara nodded: 'Perhaps, Father Abbot,' she said politely, 'everyone who was not in the church between vespers and dinner could now disperse at your bidding and those others, who did visit the church during that time, could perhaps be questioned in your parlour by my assistant and my colleague, the Brehon from the Tyrone. However, I will ask that no one leave the precincts of the abbey without my express permission. Hopefully this crime of murder will soon be solved, but in the meantime, all must stay here.' She could rely on Patrick to keep the abbot sweet, she thought. Shane, she noticed, had already been taken under Brigid's motherly wing. Without waiting for an answer she walked across to Turlough.

'Stay in the guest house until I arrive,' she said in a rapid undertone. 'Keep Fergal and Conall with you at all times. I think we will eat there tonight.'

'You seem to be in more danger than I.' Turlough looked shaken, she thought, and she hastened to reassure him.

'No, no, I'll keep Cumhal with me, but I think that was just a case of the stone rolling to the right, and thank God that it did.'

'I always did say that too much church-going was bad for your health,' said Turlough with a grin. He had obviously believed her reassuring words. He was as brave as a lion, himself, and would face any danger, but a possible danger to Mara had shaken him momentarily. She did not know the truth of that latest planned assignation but she knew that she had to ensure that he was safe.

Only her own brains and perhaps some luck could bring a happy conclusion to this Christmas-tide mystery.

Mara watched the church clear of people. She said no more until they had all gone, except Cumhal, who in response to a quick nod from her waited discreetly at the end of the church, then she turned to the mason. The carpenter had picked up the splintered chair and had carried it to his workbench close to where Cumhal stood. She had no further questions for him, but it occurred to her that there was a question that she had not asked, a question to which the mason would have an answer.

'This block of limestone that fell from the bell tower, Master Mason, how heavy would that have been?'

He looked back at her impassively.

'Not very heavy, Brehon.'

'Not for you, perhaps, but could a woman have carried it upstairs?'

He shrugged and turned his face away, sorting through some un-worked pieces of limestone. He probably did not know the answer to that question, she thought. His muscles would have been trained by this work from the time that he was a boy; a weight that would be impossible for a woman would be of little consequence to him. There was only one way to find out: she came near to him, bent down and picked up a block similar in size to the one that had tumbled down from the bell loft. The weight surprised her, but she staggered off resolutely towards the night stairs.

'No need to carry it up; that stone was up in the bell tower already.' His voice was so husky that for a moment she could hardly understand the words, but then as their import reached her she thankfully placed the heavy lump on Ardal's chair and turned back to him.

'How do you know?' she asked.

He came across the floor, lifting the block from the chair and replacing it as if were feather light, before answering.

'I know that piece of limestone,' he said with a brief glance over to where the smashed remains still lay on top of the splin-tered chair.

Mara's eyes followed his. Her attention had been fixed on the broken chair earlier and she had not scrutinized the stone that had caused the damage, but now she could see a rounded forehead, a carved eyelid and she realized that it was a large head.

'St Bernard,' said the mason. 'You find him a lot in Cistercian abbeys. The wooden bell tower was only put up fifty years ago. That head was probably moved then and never replaced. The tower has not been finished; the plans are to build it from stone and to extend it down here to ground level. The head will probably be replaced when that happens.'

Mara pondered. If that heavy block of limestone were already in the bell loft, then it would have been a matter of minutes for the assassin to put it in place.

'But no one was seen to go to the bell loft,' she said aloud, almost speaking to herself.

The mason had already begun to chip at his block, but he stopped at the sound of her voice.

'No one,' he said in husky voice, 'that a wise man would see.'

Mara considered this. It was perhaps an invitation.

'A wise man would tell what he saw and leave it to the Brehon to protect him,' she said neutrally.

'Who can protect against the king's son,' he said. And now his voice was almost inaudible.

Mara moved closer to him and said a rapid undertone, 'There is no danger. I would never betray your confidence. Tell what you know and tell it quickly.'

He looked at her doubtfully and then seemed to make up his mind. 'The king's son, he who disguised himself as a pilgrim . . .'

'Murrough,' she said and he nodded.

'He came into the church. I heard him with the abbot. I think they were putting away the bow and arrows. He, Murrough, lingered. I was in the vault, measuring up the space. I don't think that he saw me. I thought nothing of it at the time. What is the old saying? 'A king's son may go, where a humble man may not follow.' It was not for people like myself to question him.'

'He lingered?' queried Mara. 'In the nave? By the altar?'

'I heard him go up the steps to the bell loft.' The mason's gruff voice was emphatic. He stroked his white beard, turning his head away from her glance and bent over his work again. She thought he would say no more, but then he added in a curiously formal phrase: 'I know not what he did up there.'

Thirteen

Din Techtugad
(On Legal Entry)

False witness is one of the three falsehoods which God avenges most severely on a Tuáth (kingdom).

Di Astud Chirt Agus Dligid
(On the Confirmation of Right and Law)

The three worst afflictions in the world are:
- *Famine*
- *The slaughter of a people*
- *Plague*

To avoid these disasters no man must swear false oaths or give false testimony.

It was quite dark by the time that Mara emerged from the church. A faint watery strip of moonlight showed through the speeding clouds, just enough to cast a dim light on the shadowy path that skirted the cloisters. From behind her she could hear the voices of the carpenter and the mason; night was closing in now and their work would be finishing. Candlelight sparkled from the closed shutters of the abbot's house and the sound of voices came from within. Mara rapped on the door and Teige O'Brien immediately opened it.

'How's Turlough?' he whispered with a quick glance over his shoulder to make sure that his words were heard by her only.

'I don't know,' she said, surprised. 'I've been in the church. Why? Have you heard anything?' Despite herself, she could not help a note of alarm. It was only about ten minutes since she had seen Turlough, but she had a feeling that events were leading up to a climax.

'No, nothing.' He hastened to reassure her. 'It's just that so many things seem to be happening so quickly. It's hard to believe that Mahon's death only happened nine or ten hours ago. Come inside by the fire. Let me take your mantle.'

He bustled around her, helping her to shed the heavily furred mantle, hanging it up on one of a row of pegs in the narrow passageway that led to the stairs and then ushering her into the parlour.

All voices ceased when she entered. Teige took her over to the fireplace and plumped up the cushions on the padded bench that stood at right angles to the blazing fire. There was a flagon of spiced ale standing on the stone hob beside the chimney and he poured her a cup and handed it to her. Mara accepted it gratefully; the church had been icy-cold. She sipped it eagerly and then glanced around.

The abbot's parlour was a small room and yet the groups of people seemed to keep at a distance from each other almost as if they feared the thrust of an assassin's knife if they stood too close. To her amusement, most seemed to stand with their backs firmly pressed against one of the walls. Finn O'Connor and his wife were chatting loudly together about a long-past Christmas. Father Denis was pretending to leaf through a prayer book; though his eyes flashed from beneath his lids as he took quick surreptitious glances around the room. Brother Francis stood beside him, muttering in his ear. Ardal, near the window, was being gallant to Flann, shielding her from the cold wind that blew through the shutters, while his cousin, Banna, standing against the opposite wall, glared at him furiously and then turned to mutter to Teige's wife, Ciara O'Brien. Strange, thought Mara. Neither Frann nor Banna had admitted visiting the church and yet here they both were, doubtless to give their evidence.

'The two wives of my poor cousin have remembered saying a prayer for his soul,' whispered Teige, following the direction of her eyes.

'I see,' returned Mara, her voice as low as his. 'Who remembered first?'

'Frann, I think. When Ardal left her to go into the abbot's house she suddenly remembered.' Teige had turned so that his back was now to the room. There was an amused smile on his lips.

He reminded Mara of Turlough. He had the same mischievous twinkle in his pale green eyes and the same generous mouth under the large war-like moustache. It was interesting how alike all these cousins were, and yet how different their destinies. Turlough, Teige, Mahon and the abbot were all cousins, all grandsons of the same man, and yet the one was king of three kingdoms, two were mere *taoiseach*s of minor clans and the last was just a head monk of a small obscure abbey.

Mara turned her head back to look all around the room again. There was no sign of the abbot. He must be in with Fachtnan and Patrick. She would not interrupt, she thought. It was good for Fachtnan to have this responsibility. Hopefully he would pass his final examination this year and then he would be a qualified lawyer. Conducting an investigation like this would be valuable experience for him, if he ever managed to become a Brehon.

'Teige,' she said. 'Would you go and fetch Ellice over here? Father Peter will be with Conor so she can leave him for the moment.'

I'll deal with her myself, she thought. This matter has to be cleared up by tomorrow. She leaned back for a moment and closed her eyes. Banna was whispering loudly to Teige's wife, Ciara, saying something about a son – perhaps Mahon had told her that Frann was expecting – perhaps this business with dangling a ring above a pregnant stomach was a well-known way of forecasting the sex of the unborn child.

'I know,' said Ciara in a low, soothing voice. 'That's men for you; a son is all-important to them. Take Teige, for instance. You wouldn't believe what he's like with Donal, our eldest. He'd give him the moon and stars if he could. Anything that boy wants, he has to have immediately. Sometimes, I think that the rest of us matter less to him than Donal's little finger.'

'Mahon was saying that . . .' Banna was beginning to sound more cheerful. No doubt the familiar gossip about the short-comings of husbands was raising her spirits. From under her eyelids Mara could see how the bereaved widow cast a quick glance in the Brehon's direction and then, apparently reassured that she would be unheard, went on in a sibilant whisper:

'Mahon was saying that Teige only wanted to be *tánaiste* so as to pass the office on to his son. Many of the *fine* and two or three of the septs wanted Mahon for *tánaiste* and as many wanted Teige.'

'That's true,' agreed Ciara. 'Well, as God is my witness, Banna, I wouldn't say this to many, but I've heard that no one wants a boy dying of the wasting sickness for *tánaiste*.' Frann was now laughing uproariously at a remark by Ardal so Ciara obviously saw no reason to lower her voice as she added: 'Of course, if Turlough had been killed this morning, then Conor would have been king and Teige the *tánaiste*.'

'You're probably right,' agreed Banna, indifferent to the claims of her erring husband. 'Though I'd say that the chances would be that Teige would have been elected king and then young Donal would have been the *tánaiste*.'

Interesting, thought Mara, more amused than shocked at the casual way that these two middle-aged matrons discussed the death of their king. Would Conor really have been rejected? And if so, would Murrough, rather than the easy-going Teige, have been elected?

'I'll tell you something else . . .' whispered Ciara and then stopped abruptly as the parlour door was opened and the un-assuming figure of Fachtnan appeared. Every eye immediately turned to him and all conversations ceased.

'Would you come in now, *ban tighernae*?' he said, looking over at Banna and Ciara. Both rose to their feet and then Banna sank down again as Ciara swept past her. Of course, Banna was no longer to be addressed as *ban tighernae*: that title ceased at the death of her husband.

The parlour was very silent for a few moments after she had gone. Mara looked around. Had anyone overheard that conversation between Ciara and Banna, she wondered. She thought not. Murrough was the nearest as he stood leaning on the mantel-piece over the fireplace, his face imperturbable and his mouth curved in a mocking smile as he surveyed the huddled figures around him. He might have heard, she decided; his smile seemed to show that he had not thought much of the surmising. She gazed at him speculatively and he turned and faced her with his eyebrows raised interrogatively. She lowered her eyes, but under her eyelashes she saw him leave the fireplace and cross the room to join Ardal and Frann by the window.

So what was the solution to this mystery? A small number of people, all within the one enclave: this should be an easy crime to solve. And yet her mind had gone through all the evidence, again and again, but without a solution. Deliberately she shut her eyes quite tightly, this time. In her mind she imagined names written in black charcoal on the whitewashed wall of the schoolhouse at Cahermacnaghten. Each name had a large black question mark beside it. Suddenly Mara seemed to see her way clearly. She stayed very still and then, one by one through her closed eyelids, she could see the names being wiped off the wall by the damp sponge that she kept on the window ledge beside it; soon only one name would remain and then she would know the truth. She remembered Father Peter's words. '*The truth will come to you,*' he had said. '*Trust to God; He will open your eyes.*' He had looked at her keenly and then added: '*Your mind may already hold the key and some word, some sign, will reveal all to you.*' A wise man, thought Mara. He had the wisdom that sometimes comes from a life of self-sacrifice and prayer. And he was correct; the truth had been there all the time, right at the back of her mind.

'Ah, Brehon, I hope you have been looked after. I've just been talking with the Brehon from Tyrone, telling him all the details of this terrible affair.' The abbot was looking pleased with himself, she thought, as she opened her eyes and smiled sleepily at him. No doubt Patrick had handled him carefully and Fachtnan, always a boy of great tact, would have played the role of silent, young assistant very carefully.

'The Brehon decided to take the kitchen for the private conversations – does that suit you?' he continued. 'He would like to speak to Father Denis now.' He raised an imperious finger and Father Denis hastened to leave the room. His young, narrowly handsome face looked tense, thought Mara, stealing a quick look at him while the abbot's unfriendly eyes were on his son. She moved up the bench, hospitably leaving room for the abbot near to the fire. He took his seat gratefully and stretched his long thin fingers out to the fire. The kitchen was probably chillier than this room and he seemed to luxuriate in the heat for a moment before adding: 'Do you wish to join him?'

'No, no,' Mara knew she sounded sleepy and relaxed. There was a question that she needed to ask and she thought now was the moment that she could insert it without too much significance attached.

'So was Turlough embarrassed when he told you that he had changed his mind about taking the first hour of the vigil?' She allowed a slight tinge of amusement to colour her voice and, listening to her question critically, she thought it sounded the right note.

The abbot smiled in return. 'I don't think he wanted to tell me himself – perhaps he had a little too much to drink that night. He left it to his cousin to tell me.' His voice was indulgent – a man without faults making an allowance for a man with many.

'Mahon, your brother?' queried Mara.

'No, no, it was Teige who came to me with the message from the king. I must say that I was a little upset. I asked Teige whether he could take the king's place. He laughed it off; he said that he intended to sleep until ten in the morning,' explained the abbot, a slight crease of annoyance deepening between his brows. 'I asked him to tell the king that I felt that he should honour his promise given before so many witnesses. I did not receive a message back, but then I thought that I should ensure that someone was there in case the king defaulted. So I sent a note to Mahon. I thought it was the least he could do.' For a moment his face darkened and then he made a perfunctory sign of the cross on his breast and added: 'May the Lord have mercy on his soul.'

'I see,' said Mara thoughtfully. She decided not to question the abbot about why he felt his brother owed him a favour. She had heard Father Peter's evidence about the quarrel between the brothers and Frann had corroborated that. There was a knock at the door and she rose to her feet.

'That will be Teige with Ellice,' she said. 'I'll let them in; don't disturb yourself. You've had a hard day,' she added solicitously and he looked back up at her gratefully.

Ellice was alone when Mara opened the door to her. She appeared white-faced and uneasy.

'Here, let me take your cloak. You shouldn't have come out on that wet ground in such thin shoes. And look at your hair; it's all wet. You should have put up the hood of your mantle,' she scolded, drawing the girl inside and warming the icy young hands

within her own. The motherliness wasn't feigned; by the light of
the torch on the wall of the small entrance hall to the abbot's
house Mara could see the depth of unhappiness and almost desper-
ation in the thin young face and the black eyes seemed filled
with misery. There was no doubt that the girl was suffering.

'I'm all right.' Ellice gave her usual shrug.

'You must look after yourself. We can't have you falling ill as
well. And you had no cloak on either when you went out to
fetch something for Conor while your servants were at vespers,
did you?' Mara moved slightly so that the full torchlight was on
Ellice. She watched carefully, but there was nothing but bewilderment to be seen.

'I didn't go out then, Brehon,' she said in a puzzled tone. 'I
stayed with Conor the whole time. Why do you think that I
went out?' Suddenly she caught her breath. 'I know what it is.
Someone is trying to put the blame on to me. You don't think
that I had anything to do with that stone crashing down, do
you?'

Mara said nothing. The tone sounded genuinely surprised, but
Mara did not respond. She had learned the value of silence when
interrogating. Sooner or later, the guilty person usually said too
much.

'Who is it who is supposed to have seen me?' Now Ellice's
tone was aggressive. 'Whoever they were, they must be lying.' She
faced Mara angrily. And yet, thought Mara, there is something
feigned about that anger. Somehow there was a shadow of guilt
over the girl. But was it guilt because she was betraying her sick
husband and allowing another man to court her, and perhaps
make love to her? Or was there perhaps a graver reason for this
guilt? In either case, there was no point in prolonging the conversation. She would get no more out of Ellice. From outside came
the sound of heavy footsteps and then a tap at the door. That
would be Teige who had probably lingered to have a word with
his cousin.

'Ellice, you go into the abbot's parlour,' she said. 'My assistant
and the Brehon from Tyrone are taking notes about each person's
movements during the day. They'll call you when they are ready
for you. Father Denis is in there at the moment.' She watched
the girl's thin face colour up and the dark eyes cloud over at that

name. With desire? With fear? Mara wasn't sure but she knew
that Fachtnan would be careful and methodical in his fact-finding
and Patrick would ask any question that he missed. Ellice could
be safely left to them. She waited until the parlour door closed
before opening the outside door and saying softly: 'Did you see
Turlough, Teige?'

Teige shook his head. A genial, happy man, she thought. His
wife, Ciara, was genuinely fond of him and he appeared to idolize
all of his children, though, of course, young Donal was the
favourite. 'No, I didn't,' he said, 'but you need not worry about
him. His bodyguards are keeping an excellent watch at the Royal
Lodge. Fergus was at the window of the king's room when I
passed the Royal Lodge, I could see his shadow through the gap
in the shutters, and Conall was marching up and down outside.
I saw your own servant, Cumhal, looking out of the kitchen
window when I knocked on the door of the guest house.'

'And Conor?' she asked. 'How is he?'

'Not too well, poor lad,' he said. 'He was sleeping, but he was
as white as snow. I think,' he said echoing his wife's words, 'that
Turlough will have to face the possibility that a sick boy like that
cannot be *tánaiste* – even if he lives for a while longer, he's just
not suitable.'

'So it may be that the king will have to call a meeting to elect
a new *tánaiste*, in the New Year.' Mara sounded thoughtful. 'Do
you think that, now Murrough has come back, he will be the
choice of the clan?'

His face darkened with anger. 'Never,' he said emphatically.
'I'm not saying that because I would hope to be king myself.
What good would it be to me to be king? Turlough and I are
the same age. The chances are that I will die before him, or not
long after him. All the same I would hate to see the O'Briens
ruled by a man like Murrough.'

Mara nodded in a satisfied way. He had told her what she
wanted to know. 'Do you know whether Murrough has been
interviewed?'

'He was the first,' said Teige shortly. His tone was harsh. Did
he dislike his cousin's younger son because of former wrong-
doing, or was it because of a certain rivalry for the position of
tánaiste?

'In that case, I think I'll take Murrough over to his father now. Hand me that torch, Teige. It's quite dark out there and there are patches of ice everywhere.'

'Take care,' he said uncomfortably. He turned and lifted a pitch torch from its stone socket on the wall and handed it to her carefully. For a moment he looked as if he was going to say more, but then he just repeated the words and by the fierce light of the flaring pine pitch she could see how a worried frown pulled his heavy brows together before he turned to open the parlour door.

'Murrough, come here,' he said roughly. 'The Brehon wishes to speak to you.'

Ardal, to Mara's amusement, had retreated and now Murrough had been left in full possession of the lovely Frann. Despite the disapproving presence of the abbot by the fireside, the two at the window were enjoying themselves. He was whispering something into her ear. Her scarlet mouth was curved into a broad smile and her green-blue eyes shone with youth, vitality and a joy of living.

Murrough took time to whisper something else, which elicited a delightful chuckle from Frann, before he obeyed his cousin's command. Frann looked after him regretfully as he strode across the room looking handsome and alert, his short red cloak swinging from his broad shoulder and contrasting well with his green, tight-fitting hose. There was no doubt that he was a fine figure of a man.

He was everything that a father could want in a son, thought Mara. He had charm, good looks, fine physique, brains, good health – he had everything, except the most necessary thing of all. He lacked integrity. She shared Teige's feeling, no, Murrough would not be a good choice for *tánaiste*, but would Turlough agree to anything else? Somehow in his grief for his sick son, the faults of the other son were being overlooked.

'My lady judge,' he greeted her with his usual charm. 'How very well you are looking! I must say that purple gown so suits you.'

'I was thinking that you and I should have a quick chat before we go across to see your father; it is only right that you should know my feelings and that you should hear what I wish to say to your father about you,' said Mara, firmly, reaching up for her mantle as she spoke.

'Allow me.' He was quick and adroit and obviously schooled in courtly manners. He took her mantle from its peg and arranged it solicitously around her shoulders. He had the front door of the abbot's house open in a second and was bowing gracefully to her as she passed through.

'I meant what I said, you know,' he said as soon as they had started to walk beneath the cloisters' roof. The grass of the central garth was now soaking wet and it seemed easier to walk all the way around the square in front of the chapter house, monks' dormitory and abbot's house on the east side and the refectory and the kitchen on the north side.

'Meant what?' She turned a preoccupied eye on him, holding the torch aloft. All her thoughts were on the interview ahead. What would Turlough say? More importantly, would she wound him by her words?

'How beautiful you are looking?' he said with a smile. 'In fact, as you were sitting by the fire there with the abbot, I was just imagining you on your wedding day with your husband, what was his name?' He pretended to think for a moment while she watched him with amusement. 'What was his name? D . . . D . . . something . . . Dualta, wasn't it?'

'Your memory is getting poor,' she said with a grim smile, walking on ahead of him. 'You knew the name well enough this morning when you were writing that letter to the abbot.'

'Yes,' he went on thoughtfully, ignoring her words, but pausing to snap a last spike of ice from the roof over their heads, 'I was just imagining you, aged fourteen, with your black hair hanging over your shoulders and your green gown matching those lovely hazel eyes, yes, you must have been very lovely.'

'Murrough, stop this nonsense,' said Mara, pausing to allow him to walk beside her. 'You are not impressing me in the least. I need to discuss your future in the kingdom with your father, but first of all, there are a few questions that I need to ask you.'

'I'm listening,' he said with a wide smile.

'And you will give a truthful answer.'

'Of course.' His smile was as false as the rest of him, she decided, but for Turlough's sake she would endeavour to find the truth. If he were not guilty of this killing, and of the attempted killing, then that at least had to be established in deciding where he should make his home now that he was back in Ireland. She walked on, holding the torch to illuminate the stone flags of the path around the cloisters.

'So,' she said lightly, 'you helped the abbot to put away the bow, arrows and target today after dinner?'

From the corner of her eye she saw his head turn. He looked at her guardedly.

'Yes, you saw me yourself. You were the one that declared the pleasant hour of recreation was at an end and, of course, we all as usual instantly bowed to your command.'

There was definitely a note of resentment in his voice. Did Murrough hate her? she wondered. He had been a great favourite with his mother, she remembered Turlough saying. A favourite with both parents, then. He was definitely unhappy at the prospect of this late marriage between his fifty-year-old father, the king, and Mara, the Brehon of the Burren. But did he hate his father, also? She stopped again. She wanted to be able to see his face when she asked her next question.

'So when you put the shooting equipment away, where did you put it?'

'In the press,' he said readily. 'The good abbot, a man of God, keeps his weaponry close to hand in that little wooden press just inside the church.'

'So why did you need to go up to the bell tower, then?' Her question was quick and she hoped to catch him off guard. Indeed, he did look taken aback, but only for a moment. He gave a light laugh and then stepped back and waved to her to precede him through the archway leading from the cloisters to the garth in front of the Royal Lodge.

'So, that's the way of it,' he said in amused tones. 'I see where your questions are leading; you are trying to pin the blame on me for the attempted murder of my father, the king. No, I never went near the bell tower; you're confusing me with the abbot. In any case, why should I try to murder my father? What could I gain by that? Remember Conor is the *tánaiste,* not I. No, I certainly didn't attempt to murder my father, the king, today either in the early morning or at vespers.'

'But perhaps your intended victim this afternoon was me,' she countered quickly, turning around to look directly into his face.

He faced her blandly, his feelings well under his control.

'Who could possibly want your death, my lady judge?' he asked mockingly.

'Because I am Brehon of the Burren,' said Mara steadily. She did not move but stood facing him under the narrow stone archway. 'Because whoever murdered the man this morning may well suspect that I now know who did the deed.'

'And do you?' He made the enquiry smoothly in a carefree voice, but his eyes, so like his father's, watched her intently.

Mara walked on. 'You would not expect me to tell you that,' she said over her shoulder.

'I suspect that you do.' His voice sounded amused, but now she could no longer see him as he was behind her. Fergal, the bodyguard, had opened the shutters of the king's room. She could hear his voice faintly. He was saying something; no doubt telling the king that she was coming. Then the bulky figure of Turlough joined him at the window. Mara caught her breath in a moment's apprehension. How imprudent he was, standing there at an open window with the light behind him, an obvious target for a lurking assassin! She turned sharply so that the light from her torch fell on Murrough and, at the same moment, called out to them:

'I will join you in a minute, my lord. Fergal, please close the shutters again.'

She was obeyed instantly by Fergal, who thrust his slight form in front of the king's bulk, and then closed over the shutters rapidly. She breathed more easily. Did Murrough, under that padded doublet, carry the customary three javelins? She had seen him once at the fair at Coad and his skill was startling. The javelins flew from his hand with only a second's pause between them and each one hit the precise centre of the straw-padded target. She kept the light of the torch shining on him for another moment and saw him grin mockingly. She lowered the torch and hastened towards the Royal Lodge.

'Let me knock at the door,' said Murrough, as he overtook her and then he hammered so vigorously that she only half-heard his words, but as she climbed the steps she knew that she had heard them correctly.

'Yes,' he had said. 'I think you know. I thought when I looked at you there, sitting by the abbot's fire, when you opened those sea-green eyes of yours, I thought that you looked like a marten cat who has seen its prey.'

Fourteen

Críth Gablach
(Ranks in Society)

A king who is overlord of three kingdoms has an honour price of twenty-four séts, twelve ounces of silver or twelve cows. He has responsibility for deciding alliances and for making the most profitable bargains for his people.

Conall answered the knock on the door, but Turlough was already thundering down the stairs and he immediately thrust aside his bodyguard.

'My dear love,' he said, enveloping Mara in one of his bear-like hugs, 'my dear love, I've been worrying about you. I'm a poor warrior to be hiding away in a house while you are out there in danger. The more I think of it, no matter what Fergal says, I think that rock was meant to hit you.'

Mara disentangled herself and cast a quick glance at Fergal. He looked weary. No doubt he had been having a bad time for the last half hour.

'It wasn't a rock,' she said lightly, 'it was the carved head of St Bernard himself, so the mason tells me.'

'Thank God that Brehon from Tyrone arrived and you were not there,' continued Turlough, eyeing her anxiously. 'There's been no threats, no more near escapes, have there? You have been careful, have you not?'

'So careful,' said Mara, 'that I did not even cross the cloister garth by myself. I took your son with me as a guard and protector.'

There was a gleam of humour from Murrough's green eyes, but Mara looked away quickly and kept her face serious as Turlough nodded approvingly.

'Let's go into the parlour,' she said. 'Conall, will you ask Brigid to bring us supper whenever she likes? There is no hurry. You might have yours quite soon, though, while Fergal stays on guard outside the parlour door, and then Fergal can have his. After that will be plenty of time for us.'

'I hope I am invited also,' said Murrough meekly. 'I've heard much of Brigid's famous suppers from my lord.' His beaming smile swept from Mara to his father and Turlough smiled in return. There was an air of relief about him as he looked at his broad-shouldered, handsome son. Mara thought of Teige's words about the unsuitability of the fragile Conor for the position of *tánaiste* and knew that Turlough would have the same thoughts in his mind. He was very fond of his cousin, Teige O'Brien, but every man would prefer a grown son to succeed him.

'Come on,' he said, clouting Murrough affectionately on the shoulder just as if he were a small boy who had been caught stealing apples from the orchard. 'Come in and sit down and behave yourself.'

Murrough meekly took a stool, allowing his father and Mara to occupy the cushioned bench in front of the fire. The parlour was beautifully warm. Brigid had obviously made good friends among the lay brothers and the brazier was heaped with a month's allowance of charcoal. Turlough leaned back with a satisfied smile and slipped an arm around Mara. She allowed it to stay, but sat a little straighter. She wished that Turlough would realize that she was working. However much one side of her wished just to be his wife, there was no denying the decade of training and her years of office as Brehon of the Burren.

'Murrough,' she said crisply. 'I would like to take you back to your arrival here at the abbey yesterday. You came in disguise as a pilgrim. Why was that?'

He turned a lazy eye towards her. 'Because I wasn't sure whether my father would forgive me or not,' he said.

'That doesn't make sense,' said Mara. 'As a pilgrim, there would be no way that you could probe the king's feelings for his disgraced son.'

He winced a little at the word 'disgraced'.

'Perhaps he was afraid that the abbot would not admit him,' interposed Turlough helpfully.

Murrough bowed his head. 'That was it, my lord,' he said meekly.

'And yet, having successfully entered and having seen your

father and your brother, you still did not declare yourself,' she said sharply. This was like a game of chess, she thought, and felt that slight exhilaration that she always experienced when battling with a worthy opponent.

'I was unsure . . . I wondered what to do . . . I wasn't sure whether . . . I wasn't sure if I would be forgiven . . .' Murrough tried to make his tone sound broken and he still hung his head, but Mara was sure that behind the lowered eyelids his eyes would be sparkling with amusement. He, like she, was almost enjoying this encounter.

'Let me put the case, as we say at law school,' she said rapidly. 'You came here in disguise, you kept that disguise all yesterday evening, you made no attempt to make yourself known, not even to your brother or to one of your father's cousins, who might have been able to intercede for you. You hid behind the pilgrim's gown and then, this morning, having heard your father publicly declare, last night, that he would spend the first hour of the day alone, kneeling in front of the tomb of his ancestor, Conor Sudaine O'Brien, you entered the church, swung the mason's mallet and killed the man. What do you say to that?'

From beside her Mara felt Turlough stir uneasily. His arm dropped down and from the corner of her eye she saw him turn to stare into the fire. As always, every fibre of her body was aware of him and she felt his distress as if it were her own. However, this matter could not be swept into a dark corner with the dead rushes; it had to be brought forth into the light of day and examined carefully.

'Why should I want to kill my father?' Murrough's voice was calm and polite.

'Because if your father were dead, the clan would probably instantly elect you as *tánaiste* and then, if Conor died, you would be king.'

Murrough thought about that for a moment and when he spoke there was a note of passionate sincerity in his voice.

'I don't want to be king,' he said flatly.

Beside her, Mara felt Turlough give a start of surprise. She did not look at him but continued to study Murrough. The small parlour was well lit with two large, many-branched candlesticks, each holding a dozen beeswax candles, and she could see his face clearly. For once the mocking look was absent and he looked, not at her, but at his father. His voice was earnest and confident.

'I suppose this is the real reason why I've come,' he said. 'I wanted to talk to you, father. I even wondered whether I could talk to you without you knowing who I was, perhaps disguise my voice or something.'

'Talk now,' said Turlough with an effort. 'I'm listening.'

Mara sat back. This was between father and son. She would listen and judge and afterwards perhaps take up the questioning again. She could see from Murrough's thoughtful face that he was marshalling his arguments.

'You see, father,' said Murrough eagerly, 'I've spent the last few months in the court at Whitehall Palace, in London, and I've listened and I know how things are moving. There is no future in hanging on to this kingship. England is not going to allow Ireland to slip away from under its control. There is money in the coffers now. The re-conquest of Ireland is just a matter of time. Many of the clan leaders already recognize this. You should make terms with the king.'

'I am the king.' Turlough's voice was hard as iron.

'A petty kingdom! No, I meant King Henry VIII of England.'

'I know what you meant, but I still say, I am the king, and while God preserves the breath within my body, I will stay king.'

'No, but father,' Murrough's voice took on a pleading note. 'Just listen to me. If the English decide to conquer the west of Ireland, you cannot stop them. You can't win.'

'I will fight,' said Turlough passionately. 'The O'Donnell will fight, so will Clanrickard; the O'Flaherty will fight until not a drop of blood is left in his body. The MacCarthy and O'Malley of the ships, they will be there. Even O'Kelly, God rot his soul, he would not be absent if our way of life was threatened. We will all fight together.'

'Fight! With what?'

'With swords, javelins, arrows, daggers, with our bare hands if needs be.' Turlough's voice rose to a roar.

'Father, be reasonable. What good are swords and javelins against handguns and cannon? You've seen what a few handguns could do at the battle of Knockmoy! You haven't seen cannons in action, though. I have. One blast from a cannon could reduce this abbey to a pile of shattered stone in two minutes.'

'Cannon,' sneered Turlough. 'I've heard from Kildare about them. How do you think that this Henry VIII of yours will get them across the sea? Swim them? Swim them like the men from the islands swim their cattle?'

'You spoke of O'Malley of the Ships,' said Murrough evenly. 'I have seen ships in England and they make O'Malley's ships look like the toys of a young child. These English ships can hold cannons; they can hold thousands of men armed with guns. They will be coming over here.'

'We'll fight them,' repeated Turlough, but his voice had begun to lose some of its conviction.

'Who's we?' demanded Murrough. 'You name names, but you know in your heart and soul that these men are forever at odds with each other. This is the way of life over here. There is continual rivalry, continual strife – cattle raids, disputes over territory. This is happening all the time. You are a king, yes, but only king of three small kingdoms. Will the McCarthy, the O'Kelly, the O'Donnell, the O'Malley, will any one of them accept your leadership? No, they will all fight in their own way for their own little kingdoms. And then the English will pick you off, one by one. They will bribe some, crush others; that is the way it will go.'

'We will fight for clan and land,' repeated Turlough. 'And we will win. The English came over here four hundred years ago and now look at how little of the country that they own – a few cities, a swathe of land around Dublin and Wexford, that's the extent of their possessions.'

'You will fight,' said Murrough, ignoring this. 'You will stand up there, you and your clansmen. You know how they will all be dressed, in quilted leather – enough to turn an arrow, but not a bullet. They will hold their bows and arrows, they will ride their horses without stirrups, just like they did down through the ages, they will let fly their javelins against men wearing armour, carrying guns and men massed behind cannons. You will all be slaughtered and for what? An earl, in England, would have more power than you do. If you made obeisance to Henry VIII now he would make you an earl – perhaps Earl of Thomond, and your safety and the safety of your territory would be guaranteed.'

He speaks with utter conviction; he believes this, thought Mara. But does it make it less, or perhaps more, likely that he would attempt to end the life of his father? Murrough was a young man. Young men are impatient. He sees the future; he will not want to wait patiently for it to arrive. He came over perhaps to persuade, but did he, when faced with the physical presence of his father, decide that the easier path would be to simply remove this obstacle to what he sees as progress?

'You can talk all night if you wish,' said Turlough, rising to his feet and throwing some more charcoal on to the already glowing fire. 'You can talk all night, and you still will not convince me. I won't listen to another word.'

'In that case,' said Murrough, in a low voice, 'I'll return to England tomorrow.'

'Not until this murder is solved,' said Mara tartly. 'Remember this is still the territory of your father and as his Brehon I say that no one leaves this abbey until the crime is solved and preparations made for it to be admitted and paid for at the judgement place in Poulnabrone.'

She looked at him keenly, but he said nothing, just bowed his head in a weary way, so she rose to her feet with a quick pat of Turlough's shoulder. 'Now I must go to see Brigid to tell her that we will be three for supper and, with your permission, my lord, I think that Fergal should come in here out of the cold. You can tell Fergal about English weaponry, Murrough. He will be keenly interested in that. He is a very intelligent young man.'

'Yes, yes, I guessed that he would stay for supper.' Brigid eyed her mistress uncertainly. There was an unusual hesitancy about her.

'Is that all right? You have enough food? Has Shane eaten all your stores?' Mara cast a quick, maternal glance at the black-haired boy sleeping peacefully on a sheepskin rug by the fire, a half-eaten pie still in his hand.

'No, no, God bless him.' Brigid was immediately reassuring, but there remained a slight hesitancy.

'What's wrong?' asked Mara, closing the door and coming right into the kitchen.

'It's just that Brother Melduin; do you remember me telling you about him?'

'Yes, of course, he's the lay brother that is one of the O'Brien clan, isn't he?'

Brigid nodded. 'Yes, well, I went over there for some more charcoal and he told me, in confidence, mind you, that he had seen that Father Denis in the stable and from the way that he was checking everything, it looked as if he might be thinking of moving on. He was enquiring about the state of the roads and looking at the horse's shoes.'

'I see,' said Mara. Of course, Father Denis was not an inhabitant of the Burren, so in theory she had no jurisdiction over him. However, she hoped to get this case solved before any of the guests at the abbey moved on. Perhaps there was an agreement between the young priest and the abbot that the embarrassing illegitimate son should disappear before the important guest from Tintern Abbey arrived. On the other hand, Mara did not want anyone to leave until the case was solved. She hesitated for a moment, wondering what to say and Brigid gave an understanding nod.

'Don't worry, Brehon,' she said. 'Brother Melduin will keep an eye on him and will be over with a message if there is any sign of him moving.'

'That's good,' said Mara sedately, wondering what she would do without Brigid and her love of gossip. Nothing more needed to be said so she turned the conversation. 'I'm just going across to the abbot's house. I suppose that Fachtnan and Shane's father, Patrick, are finished with the questioning, now. I'll just have a chat with them. Fachtnan will come back with me, but Patrick may well be having supper with the abbot. If he is not, then would it be all right if I bring him back here, also?'

'Plenty for everyone,' said Brigid, with a quick glance at her pots and pans and at the baskets piled up in the corner of the kitchen. 'Bring him or don't bring him, Brehon. There's no problem either way.'

As Mara went towards the door, Brigid called out: 'Wait a moment, Brehon, let me call Cumhal, no sense in taking any risks. He'll walk across with you. There may be someone out there who wants to get rid of you. That stone would have killed you, you know, if you had been in your usual place, and what would we have said to your father then when we meet him in heaven?'

'Very well, Brigid,' said Mara meekly. A scolding from Brigid, when she was a child, usually ended with the words, 'what would your father say to me if he knew about this?' Obviously, the fact that her father had been dead for twenty years meant little to Brigid.

There was a murmur of conversation from the warming room as Mara followed Cumhal along the dark path through the cloisters. This was the monks' one hour in the day of recreation and normal living – a time when they could rub their frozen hands in front of the fire and gossip with each other. A strange life, thought Mara. In the time of her father many of the Cistercian monks had lived in small houses with a wife and family outside the walls of the abbey, but since the arrival of the abbot, Father Donogh O'Brien, this had all ended and now the abbey of Our Lady of the Fertile Rock had become a model of propriety and strict adherence to the laws and rules of the Roman church. No wonder that the abbot wanted all traces of that violent death cleared from the church and the body quietly reposing in the vault before the visitor from Tintern Abbey arrived on his tour of inspection.

The abbot himself opened the door to them.

'Ah, Brehon,' he said in a friendly tone, 'I was just on my way over to the warming room; I like to drop in there every evening, the brothers expect it, but your assistant and the Brehon from Tyrone are by the fire in the parlour.'

'I'll wait for you in the kitchen, Brehon,' said Cumhal, as the abbot disappeared with a twirl of his long grey cloak.

'I'd prefer if you went back to the Royal Lodge, Cumhal,' said Mara. 'Conall and Fergal are devoted, but they are very young and they might be tricked. Make sure that the king does not leave the lodge for any reason and that no one is admitted without yourself and the bodyguards being present. Don't worry about me; I have Patrick and Fachtnan.' It was as far as she could go in saying: *Trust no one, not even a close relative; the king may still be in deadly danger,* but by the light of the torch in the small hallway she saw Cumhal's thoughtful face and knew that she had been understood.

He went with a quick nod, closing the door quietly behind

him, and Mara turned into the parlour. Patrick and Fachtnan were at a table by the fire, poring over a piece of vellum, Fachtnan pointing to names with a rather battered-looking quill. Their faces brightened when they saw her.

'You've made the list, Fachtnan?' Mara bent over the vellum. She had trained her students to tabulate the evidence gathered and here it all was: names, times, cross-references: all carefully done.

'We were just seeing whether we could cross anyone off the list on the basis of the evidence,' observed Patrick.

'The wife of Mahon, Banna, is it? The fat woman.' Fachtnan pointed with the quill and then took out his knife and sharpened it vigorously, his face thoughtful. 'I just popped across to the guest house and checked on her evidence and it's true. So she can be crossed off.'

'And what about the other wife?'

Patrick chuckled. He took the pen from Fachtnan and drew a neat circle around the name of Frann.

'The little lady's evidence and Ardal's didn't quite tally. Her account said that she met him at the door to the guest house, his that he met her at the door to the church. Which do we believe?'

Mara smiled. Patrick had not drawn a circle around Ardal's name; he knew quite well which to believe. She gazed at Frann's name in an interested fashion. Perhaps the lie was of no consequence. Frann was a storyteller and storytellers had an imperfect relationship with the truth.

'I'd say that she just thought it sounded better,' observed Fachtnan before she could voice her thoughts. Mara smiled at him. As a student of Latin and of the vast intricacies of Brehon law, Fachtnan had his weaknesses, but when it came to human nature, not a single one of her scholars could exceed him.

'Any other discrepancies, or interesting points?' she asked, gazing down at the vellum. The roll was being held open by the inkhorn and a heavy silver cross, studded with jewels. The abbot certainly had the best of everything in his house. Even the inkhorn was banded with hoops of silver and held upright by a silver stand. It did not seem to go with the Cistercian ideal of poverty and aestheticism.

For an answer, Patrick drew another neat circle around the name of Father Denis. 'His evidence did not agree with the abbot's,' he remarked.

'What did you think of him?' asked Mara. She spoke to Patrick, but her eyes went to Fachtnan's face.

'Keen to impress,' said Patrick.

'Lying,' said Fachtnan bluntly and then added more thoughtfully, 'but I think the abbot was lying also.'

'Ah,' said Mara with satisfaction. She beamed from one to the other.

'It's this matter of accounting for the time between that couple of hours between dinner and vespers,' said Patrick. 'The abbot says that he and the king's son, Murrough, put away the bow, arrows and target in the wooden press and then he left the church.'

'And Murrough?'

'Well, he says that he did the putting away and that the abbot strolled off as soon as they entered the church and he went up to the chancel and had a word with the mason. That was the last he saw of him as he, Murrough, left the church after he had shut the press,' explained Fachtnan.

'And which did you believe?'

Fachtnan glanced politely at Patrick, but the latter just pursed his lips and lowered his eyelids, looking enigmatically at the fire, so Fachtnan fixed his honest brown eyes on Mara and said hesitantly:

'I know that Murrough has lied before and that would give a prejudice against him, but do you know, Brehon, I think he might have been speaking the truth here. You see, he didn't try to say that it was the abbot who had gone up into the bell tower. He just said that the abbot went off to talk with the mason.'

'I see,' said Mara thoughtfully. 'And what about Ellice? What did you make of her?'

'Defensive,' said Patrick unexpectedly. His eyelids snapped open. 'She has something on her mind, that young woman, don't you agree, Fachtnan?'

'I agree,' said Fachtnan. 'She was wary of every question that we asked her, and yet,' he hesitated and Mara took up the phrase.

'And yet?' she queried.

'And yet, I don't know whether you agree with me, Brehon,'

he looked deferentially at Patrick, 'somehow I felt that she was not worried about our questions, more about whether she had been with her husband all of the time.'

'I think you may be right,' said Patrick after a minute. 'You may be right, but where could she have been? I presume that this Father Denis,' he turned to Mara, 'I presume that he was there in church for the service of vespers?'

Mara thought for a moment. 'I think it is unlikely that he was missing,' she said after a minute. 'Someone would surely have noticed. There are just two rows of choir monks, one on each side of the chancel. If no one else had thought to mention the absence, I'm sure that Father Peter, the prior, would have done so and I had an opportunity of a private talk with him.'

'And he said nothing?' queried Fachtnan.

'He said some very interesting things,' said Mara, thinking back to her conversation with Father Peter. 'In fact, his words pointed me in a new direction, but, no, he did not mention any absence of Father Denis from vespers. Perhaps Ellice went down to see her horse. She's very fond of the animal, Turlough told me.'

'So that's it,' said Patrick. 'It's all still wide open. There are still mainly the same suspects: perhaps not Banna, but Frann, Father Abbot, Father Denis for Mahon O'Brien and Murrough, Ellice and perhaps Conor for the failed attempt on the king's life and any one of them for the failed attempt this afternoon on either your life or the king's. You are no nearer to a solution than you were earlier this afternoon.'

'I wouldn't say that,' said Mara sombrely. 'I think I might now know who the assassin is, but I must think it over carefully.'

Both looked at her in startled manner and she added lightly: 'Let's go across to the Royal Lodge now; Brigid is ransacking her stores for a worthy supper.'

She took her mantle from the chair and allowed Patrick to help her into it. It was only after they had closed the abbot's door and had begun to make their way along the darkened cloister walk under the faint, misty light of the moon, that he spoke.

'Have a care,' he said. 'If the assassin suspects that you have guessed, then you are in grave danger.'

Fifteen

Bretha Étgid
(Judgements of Inadvertent Events)

If a man is killed by going too near a blacksmith's hammer no blame is attached to the blacksmith. The same applies to a miller or a carpenter at work.

Anyone travelling in a ship or a boat must accept the risk posed by the ocean or river and no liability is borne by the boatman for any accident.

'Brehon!' The voice was soft but insistent and Mara woke with a start.

'Brigid! What's wrong?'

It was just as well that Turlough slept in his own room, well-guarded by Fergal and Conall, as Brigid had come right into the bed-chamber and was now standing above Mara, candlestick in hand. Brigid still wore her nightgown and her pale sandy hair hung over her shoulders so presumably it was as early as it felt. Mara sat up in bed and tried to collect her thoughts.

'What's wrong?' she asked, and the breath caught in her throat at the thought of all that might be wrong.

'It's happened!' Brigid's tone was as gloomily exultant as one who, expecting little of the human race, is pleased to see those expectations fulfilled.

'What's happened?' Mara swung her legs over the side of the bed.

'Brother Melduin has just come over. He's always the first to get up because it is his duty to pump up water for the cooking and washing.'

'Ah,' said Mara. Now she could guess what was coming next and the hard hammering of her heart slowed down.

'They've gone!' said Brigid.

'Who's gone?' said Mara. She might as well play her part now, but she knew who had gone and she looked around for her clothes.

'Father Denis and the wife of the *tánaiste*,' said Brigid. 'I told you, didn't I? Mark my words, I said it, didn't I, Brehon?'

'You did, indeed, Brigid,' said Mara patiently. 'I think I'd better talk to the king. Is that water hot?'

Brigid, recalled to her duties, rushed across to the jug on the hob by the brazier and poured the water into a wooden bowl on the small table against the wall.

'What will you wear, Brehon?' she asked, going to the chest at the bottom of the bed. 'I think your woollen purple gown will be the best for riding. It's good and loose and it's warm. There's a cold wind out there, this morning. Yes, the purple will be best.'

'You're probably right,' said Mara, trying to conceal a smile. Brigid, as always, had unerringly seen into her mind. Her first thought had been that she would go after the pair. After all, she had stated that no one was to leave the abbey until she had declared the crime solved. Of course, she could send some servants or lay brothers, but, no, she decided, I'll do this myself.

'Perhaps, you could have a word with one of the bodyguards, just say that I wish to speak with the king, don't say any more; we'll try to keep this matter a secret.'

'I'll get Cumhal to do it,' decided Brigid. 'I'll go back to the kitchen and get you some breakfast. Just a couple of pies and a cup of hot ale: that will keep you going. It's not raining yet, but that there sky doesn't look good.'

Where would they have gone? wondered Mara as she rapidly washed and dressed. She went to the window and unlatched the heavy wooden shutters and then pushed open one of the casements. Brigid was right. Already the trees were bending before the force of the wind. There might even be a storm today. Her window faced east and she could just see the sun rising above the swirling silver terraces of Abbey Hill and the sky was striped with long slanting lines of crimson and purple against a pale yellow background; the sun, itself, perched on the rounded summit of the hill, was like an enormous copper platter.

'Red sky in the morning is the sailors' warning,' quoted Mara as she turned away from the window and pulled on an extra pair of footless woollen stockings before picking up her leather boots. A sound of voices outside made her return to the window, boots in hand.

It was the abbot. She could not mistake those tones of authority. She leaned out of the window as far as she could go. He was over by the stables near to the gate; she could just see the top of his head. His back was to her, but by his voice she knew that he was furiously angry.

'Make all the speed that you can . . .' She just caught those words but the strength of a sudden blast of wind from the west blew away the rest of the sentence. And then the abbey gate swung open and there was a noise of horse hoofs striking the limestone road.

Mara quickly pulled on the other boot and plaited and coiled her hair with the speed of one who often had to respond to emergencies. In a moment she was down the stairs, smiling affectionately as she heard the sound of Turlough's sleepy voice from his bedchamber. In a few minutes this would turn to a roar of rage, she knew, but she did not wait.

The abbot was striding across the wet grass, his mantle sailing vigorously in a straight line behind him. He had seen her; she was sure about that, but it did not look as if he were going to stop so she called to him peremptorily. Even then he paused and looked at her with an expression of annoyance on his face, a busy man detained when he had serious matters on his mind. She ignored the expression and drew near to him.

'Father Abbot, how did they get out? I thought the abbey gate was to be kept locked until I gave the word?'

His thin lips tightened, but then he said in a resigned tone: 'Father Denis stole the key from my chamber. I noticed he was missing at the service of prime. I only realized that when we were halfway through the service. I thought he had overslept. Once I came back to my house, I looked for him and found that his chamber was empty and then one of the lay brothers came running to tell me that the gate was wide open and two horses were missing.'

'Two?' queried Mara. Did he know about Ellice, she wondered, or was there any possibility of keeping this matter of the *tánaiste's* wife a secret?

He nodded solemnly. 'I'm sorry to have to tell you, Brehon,' he said with a return of his usual pompous manner, 'he did not go alone. The king's daughter-in-law went with him. I have sent after the guilty couple, but whether we will catch them in time to prevent another sin, I don't know.'

'Another sin?'

He bowed his head in an expression of humility but his nostrils flared like those of a warhorse and his grey eyes were as cold as the stone around them.

'It's obvious, isn't it? You gave many people the impression yesterday that you might have solved the case; the king's younger son was saying that he thought it was all settled in your mind, and now the guilty ones have fled. So this man as well as being guilty of adultery and theft has probably also killed. He has broken almost every commandment in the laws of God. He should hang!'

'Hang!' For once Mara was taken off guard and her voice rose with astonishment. 'Your own son!'

The abbot said nothing, but his eyes spoke for him. There would be no forgiveness, no compassion to be expected from this man.

'Your own son,' repeated Mara quietly. She wondered whether he might be about to deny paternity, but he didn't.

'I live my life by the law of God, Brehon,' he said loftily. 'Justice has to be impartial.'

'And how did they get out? Surely no lay brother disobeyed your instruction.'

'Certainly not! I told you, the key was stolen. And from my own chamber! They must have seized the opportunity of Brother Porter's absence at prime. And that's not all, he also opened the wall cupboard in my own room and stole a valuable communion cup which is worth a hundred marks.' The abbot, a thin man, seemed to swell with anger just as his clothes swelled with the wind. Then he rearranged his features into their usual stony calm. 'However, Brehon,' he continued, 'you need not concern yourself further about this matter. I have told the lay brothers to bind the guilty man and to bring him before the judge in Galway. The crime was committed here at the abbey and should be judged by Roman law, not Brehon law.'

'The crime was committed here in the kingdom of the Burren

and as such will be judged by me,' said Mara firmly. She eyed him steadily. Yes, there was no doubt that the abbot wanted to get rid of Father Denis as quickly as possible, but he was not prepared to see one of the most valuable possessions of the abbey disappear with him. This unwanted son could languish in a jail in Galway until the visit of the abbot of Tintern Abbey was over; that was obviously the plan.

'Mara!' The king had undoubtedly heard the news by now. His tousled head with its rough iron-grey hair was protruding out of the window and Mara hastened to obey the summons before any further indiscretion could betray the matter to the whole world.

'I'll see you in little while, Father Abbot,' she said. 'I must speak with the king first.'

He said something, but the wind was rising now and his words only faintly reached her. She turned back to look at him and he repeated the words, loudly enough to be heard by the king at his window.

'He will hang!' he shouted. 'I will allow nothing else. He is under the rule of Rome.' He stopped for a minute and then said, more quietly, 'As for her, the wife of the *tánaiste*, the king may deal with her as he wishes.'

'So far as the theft of the communion cup is concerned, the abbot may be within his rights; it is a difficult point. We were discussing this at the last Brehons' convention. The consensus of opinion was that these monastic communities could rule themselves according to their preferences, and could, if they felt it to be right, reject Brehon law and be subject to the law of England or Rome as they themselves are considered to be daughter houses of English abbeys and monasteries. However, where the murder of Mahon O'Brien is concerned, that is my affair to deal with.' Mara kept her voice very quiet as she poured some more ale for Turlough and took another oatcake for herself. They were alone. Brigid had gone to fetch Fachtnan and Shane to tell them to saddle their ponies and even the two bodyguards were outside the door discussing the weather with Cumhal. 'He seems determined that Father Denis will hang, one way or another,' she added.

'What!' Turlough gulped down his ale. 'He's not going to bring English law into the Burren, not while there is a breath in my body. If this Father Denis is guilty of anything then he can be tried at Poulnabrone and can pay a fine. That will be more use to everyone than a dead man swinging by the neck.'

'And what about Ellice?' asked Mara, gulping down the last of her cake and taking down her mantle from the peg.

'She had nothing to do with the murder,' said Turlough defiantly, wiping his moustache with the back of his hand. 'As for the other, well if she fancies this young priest, then that's her affair. I'd like to have a word with the girl, though, before too much gets out. Give her a chance to think again. It's not a good thing for her. I didn't like the look of that fellow. She's better off with Conor; he's a decent lad, poor fellow.'

'If we can catch up with them,' said Mara, 'you can do all the talking that you like, but there is no way that they can be allowed to ride off together now. I have said that no one was to leave the abbey without my permission and I am not going to have my authority flouted like that. In any case, you're right; I don't like the look of that young priest; Ellice should be given the chance to think again. We'll take Cumhal as well as Fergal and Conall and then there will be Fachtnan, and Patrick will come too. I've sent over a note to him.'

'He's on his way across. Can you see him? He's under the archway to the cloisters and there's Father Peter outside the window. I wonder what he's come for?'

'I'll go and talk to him.' Mara quickly left the parlour and slipped past the group of men outside and opened the front door. If Conor's condition had worsened during the night she wanted to be the first to know.

Father Peter, however, was beaming sweetly, his small, thin face alight with pleasure.

'Ah, Brehon,' he said. 'Could you tell the king that his son is very well this morning.? He woke with no fever and he even talks of going out and walking by the seashore today.'

'Thank God,' said Mara sincerely. 'I even feared you were coming to tell the news of his death.'

'No, no,' Father Peter seemed genuinely shocked. 'Who is talking of death? We've had a few setbacks during the last few days, that's true, but it is understandable. A week ago I would have said that he would definitely live. He was putting on weight, regaining his strength. But, with the help of God, this is just a temporary business. He's had a few shocks, but I'll get him back to health again. With the wasting sickness, it's just a matter of giving the patient time, good food, good air and rest. This is all very bad for him. The sooner it is all solved, Brehon, the better for everyone.'

What will happen, though, if he finds out that his wife has left him for a young priest? wondered Mara. She cast a quick glance around. Patrick, seeing her occupied, changed direction and was now making for the stables. After he passed, the monks working in the cloisters had moved closer as if sharing a conversation. A couple of lay brothers, engaged in sweeping the paths, had heads together while the brooms stayed idle in their hands. When they saw her glance over at them, they took up work again, but she could guess what they were gossiping about. Soon everyone would know that Ellice had left the abbey in the company of Father Denis. Would there be any way of protecting Conor from the news?

'The *tánaiste's* wife has gone for a ride but when she has returned she will be delighted to hear that news,' she said, looking at the small monk intently.

'Gone?' Father Peter's thin lips puckered on the word, showing the toothless gums behind, but his voice was barely audible. A slight frown appeared between his brows and his sharp grey eyes looked a question at Mara and she nodded slightly.

'The king and I are about to set off to meet her,' she said, allowing her clear voice to rise and reach listening ears.

Father Peter nodded solemnly. 'The *tánaiste* and I might come and meet you on the way back,' he said, raising his gentle old voice. 'Perhaps not too far! Let us know when you are on your way back. When you get near you could send the boy.' He beamed at Shane who had emerged, dressed for the journey, and was making his way towards the stables.

Fachtnan was already holding Mara's horse by the time they made their way to the stables. Turlough took the reins from him and assisted Mara into the saddle.

'Thank God you're here,' he said softly. 'I don't think I could cope with all these things if you were not by my side. Why don't we just leave the lot of them, ride away and spend Christmas at Cahermacnaghten?'

'Let's get this matter uncoiled first,' said Mara lightly. He was not in earnest; she knew that. This murder had to be solved; it was not in his nature, no more than in hers, to shirk a duty.

'Which way do we turn at the bottom of the road, Brehon?' Shane's clear, joyous voice came back to them as they started to ride through the gate.

'Turn right,' called Mara. Left just led to the small harbour at Béal an Chloga; right would bring them on to Cleric's Pass and then, down the steep hill, on to the road to Galway.

Shane and Fachtnan were still waiting, though, when they reached the bottom of the road that led out from the abbey gates.

'There are some horses coming from the left, riding fast, Brehon,' said Fachtnan as they drew near. 'I thought we should wait to see who they are. Here they are now, coming around the corner.'

'It's that party of lay brothers that I saw setting out a while ago,' said Mara in an undertone to Turlough. 'They've given up the chase quickly. And why did they take that road?'

The brothers were riding slowly, the foremost one with a long length of coiled rope clearly visible from his satchel. The abbot had thought quickly. Once surrounded, Father Denis could have been tied up and taken to Galway. There would be no mercy now for this son who had betrayed him and stolen from him.

'They look as if they've lost the scent,' observed Turlough.

'Strange,' observed Mara. 'The abbot won't be too pleased with them if they return so quickly without their quarry.'

'Any sign of them?' she asked crisply as they drew near to her. They looked startled and glanced from one to the other, but, impressed by the note of authority, the brother with the rope nodded his head and then shook it.

'We've seen them, Brehon,' he said. 'But it's no good. We were too late.'

Mara frowned and he hastened to add: 'They've taken a boat, Brehon. They were already out on the sea by the time we saw them.'

'We saw the boat from the top of the hill and we could see two horses in it.'

'We went right down to the harbour to be certain.'

'It was no good. That east wind was taking them out quickly.'

Now everyone was trying to speak; doubtless, they felt their story for the abbot could do with a preliminary rehearsal.

Fachtnan licked his finger and held it up. 'A north-easterly wind, now,' he said.

'They'll never get to Galway against a wind like that,' said Shane. 'What do you think, Father?'

Patrick nodded. 'Even on a lake it would be hard to make progress against a headwind like that; with a heavy sea running like it is today, it will be nearly impossible.'

'I know whose boat they have taken.' A young brother who had not previously spoken took up the tale. 'That boat belongs to Tearlach, you know, the son of big Séan.' He turned to the brother with the rope who nodded knowingly.

'This Tearlach is a *druth*, a half-wit, Brehon. I wondered who would be mad enough to take a boat out in a sea like this.'

'They may be driven back on to the shore, Brehon,' said Fachtnan thoughtfully. 'Would it be worth riding towards the sea and looking for a likely spot?'

'That's worth a try.'

'Yes, that's the thing to do.'

'We'll come with you.'

'They'll probably come ashore at Baile Bheachtain.'

All the voices were enthusiastic. No doubt this was a welcome break for these hard-working lay brothers. Also, it saved them from the abbot's wrath if they returned so early with only failure to report.

'They couldn't be thinking of going to the Aran Islands, could they?' asked Mara as they set off riding behind the lay brothers and the two boys.

'Unlikely,' said Turlough. 'After all, Aran is mine. I don't think anyone would shelter them there. No, they will be going to Galway; that's out of my jurisdiction.'

'He may have arranged the boat yesterday when the wind was slack, and then, this morning, he did not want to change his plans. He probably prevailed on this unfortunate Tearlach to take him,' said Patrick shrewdly.

'And, of course, Father Denis is from east Galway; he would not know too much about the sea.'

'And the girl is quite reckless,' said Turlough. There was a note of affection in his voice and Mara turned to him with an indulgent smile. He was such a kind man, she thought, so very different from his cousin, the abbot. She wondered whether there had been an agreement between the abbot and his son. *You put no obstacle in the way of my becoming abbot of Knockmoy and I will disappear before your important visitor from Tintern Abbey arrives*, he might have said. Or even: *help me to achieve my ambition and I will not get in the way of your ambition*. Like father, like son, she thought.

They could see the boat clearly when they reached the harbour. It was a solid, heavily made wooden boat, what they called a Galway hooker. It was built for heavy seas: clinker built, and well painted. It had room for three sails, a main sail and two fore sails, but only one of them bore canvas.

'*Druth* or no *druth* he's handling that boat well,' said Fachtnan appreciatively. 'He's doing the right thing; isn't he, Cumhal?' he called back. 'He's heading into the waves, not letting them hit him broadside.' Cumhal had taught all the boys to sail in the choppy Atlantic waters between Doolin and the Aran Islands, so he was an authority on all things to do with boats for the law scholars of Cahermacnaghten.

Mara glanced back at her farm manager now and saw him shake his head ominously.

'He's doing his best,' he grunted, 'but no boat is going to last too long on a sea like that. His only hope is to head for the shore as soon as possible. He can't possibly make Galway.'

'Wind's shifting,' said Fachtnan, holding up a wet finger. 'What do you think, Cumhal? It's going around to the north again, isn't it?'

Everyone drew to a halt and all eyes were now on Cumhal, who moved his face around thoughtfully. 'North-north-east,' he said eventually. 'Now's his chance. If he turns his boat towards Drumcreehy Bay now they might all escape with their lives.'

Could anyone escape from a sea like that? thought Mara. There were clouds of breaking white spray over the rocks at Black Head point; the sea was a dark green and churning like yeast moving in a beer cask and the thunder of the waves on the shore below almost deafened them.

A sudden gust of wind had ripped the sail and only left tattered ribbons fluttering from the mast. Now the sea lashed the boat unmercifully. It was moving backwards and each giant wave, mountain-high, lifted it up, carried it to the pinnacle and then cast it down into a trough. The air was clear, with that strange yellow light that comes just before a storm, and Mara could just make out the figure of Ellice standing beside the two horses that were tied to the side of the small cabin. No doubt the animals were maddened by fear and Ellice was trying to soothe them. Turlough had said that she was a great horsewoman. Mara breathed a quick prayer for the girl's survival from this terrible adventure.

'Let's go down to the bay,' she said, and signalled when she saw that her words had not reached them.

'Look!' screamed Shane. 'Look at the two men!'

Mara peered, but his young eyes were more long-sighted than hers. She could only see Ellice. She waited for a moment, her eyes straining through the distance.

'They are fighting,' yelled Fachtnan. 'Look, Brehon, the two men at the tiller.'

'What's happening?'

'The monk is trying to wrestle the tiller from Tearlach.'

'He'll have the boat over!'

'Look at the way it is spinning in the waves.'

'He's mad, that monk; he should leave the tiller to the man in charge of the boat. He's crazy, look! He's dragging Tearlach away from the tiller.'

Now the boat was broadside to them and Mara could dimly see the two figures. A huge wave swept over the boat and its prow plunged straight down into the trough that was sucked out of the sea when the wave passed on rapidly towards the shore. For a moment it looked as if it would capsize, but then it was afloat again.

'They've gone overboard.' Fachtnan's yell was loud enough to be heard over the thunder of the shingle.

'They're gone, Brehon,' shouted Shane, turning around to her. His young face had turned white and his dark blue eyes were wide with horror.

'They're gone all right,' said a lay brother gloomily in the calm before the next crash of the breakers. 'Poor Tearlach, that will break his father's heart. A harmless poor soul, no trouble to anyone and a great boy with the boat.'

'Let's get down to the bay,' shouted Mara, urging on her horse and letting them follow her.

As they galloped across the hill they could see the boat. Oddly enough it now seemed to be steering a steady course inland going straight in towards the shingle beach.

'It's the girl is at the tiller, Brehon.' Fachtnan gasped. The wind was now blowing directly in their faces, making voices almost impossible to hear, but Mara thought she heard Turlough's voice uttering something like a cheer.

Within ten minutes, they were down on the flat land of Drumcreehy Bay. They were not alone. People were streaming out of the fishermen's cottages, many carrying ropes, others nets, a few women with blankets. By the time that they reached the beach, a fire had been kindled of driftwood, its flames shooting out flickering tongues of blue. The men were beginning to line up along the shingle, lashing themselves together with a long rope. The man at the head of the line, a huge fellow with a weather-beaten face, held a spare rope in his hand. The noise of the breakers was now diminished; the tide had begun to turn and there was an ominous sucking noise as each wave retreated from the beach.

'I'm going down there!' In a moment the lay brother was climbing off his horse, pulling out the rope from his satchel. Rapidly he stripped off his monk's gown and cloak; clad just in his *léine,* he raced down the beach and lashed himself to the end man, holding out the rope as another and then another lay brother joined him.

'No, Fachtnan!' Mara spoke sternly. 'I am responsible to your father for you.'

He gave her a quick nod of acquiescence; he was always a biddable lad, she thought.

'There are probably enough men on the rope now, anyway. If anyone does make the shoreline, these will be enough to be able to haul them in. Come on, Shane; let's find some more

driftwood for the fire. They'll need warming when they are
hauled ashore.'

The optimism of youth, thought Mara. Her eyes were on the
heavily swelling cauldron of the sea and she doubted whether
anyone could emerge alive out of that.'

'They don't light the fire for that reason,' said Cumhal, after
the two boys had gone. 'There's a sandy spit goes out here. If the
boat can beach on it, it might be saved. They may not know yet
that the boat has lost its master. It would take great skill to bring
that boat ashore and there's just that girl at the tiller.'

'Look at her!' said Turlough. 'There's breeding for you! There's
courage, too! What a queen she would make!'

All that Mara could see of Ellice was a figure standing resolutely
at the tiller and a skein of black hair whipping around her head.

'By the grace of God, she's pointing the boat towards the sand,'
continued Turlough. His voice rose to a roar: 'Come on, girl,
come on! You can do it!'

In a moment, everyone on the beach took up the cry: all arms
began to gesture. Some of the women fell to their knees, praying
aloud the passionate Gaelic words calling on St Brendan, the saint
of the sailors, on St Patrick, and on the Blessed Mary, Star of the
Sea.

'She knows what to do; someone must have told her about
the spit of sand. She spends hours on this beach,' said Turlough.
He made an impatient movement as if to get off his horse, but
Mara put her hand on his with a quick glance towards the two
bodyguards still watchful beside him.

'There is nothing you can do, my lord,' she said. 'Ellice is in
the hands of God, now.'

There was a new danger, she could see. The tide had turned.
It was retreating and every outgoing wave sucked the boat back.
The wind, just when it was needed most, seemed to drop a little
and the incoming waves did not have so much force behind
them. There was nothing Ellice could do but hang on to the
tiller, though Mara could see how she cast glance after glance
upwards at the useless pieces of sail snapping in the wind.

'Look, Brehon!' Shane was running up towards her, 'Look, look
out to sea!'

Mara followed the direction of his raised arm and saw what

he pointed at. Right out far, outside the curve of the bay, there was an enormous wave, mountain high and approaching with frightening rapidity.

'Move back, everyone,' shouted Turlough. 'Move back; you'll all be drowned.'

No one obeyed him, though. The line of men stood solid and unyielding. They knew this shore, thought, Mara. This was the last opportunity to rescue anything alive out of that rampant sea.

'That's Tearlach's father, one of the women has just told me,' said Cumhal, pointing to the giant figure standing resolutely at the front of the gallant line.

From out at the edge of the bay the great breaker travelled towards them. It was about halfway in when, close on its heels, came another, so much higher that it seemed to look down upon the first. A cry rose up from the crowd on the beach as the two waves merged forming a foam-fringed monster that swept rapidly in towards the shore.

For a few minutes it seemed as if the air grew very quiet. No one spoke. The last wave had sucked out a channel from the shingle and retreated with a terrible roar. The line of roped men advanced in its track, step by step, into the yellow foam. Only the lay brothers, on the end of the line, were standing on the shoreline now. The fishermen were up to their necks in the surf frantically searching amongst pieces of broken wood.

And then the wave hit the boat. For a moment it seemed as if all would be well as the wave lifted the boat and seemed to bear it towards the beach. But then the vast green hillside of the monster wave met the smaller retreating wave, and this seemed to curl up its side. The boat twisted and spun, and then its mast disappeared. Its black keel appeared for a moment and then that, also, was lost beneath the swelling water. The line of men turned and scrambled for the shore, clawing their way up the shingle bank with a terrible urgency written on every face.

They were no sooner on the top of the bank than the monu-mental wave hit the beach with a sound louder than any clap of thunder. It seemed to gather breath for a second and then came the awful scouring, sucking noise as it clawed a channel of shingle back into the sea again. The men hesitated for a moment, but then, with no word spoken among them, they turned, ran back down the shingle and allowed themselves to be sucked back out into the seething cauldron of the ocean.

'Brave fellows,' shouted Turlough in Mara's ear. He put both of his arms around her and she stood there, glad of the warmth of his body, but filled with horror at the terrible waste of life which now seemed certain to be the result of that silly, amorous adventure. Once again only the lay brothers, on the end of the line, were standing on the shoreline now. The fishermen were in the boiling sea searching desperately for any bodies that might come ashore. Every second or two their heads turned out to sea to watch the progress of the next wave.

And then just as they started to move back towards the safety of the shore again a great shout went up. The women on the beach redoubled their prayers and Mara strained her eyes, opening them as widely as she could. A bundle of clothing floated on the foam of the incoming wave. In a moment the last man on the rope snatched it up and then was towed to safety by the other strong arms pulling. Mara broke free from Turlough's arms and ran down the beach. He was behind her, she knew, but in a minute Fachtnan and Shane overtook them both. By now they all knew who had been snatched out of the seething sea. The long mane of sodden black hair hung down the fisherman's back before he put her on the beach into the arms of a waiting woman and turned back to the sea again.

Ellice was crying with heartbroken sobs and the woman was rocking her like a baby. She set the girl on her feet and urged her up the slope towards the fire, but Ellice resisted, turning her tearful face towards the sea.

'We'd better get her back to the abbey,' said Mara in Turlough's ear, but her own eyes were fixed on the crashing, tossing waves and she could not turn them away.

'You take her back.' Turlough's eyes, like her own, were locked on to that heroic line of men, advancing and retreating at the pace of the breakers, and he did not look at her, but after another agonizing, empty-handed retreat he added: 'How could I ever call myself by the name of king if I turned my back now on that poor father searching for his unfortunate son.'

Sixteen

Heptad Thirty-Five

There are seven cases in which the shedding of blood does not require a fine.

1. *No penalty is incurred by a man who kills in battle with an unfriendly clan*
2. *No penalty is incurred by a man who kills a captive from an unfriendly clan if his* tuáth *or clan refuses to ransom him*
3. *No penalty is incurred by a man who kills a thief who will not desist from the crime when challenged*
4. *No penalty is incurred by a man who kills when his own life or another's is challenged*
5. *No penalty is incurred by a man who kills in battle someone from a friendly clan or* tuáth *whose identity was not known at the time*
6. *No penalty is incurred by a physician who kills if his action resulted from an honest effort to cure*
7. *No penalty is incurred by an insane man who kills if he is out of his mind at the time*

'I'm afraid news has come at last. He's dead,' said Mara, watching Ellice comb out her long, wet hair over the heat from the brazier in the bedroom in the Royal Lodge. They were alone. Ellice had changed her drenched clothing and was now wearing a borrowed gown of Mara's. She seemed dazed and had not spoken a word since the ride back from the beach. Mara looked at her keenly and then repeated the statement.

Brigid, who had just whispered the news to her mistress, departed quickly leaving Mara alone with the girl.

'Who's dead?' Ellice spoke almost mechanically. Her voice was toneless and the words were spoken without curiosity.

'Father Denis,' said Mara, and added quietly. 'And the poor boy, Tearlach, he's dead also.'

There was no flicker of emotion on Ellice's face and she continued to comb her hair.

'What was the plan?' asked Mara.

'What?' Ellice sounded confused, almost as if the words did not make sense to her.

'What had you planned to do, you and this Father Denis? Where were you going?'

'Oh.' Now Ellice turned to face her, but her dark brown eyes were still dull and unresponsive. 'We were going back to Knockmoy. Now that Mahon was dead, Denis thought that he could prevail on O'Brien of Arras to make him abbot. He had that in his mind. That mattered to him more than I mattered. He's like the rest of the O'Briens – power-hungry – it's bred into them.'

'What was the hurry? Surely that could have been done after Christmas? Why did you run away?'

Ellice did not answer. She looked confused. Possibly her head had been struck by the mast, thought Mara. For a moment she thought to abandon the questioning, but then she hardened her heart. This affair had to be tidied up today. The guilty had to be accused and the innocent set free of any shadow of blame. This could not be done unless there was no shadow of doubt in her mind.

'Who made the plan?' she asked gently.

'Denis,' she said dully after a moment. 'He said that he had to leave this place by before Christmas night. He had promised, he said.'

I was right, thought Mara. The abbot says nothing and Denis goes. However, he was too greedy when he stole the communion cup. This was the prize possession of the abbey and it would have to be shown to the visitor from Tintern Abbey. That was one of their functions, she had heard; they were supposed to check on all recorded goods. In the past, many of these handsome gifts had been melted down and the abbots had become wealthy, so now the Cistercians had set in place this programme of inspections by mother houses.

'What drew the two of you together?' she asked.

'I suppose it was me,' said Ellice after a long pause. 'Yes, I wanted something to do, a bit of fun, a bit of excitement. I was sick of it all, sick of pretending, sick of doing nothing, sick of being tied here and my youth departing from me. I had nothing to do, nothing to look forward to.'

'And then this Father Denis arrived, is that how it happened?'

'That's how it happened, I suppose,' said Ellice, looking as if she was not quite sure of her words.

'You were lovers?' Mara made her voice sound casual and Ellice nodded just as casually.

'Yes, of course,' she said indifferently. 'What else is there to do around here?'

'And which of you was the one that murdered Mahon O'Brien?'

Ellice rose to her feet. 'Neither of us,' she said steadily. 'That was just a bit of good luck for Denis . . .' There was a long pause and Mara thought she had completed her sentence when Ellice suddenly, violently, threw the comb across the room and made for the door '. . . and now Denis is dead, so what can I do? I know what you are going to say,' she said explosively. 'And I suppose you are right. There is only one thing left for me to do now. When the fox is cornered he runs for his den, and I am going back to Conor.' She pulled open the door and ran down the stairs so noisily that the bodyguard dozing on a chair in the small hall jumped to his feet in alarm and Brigid shot out of the kitchen. Both of them gaped as Ellice pushed her way past them and violently slammed the front door behind her.

'Brigid, you could make a bundle of these wet clothes and send them over to the guest house,' said Mara serenely. No need for Brigid to spend her time washing and drying the sea-soaked garments, she thought. Then she changed her mind. 'No, just give me a basket and Shane and I will take them over.' There was one more question that she wished to ask Ellice and this would make a good opportunity to do so. With some luck, the young priest had chatted with her.

Patrick, from his position at the window of the abbot's parlour, saw her coming after she had left Shane at the guest house. He came to the door immediately.

'I'm the only one in the house,' he said as he admitted her. 'Father Abbot has gone over to the church to receive the body of Father Denis. I've been sitting here by the window, studying Fachtnan's list.'

'I've a few things to add to that,' said Mara when they were both back in the parlour and the door closed against any curious lay brother who might come in through the kitchen door.

Patrick looked at her curiously, but he did not question her, merely pushing the vellum and the inkhorn across the table to her. She read through the notes carefully, adding some more pieces of information, and then drew a neat straight line under Fachtnan's notes. She sat back for a moment, leaning against the hard wood of the bench. She felt unutterably weary and an immense sadness was robbing her of her energy. She had known the truth last night, and if she had not shirked the revealing of it, telling herself that she had to be quite certain, perhaps she might have been able to save those two lives. Her mind went briefly to 'Big Séan' as they had called him. By now he was mourning the untimely death of his son and this death could perhaps have been prevented if she had acted decisively last night. With a sigh she sat forward. There must be no more deaths. The truth had to be revealed this afternoon. She made some additional notes; her training and her lifelong practice impelled her to do this, but her mind knew it was unnecessary. Every detail of her reasoning was seared into her brain.

Patrick watched her in a puzzled way, but did not attempt to question her. Never had she been more grateful for the taciturnity of a companion. When she had finished, she rolled up the vellum, tied it with a piece of pink linen tape from her pouch and then melted some wax in the heat of the candle and sealed the roll.

'Keep this,' she said to Patrick. 'Keep it and only open it if the necessity arises.' This was as far as she was prepared to go to admit that she knew she could be going into danger and, by the sudden raising of his eyelids, she knew that he understood. He said nothing, though, just nodded.

'So,' she said in a businesslike manner, 'I think after the funeral the monks will have their usual time for recreation and then you can gather them all into the church. I'll ask the abbot's permission for this, but that is the best place. It's the one room that will hold everyone and everyone must be there. Everyone must know the truth now, as some may wish to leave the abbey today.'

'And what about you, will you need any help?' he asked, looking at her keenly.

'No,' said Mara bleakly. 'This matter I must handle myself,'

★   ★   ★

Father Denis's body lay in the church. The storm was over and the hammer blows sounded clearly across the garth; the carpenter was hastily nailing the last board to the makeshift coffin. He would be buried quickly and quietly in the monks' cemetery, and without the presence of anyone, other than the abbot himself and a few lay brothers to bear the coffin. This would take place before the funeral service for Mahon, the abbot, stony-faced, had decreed. Mara spoke with him briefly and then left him looking down soberly at the body of his dead child. The communion cup, battered, but still with all its jewels in place, had been retrieved from the leather satchel that was strapped firmly to Father Denis's body, under his cloak. Would that be any consolation to the abbot, she wondered, glancing keenly at the icy features? Was there any compunction within him that he had abandoned his son all those years ago and had never willingly recognized him? Did he truly suspect his son of murder and would he have pressed for the death penalty for him? She did not know, but left him alone in the church to say his farewells.

'I don't care if she had anything to do with the murder of Mahon,' said Turlough defiantly. 'Don't ask her. Let it be laid to Father Denis's door. He's beyond any justice of ours now. God will deal with him.'

'How was Tearlach's father?' she asked, turning the conversation away from the investigation. Turlough, himself, had insisted on waiting and following the procession to the fisherman's cottage, rather than the procession to the abbey. He had only just returned.

'As well as you could expect; he seemed resigned. They live with death, of course, these fishermen. I told him that he would be compensated for his son's death, that he would have the silver to buy a new boat, but he hardly took it all in. You'll go to see him, won't you, my love? You will be better than I. You will make him understand.'

Mara nodded. 'I will, but we'll leave it for the moment. His family and neighbours will comfort him better than we can. Poor Tearlach will have a hero's funeral.'

'And what about Ellice?'

'She's well,' said Mara, deliberately misunderstanding him. 'She's a strong girl. She'll come to no harm. Conor is with her now, and so is Shane.'

'Shane?'

Mara laughed. 'Yes, funnily enough, she's clinging to him. He admires her tremendously. He told her how wonderful she was for managing to bring the boat on to the sand, even if it did get smashed to pieces by the next wave. He thinks she was heroic to try to save the horses before the breakers swept her off the deck. He was the first to take off his mantle and wrap it around her. He had his arms around her when the body of her horse came on to the shore. He wept when he heard her sob and then she wept holding him in her arms. It's a grief that a child can understand: the loss of a beloved animal. He knows nothing else about her; she is aware of that, so they are easy with each other. She is shy and awkward with Conor and they have very little to say to each other.'

'And you will do what I say about this murder?' persisted Turlough, looking at her uneasily. 'He wasn't worth much, you know, Mahon O'Brien. Don't let his death cloud these two young lives. I'll make it up to Banna, somehow, and the other little wife, too, if she hasn't been left anything. There's no need to involve Ellice; she was just led astray by that young scoundrel. Father Peter tells me that Conor is stronger and that his body is battling against this wasting sickness. Ellice will be happier when he is well, again. You will do as I say,' he repeated.

'I will bear your words in my mind,' promised Mara. It was on the tip of her tongue to say that she never did what anyone said, unless it was what she was going to do anyway, but she kept quiet. All would be revealed shortly; time enough then to talk about open admission of the crime at Poulnabrone and retribution to the victim's family.

'We'll get the burial over first and then I'll sort this matter of Mahon's death out finally,' she said aloud. It was going to be an ordeal, going to cause pain; she knew that but nothing could be done. The truth had to be shared with all.

'That's Teige,' said Turlough as a tremendous knock sounded on the door of the Royal Lodge. 'God bless him, he said that he would come over for me and that he would be at my back every time that I stirred out of doors until the murderer was discovered.'

Teige's face, however, was beaming with relief when Fergal admitted him to the room.

'I hear he's dead,' were his first words even before he greeted either of them. 'That must be a great relief to you, Brehon, and to you, Turlough. A clean end to an unworthy life! Better for Donogh, too. Who would want a son like that! A man who would strike down a man just to gain a position for himself! It was a cowardly, dastardly crime and the world is better off without that Father Denis. Ah, there's Ardal, now. I'd know his knock anywhere. He'll be coming to congratulate you, too.'

Ardal, more cautious than Teige, merely murmured a greeting, but he cast a quick eye of enquiry at Mara. She smiled blandly at him and went upstairs to put on her black gown.

The church was full as they entered. The light had begun to fail outside, but the dark interior was lit up with hundreds of sweet-smelling candles of beeswax. Nothing had been spared to make this burial mass impressive. The long stone altar, in front of the three tall pointed windows, was draped in black velvet and so was the coffin. The church was full: lay brothers on the north side of the nave at the back of the church, servants, workmen on the south side and the higher ranking people further up in the nave.

Chairs had been found for Patrick and Fachtnan who were in the third row and Shane was sitting, like a page, on a cushion between Conor and Ellice. All rose to their feet at the entry of the king with his Brehon and stayed standing until they seated themselves. A new chair had been found for Mara, she was glad to note. It would have chilled her to sit on the original chair, no matter how well repaired. It was difficult enough to turn her mind from that terrible outpouring of hatred and malice that had sent the block of stone on its fateful path. She turned her head slightly, first to one side and then to the other. Yes, all were here: Murrough beside Conor, the four *taoiseach*s and the two wives of the dead man.

'*Subvenite, Sancti Dei . . .*' sang the abbot, sweeping out from the sacristy and standing with head bowed before the altar. Everyone stood at his entry and then sank to their knees.

The trained voices of the choir monks took up the responsory, calling on Christ to receive the soul of Mahon O'Brien and on the angels to lead him into the bosom of Abraham.

'*Requiem aeternam dona eis, Domine, et lux perpetua luceat eis . . .*' sang the abbot and the monks responded.

Not a bad man, Mahon O'Brien, thought Mara. A dull, fussy, sanctimonious sort of man, she had thought him when they met last night, but he certainly did not deserve to die there from an assassin's blow at a time of life when he was probably happier than he had ever been. He would have had his baby to marvel over, doubly precious since he had waited so long for an heir, and if this baby were a girl that would not matter – Frann was young and strong and there would be many children to come. She added her prayer that God might give him eternal rest and that perpetual light might shine upon him, but knew that it was up to her, as Brehon, to name his murderer in public, no matter what the cost.

Had the abbot received her note? she wondered, watching him walking around the bier sprinkling holy water on the coffin. No answer had come from him, but he was an incommunicative, arrogant man.

'*Domine, exaudi orationem eum,*' he sang with a steady voice and then came the final words of the Mass for the Dead: '*Requiescat in pace.*'

Then the two cousins of the dead man came from their places in the church and stood beside the bier: Turlough at the head with the abbot opposite him and then came Teige. Conor had started to move, but Turlough had waved him back impatiently and Murrough, with an expression of amusement on his face, moved forward and stood at the fourth corner. The choir monks took up their candles and led the way towards the small chapel in the north transept, standing in two straight lines to allow the coffin to be carried between them. The rest of the congregation stood up and moved to the north aisle, crowding between the piers of the transept. Banna was sobbing noisily and leaning heavily on Ciara O'Brien's arm; Frann made no sound, but her young face was solemn, its matt pallor a little whiter than usual.

One of the lay brothers, or perhaps the mason, had unlocked the door to the vault during the service and now it gaped wide open. A solitary candle flickered unsteadily from its depths. A heavy

smell of damp and decay seemed to drift upwards and several of
the congregation took an uneasy step backwards.

'*De profundis clamavi ad te, Domine . . .*' sang the monks and the
awful gaping hole of the depths before them gave to their clam-
ouring voices a hollow, ominous sound.

At the head of the steps that led to the vault the abbot made
a sign and all of the pall-bearers stopped. Father Peter, without
pausing in the chanting, jerked his head slightly and four strong
young lay brothers came forward, all of them of the O'Brien
clan, surmised Mara. Certainly Brother Melduin was amongst
them. Deferentially they took the weight of the top end of the
coffin on their shoulders, while Turlough and Father Donogh
moved back near to Teige and Murrough. Now eight men bore
the weight, but even still it was a difficult matter to manoeuvre
the coffin safely down into the vault. Mara held her breath until
it was down and, looking around afterwards, she could see the
relief on other faces.

The mason then slipped unobtrusively after them down the
steps. His would be the final task. Once the coffin was placed
within the stone chest he would seal it and then the vault itself
would be closed up again until another O'Brien of the Burren
came to be laid to rest there. What was Teige thinking, wondered
Mara, or the abbot? In all probability one of these would be the
next to be laid there in that mouldering place. She moved
impatiently. What was the point of all these stone vaults where
the body corrupted until nothing but bones were left? The monks'
cemetery, with its well-tended apple trees, was a much more practical solution. Let the dead help to nourish the living.

'*Et lux perpetua luceat eis . . .*' sang the monks once again as the
pall-bearers came back up to the lighted church, leaving the
mason, and the dead body of Mahon O'Brien, down in the dark
vault.

'*Amen*'. The final word was heartfelt. All would be glad to get
away from this gloomy moment. Already some were moving
towards the back of the church.

'I'll join you in a while, my love,' whispered Mara to Turlough.
As she spoke she beckoned to Cumhal. He came instantly and
stood by her side patiently waiting for instructions. The device
worked; Turlough went ahead, followed by his bodyguards and

by Teige O'Brien and Ardal and once they were out of sight Mara just repeated to Cumhal her instructions to Patrick and then dismissed him. She returned to her seat and waited there quietly. Soon all, monks and laity, had left and she was alone.

But not quite alone: one man remained.

Seventeen

Heptad Twenty-Five

A Brehon who hears a case is entitled to a lóg mbérlai *(a payment for legal language) of one twelfth of the amount involved in each case.*

If the Brehon's verdict is wrongly disputed, a fine of six séts, *three ounces of silver, or three milch cows must be paid as recompense for the loss of face.*

A Brehon appointed by the king is given lands and other gifts.

Mara stayed sitting on her chair until he approached her. The church was very still and very dark. Just one candle stayed alight beside the west door; all others had been extinguished. A faint gleam of daylight from the north-west came through the window above the door to the cloisters and dimly illuminated the stone piers of the chancel, showing the newly executed carvings standing out brightly against the work of long-dead masons. Above her head the raw, broken timberwork of the bell loft still gaped menacingly.

She heard his footsteps before she saw him. They came slowly, as if he were unsure. After a few moments, he stopped and she wondered whether he would suddenly break into a run and flee through the west door. He wouldn't, she decided. Oddly enough, she felt that she knew him sufficiently well to be sure that was not in his character. She said nothing and did not move nor turn her head.

He carried a simple candleholder with one candle of tallow burning smokily on it, but before he came near, he bent down and put it on the broad base of one of the fluted piers that supported the arch to the south aisle. It illuminated one small, newly carved harebell, lying on the floor ready to be plastered into its place on the frieze, but threw a shadow over the man. Now she could not see his face.

'No need for that,' she said quietly as she watched him straighten up. 'I know the truth.'

'I thought you might,' he replied. 'You are clever; I'll grant you that.'

She sighed. 'Rather more hard-working than clever,' she said. 'I've never believed in sitting around and letting things come to me. I've sifted the evidence and yours is the name that has come up again and again. The problem was that, for many hours, I just couldn't see any motive, so I dismissed the evidence.'

He got up and picked up his candle and came back to her with it in his hand.

'I'd have thought that I gave you something to think about,' he observed. 'It could have been any of them. What about the abbot, didn't you suspect him? There was no love lost between these brothers, you know. I tried to point you in his direction – and towards some others, too.'

'You told some lies, laid some false trails, but in the end the truth emerged.'

'How did you know? How did you guess? You didn't in the beginning. Don't lie. I know you too well. You certainly didn't guess yesterday morning.' His voice was rough and threatening, but she did not flinch.

'Was it only yesterday?' Mara spoke wearily. 'It seems an age. But, yes, you are right. I didn't guess in the beginning. I suppose you were watching for that. You were observing me.'

'I was alert for it, yes.' He placed the candle on the floor between them and sat down heavily on Turlough's chair.

She disliked seeing him sit there. For a moment she felt like ordering him to get off it, but what did it matter? Soon all would know the truth.

'All through the morning, I wondered, but by the afternoon, I reckoned that you had other matters to think of. I saw you, heard you . . . more than you ever realized; I listened to conversations; I knew what was going on. I thought that, as you hadn't recognized me straightaway, you would never stumble on the truth.'

'Someone said something yesterday at dinner time and this stayed in my mind,' said Mara thoughtfully. 'He said . . . it was the O'Lochlainn that said it . . . he said that it seemed to be a violent and hate-filled attack. Whenever I came up with a name – and there were certainly people who had reasons to kill the king or the king's cousin – then the motives were always for money or for power.' She was silent for a moment thinking of Ellice and of Murrough, of Teige who loved his son so much, of the abbot, of Father Denis, even of Frann. None of these had reasons to hate the victim.

'That's what I reckoned,' he said with satisfaction. 'Unless you knew who I was, you would never solve this crime. Why should I want to kill that man, what was his name? That Mahon O'Brien, the king's cousin.'

'But then you had made a mistake. You tried to cover it up, but you knew that a suspicion had come into my mind.' Mara paused and then added: 'So you attempted to kill me.'

His voice was deeper and lower now, a savage note in it as he said: 'Why not? You were trying to wreck my life forever . . . not for the first time, either. You took everything that I had and now you wanted to take my life away, as well.'

'Not your life,' said Mara. 'You know the law better than that. Open admission of the crime and compensation to the victim, that is what is required.'

'Do you believe that?' he sneered. 'You haven't heard the abbot, have you? This crime was committed on church soil; Roman law will prevail. He will want the murderer hanged.'

'I am Brehon of the Burren,' said Mara simply. 'My word goes on the Burren. You will not hang.'

'I will certainly not hang,' he said with determination, 'and I will pay no fine. You won't shame me in public, again, either.'

And when she said nothing, he added, 'I'm not going to stand there at Poulnabrone, as I did twenty years ago.'

'Why did you kill him?' asked Mara, ignoring this.

There was a silence and then he gave a short laugh.

'That was a mistake,' he said.

'You thought it was the king; I know that. This was one of the reasons why I knew it had to be you; another who might have had a motive to kill the king knew of the switch,' her mind went to her suspicions of Teige O'Brien, before she added, 'you did not. You thought that the arrangement had been unaltered, that the king was going to do the first hour of the vigil. You went down, killed him, returned to the lay dormitory and then Murrough woke up and saw you, fully clothed, even with your boots on, standing at the window.'

'What if he were lying?'

'It was possible,' admitted Mara. 'But why should Murrough lie?'

'I'm surprised that you did not recognize that he had as much opportunity to kill the king as I had, and of course, far more of a motive. And what about the stone in the bell tower?'

'So far as the bell tower was concerned, the evidence against Murrough was given by the mason, that very mason who had primed Murrough with details of my divorce. That was a mistake that you made. You had probably drunk too much when you told him that the name of my first husband was Dualta. Even the king, his father, did not know that and Murrough was only a baby nineteen years ago.'

'So, when you saw my mason's mark, that I signed my work in the church with the letter 'D' writ in stone, you guessed.'

'No, not then, although that stayed at the back of my mind and it served to verify my conclusion. No, you betrayed yourself when you said: "a king's son may go, where a humble man may not tread". That brought me back to the law school immediately. I could hear my father's voice quoting Fithail: it was one of his favourite quotations. I wondered why a mason should use those words. They showed an education either at a law school, or perhaps at a bardic school. I never knew what had happened to you, once our marriage was dissolved, never cared, I suppose, but I knew that your father had been a mason.'

'That can't be all. You recognized me, didn't you? I kept thinking that, sooner or later, you must recognize me.'

'No,' said Mara with weary honesty. 'I did not recognize you. You are very changed.'

He picked up the candle, holding it closely against his face, moving it around.

'Look at me now, there must be something of the old Dualta, the man you married twenty-two years ago.' There was a pleading note in the rough, hoarse voice.

Mara looked at him compassionately. He was only three years older than herself, but life had not been good to him. She looked at the white hair, the heavy drooping white moustache, the deeply scored wrinkles, the stooping figure. She shook her head wordlessly. Even his voice was completely changed, she thought. Years of breathing in stone dust, years of tramping through bad weather, sleeping in wet clothes, years of steady drinking had altered him completely.

'Don't look at me like that.' Now the husky voice was charged with passion. He had always had that streak of a bully in him. 'I'm as good as you any day, better. Just because I did not spend my time chanting all those silly laws and Fithail . . . I was sick of Fithail being rammed down our throats every day. I had far more brains than you ever had but you thought yourself to be something special. Your father worshipped you. He neglected the other scholars just so that he could boast about his brilliant daughter. He never wanted you to marry me, of course. I wasn't good enough for the wonderful Mara. You ruined my life between you: you and your father. I think about it every day and every night. I know what I could have been if I had never met you.'

He sounded sincere, but he had always been someone who could be convinced by the sound of his own words. For a moment she felt sorry for him, but then her eyes went to the still-gaping hole above their heads and returned to his face.

'Don't live in the past, Dualta; you have made yourself another life,' she said quietly, but he ignored this and hurried on.

'When I fixed that bell there and when I imagined it falling on you I suddenly felt free. I knew that if you were killed I would no longer have you looking over my shoulder, always telling me not to drink so much, to do this and to do that. While you lived I could never get the sound of your accursed voice out of my mind. And then you didn't come to church and now it is to do again. Unless . . .' He paused and looked closely at her. He took a long drink from his flask of *brócoit* and then upended the flask and watched the last few drops drip on the flagged floor before replacing it in his pouch. When he spoke again, Mara recognized that he was now quite drunk.

'Perhaps we could get together again?' he said flippantly. 'You owe me that, surely. Why should you go off with another man? The abbot here would tell you that it is a sin. You cannot have another husband; I'm your husband so I should save you from that sin.'

There was no mistaking his meaning and suddenly Mara was filled with conviction that she had made a bad mistake. She should have interviewed him in the presence of others, should have kept everything on a professional basis. This was an unhappy, disappointed man trying to hurt in every way possible, and more worrying, perhaps, trying to resurrect the past.

'Dualta,' she said quickly. 'There is nothing left of any feeling that prompted that marriage twenty-two years ago. However, for the sake of the bond that was once between us I will give you the silver to pay the fine. You can go back to Galway once judgement day is over. The affairs of the kingdom of the Burren will be of little interest to any there. Your life will not have changed, but the law must be upheld.'

'The law,' he sneered. 'That's all that matters to you, isn't it? That's all that ever mattered to you. You wrecked our marriage, left our daughter without a father, and all so that you could be Brehon and *ollamh* of the law school; all so that you could take your father's place.'

She made no reply. Was it true? She swept the accusation aside. She had done what had seemed to be right at the time. The past was over and could not be undone. Dualta had made his own future and so had she. She had cared for Sorcha as best she could and her daughter had grown up happy and secure. The presence of a father such as this man before her was unlikely to have added much to that security. She brushed aside these speculations. She now had a duty to perform; she was the king's representative; she would have to summon him to appear before the king and the people of the Burren and if he refused, to serve the writ of the law upon him.

'Dualta,' Mara said quietly and calmly, 'I have now solved this crime, so I shall have to lay my findings before the king, hear the case at Poulnabrone and allocate the compensation.'

She got to her feet. How long had elapsed during this conversation? she wondered. Nothing more needed to be said about the past. The future was what concerned her now. Willing or unwilling, Dualta had to admit his crime at Poulnabrone and the fine had to be paid. She glanced towards the west door. Soon the king, members of his family, the abbot, monks, lay brothers, guests and servants would all come streaming through it. She still hoped to bring Dualta to a reasonable frame of mind before they arrived.

'Our lives have parted and they can never come together again.'
She said the words resolutely and without warmth. First she had
to convince him to abandon all dreams of a future by her side.
Then she could talk about his future. She had silver in plenty.
Her years as Brehon of the Burren had brought her wealth. Her
law school was popular, the fees had accumulated and Cumhal
managed the farm so well that there was always a profit. She
would give Dualta what he needed to set himself up in Galway,
she decided. Once the trial at Poulnabrone was over and he had
admitted his guilt and the fine had been paid then she would
make him the offer. He would no longer need to be a jobbing
mason, travelling the countryside, but could have his own shop
and perhaps some pupils to train in the prosperous city of Galway.

'We are two very different people now from the boy and girl
of twenty years ago,' she added firmly.

She watched him keenly and saw the realization of the position come into his eyes. After a minute, he nodded indifferently.

'I'll go, now,' he said, and she recognized that his voice was
devoid of hope. 'Don't worry; I'll get out easily, no matter how
many instructions you have issued. I tested it myself a few hours
ago. I just told the porter that I needed a stone from outside the
gate and he handed the key into my own hand. I locked the gate
behind me when I came back in and pretended to put the key
back on the peg, but here it is now.' From his pouch he produced
a large key.

'And why didn't you go then?' Perhaps that would have been
best, she thought, though recognizing the feeling as a weakness.

He gave a short laugh. 'Why not, indeed? There speaks a lady
who has plenty of money. I wanted to finish the work and get
my payment for it. I can't live through the winter in Galway
without that. Anyway, by then I was sure that you did not recognize me and without recognizing me what would be the motive
for the crime? However, you were cleverer than I thought, so
now I will go.'

'No,' she said firmly. 'Not without admitting the crime in
public.'

'Perhaps I'll take you with me,' he said. He pulled out another
flask of *brócoit* from his pouch, emptied it in one long swallow
and then replaced it. 'You would have come willingly at one time.'

She ignored that. She would say no more about giving him money, she decided. He was obviously a very heavy drinker; there might well be no saving of him. 'If you are not prepared to acknowledge your crime,' she continued, 'then I shall order that you be bound and guarded until the case can be tried. I will find a lawyer to speak for you if you wish, but I can assure you that my evidence will convict you.'

'You were always hard,' he said, looking at her gloomily.

'Three years with you meant that I had to harden, or else break.' She flashed the words out like the thrust of a dagger, breaking her own resolution not to talk about the past.

It should not have been said; she knew that as soon as she had uttered the words. His face darkened and changed.

And yet all might still have been well if the west door had not opened suddenly, young, confident feet strode up the church and then Shane's voice, high and light:

'Brehon, the abbot has sent me to tell you that we are on our way.'

Close on his heels were a couple of young monks, one of whom, with a taper in his hand, proceeded to go from candlestick to candlestick filling the church with light. They passed the three figures at the top of the nave and the brilliance of the lights that they carried blinded Mara for a moment.

As soon as they lit the candles in the chancel, Dualta blew out his own candle. The strong, burning-flesh smell of the tallow floated beneath Mara's nostrils. Now she could no longer see him properly, but he stood very close to her and very close to Shane. And then came the sound of voices and the noise of footsteps coming across in through the west door, walking to their places in the nave. And then more footsteps, tramping in disciplined silence, of the monks entering the church behind the abbot.

At that moment Dualta acted.

Swiftly he took a step forward and seized Shane, dragging him away from Mara and up the steps towards the altar. All candles had now been lit there and their light illuminated the scene. At the same moment as Shane screamed, Mara saw the dagger at his throat.

'Keep away, everyone, keep away from me.' Dualta's hoarse,

rough voice rasped through the church and a stunned silence fell
instantly.

'What is the meaning of this?' The abbot spoke carefully and
quietly; the menace to the boy's life was obvious. Mara glanced
at Conall and Fergal; each had a dagger in his hand. Teige O'Brien
was fumbling for his, while Ardal O'Lochlainn moved slowly, but
softly, towards the north transept.

'The meaning of this is that I have accused this man, Dualta,
the mason, of the murder of Mahon O'Brien.' Mara made her
voice as loud as she could. She heard it ring from the arches and
hoped that it could cover the small, soft movements that Ardal
was making. Deliberately she moved to the opposite side of the
church, near to the door leading out on to the cloisters. Let all
attention be focused on her, she prayed, and let Ardal approach
the altar without being seen.

'This man,' she repeated, 'this man, Dualta, the mason, was my
husband once. I divorced him nineteen years ago. Yesterday, in a
fit of insanity, he planned to murder the king, rather than to allow
me to marry again.'

A murmur arose in the church and Mara heard the soft noise
with pleasure, even the brothers were turning one to the other.
Let Dualta be occupied in looking across at her, in listening to
her words, let him not look towards Ardal.

'As we all know now, Mahon O'Brien took the king's place in
the church. One hooded man, of the same size and build, looks
like another,' she went on, spacing her words to allow the echo to
return its response. Ardal had now reached the scalloped archway
leading to the small north transept chapel.

'He went into the church,' she continued. She was accustomed
to holding attention by her voice, but it was a long time since she
had tried so consciously to use every trick of oratory. She raised her
voice dramatically, 'He lifted the hammer, his own mason's hammer;
he swung it and then battered in the head of the man who was
kneeling in prayer. It was a violent and hate-filled attack,' she finished.
Now Ardal had one foot on the stone flags of the chancel.

'I call on Dualta, the mason, to answer this case,' she said loudly.
Surely he would say something now. For twelve years he had
been part of Cahermacnaghten Law School. This procedure must
be imbedded in his mind.

There was a quick exclamation from Shane, which tore at her heart. He would never cry out unless he was hurt. He was a courageous, strong-willed child. Dualta must have pressed the knife a little further into his throat.

'What do you say, Dualta the mason, are you guilty or not guilty?' she called out quickly and loudly. These words should have been saved for judgement day at Poulnabrone, but she did not care that she was going outside the legal procedure. Patrick now had started to move. She could understand that; he was, after all, the father, but he was heavily built, elderly and unfit; it would be best to leave it to Ardal.

And then everything went wrong. Dualta suddenly swung around. He had caught the movement from Patrick and had then seen Ardal.

'Stay still,' he roared. 'Stay still, everyone, or this boy will be killed here on the altar. Get back!' he signalled frantically to Ardal. 'Get back, get back into the nave.'

Ardal moved back instantly. A man who had worked all of his life with highly strung thoroughbred horses, he recognized the dangerous note of hysteria in Dualta's voice. Patrick became quite immobilized, like a marble saint standing with his back against one of the stone columns.

'Lock the west door, Father Abbot,' shouted Dualta. His voice rose to a hoarse scream. 'Lock it, I say. Lock it immediately. Yes, that's right. Don't stop. Go straight down. Lock it. Let me hear the noise of the key turning.'

The abbot hesitated for a moment and then strode down the centre of the nave and locked the door, the click sounding very loud in a silence where people almost forbore to breathe. He returned up the centre of the church and approached the altar.

'Stop there,' shouted Dualta. 'Don't come any nearer. Stay where you are. That's right. No one else move.' Like a maddened bull, he swung around from the right side to left. No one moved.

'Dualta,' said Mara calmly, her voice high and steady. 'Remember what I said to you. For the sake of that marriage that once existed I will take your debt upon me. You have nothing to fear.'

'Throw the church keys up here on the altar, Father Abbot,' shouted Dualta. 'I am going now by the cloister door and I will lock you in. I don't want any pursuers.'

'I shall not give you the keys,' said the abbot, his voice steady and low.

Dualta ignored this. 'I'll leave the keys somewhere outside the gate. Sooner or later someone will release you. But I am taking the boy with me. He'll be my safeguard, I may leave him, also, somewhere, or I may cut his throat on the way. I don't know.'

From the corner of her eye, Mara knew that Ardal, once again, was braced and ready. Cumhal had begun to steal softly from the back of the church and was directing his noiseless route towards the cloisters' door. Turlough had his dagger out and the body-guards had moved a silent step forward. There was no way that Dualta could leave the church unscathed. But what about Shane? No one wanted to put his life in danger.

'Throw the keys,' suddenly screamed Dualta with a hasty glance around. 'Throw the keys now. No more talking, no more waiting.'

'Give him the keys, Father Abbot,' said Mara in a loud clear voice. Anything to keep the talking going, she thought! Surely the man had enough wit to throw them awkwardly, to make Dualta shift, bend down, move that deadly dagger from Shane's neck. She turned to look at the priest and her heart sank. His face was set in obstinate lines and his grey eyes were ice-cold.

'No,' he said loudly. 'No, I will do nothing to allow this man to escape. This man has murdered my brother. This man must hang.'

'I will kill the boy.' Dualta's voice was hoarse, but everyone in the church heard the words and there was a low murmur and a restless stirring of feet.

'Keep still!' The scream was so loud that the sound echoed through the stone church. Instantly the church was as silent as if it were empty of all but the graven saints.

'I tell you once again,' Dualta's voice was all the more sinister for the low tone in which he now spoke. He stopped and then started again. 'I tell you that I must leave this church now. I will take a horse from the stable and I will never be seen in the Burren again. Now I give you one last chance. Throw those keys to me, or I shall come and get them from you, but before that I will leave another dead body in this church.'

'No,' said the abbot. 'You will not escape. You are one man

against many.' Quickly he went over towards the cloisters' door and locked it rapidly. 'Put down that knife and let that child go.'

'Give him the keys, Father Abbot,' said Mara urgently. 'Stand back from the door, everyone.'

'No,' said the abbot. 'I will not allow the man who killed my brother to escape. Brehon law holds no sway here; this case must be judged by Roman law and the culprit punished according to its rules.' Deliberately he reached up to the full extent of his very tall figure and placed the keys on top of the fluted column, where they rested on the frieze of poppy heads.

'Now you have left me no way out; now the boy will die,' said Dualta. His voice was deep and resolute. With his left hand he grabbed the heavy *glib* of black hair that overhung Shane's brow and bent the child's head back so that his skull rested on the altar and his white throat was exposed to the knife.

Eighteen

Senchas Már
(The Great Tradition)

A king may make a treaty with another kingdom. If a crime such as murder, wounding, theft, rape or satire is committed by a member of this other kingdom then restitution will be paid.

The nave of the church was almost in darkness. It was only a couple of hours past noon, but it was a dark day and very little light entered the church, just one pale gleam slanting in through one tall, narrow window at the end of the south aisle. The chancel, however, with its rows of candles, was now brightly lit and all eyes were focused on the altar with the two figures in front of it: the man with the knife and the boy with the dangerously exposed throat. There were nearly sixty people in that church and yet the silence was intense. No one moved, no one spoke; hardly a breath disturbed the air.

There had been no noise, nothing to alarm: no creak of a door, no whisper of wood sliding on wood, no rippling of string.

So the sound, when it came, was startling in its intensity: almost like a jangled chord from a lute, a sudden, ping-like sound that made all heads turn, all except one.

From the altar came a scream.

Mara, like the others, had turned, saw, and then instantly turned back. In a moment she had reached the steps to the altar and held Shane in her arms for a minute before handing him to Patrick.

Dualta's body, face down, lay slumped on the steps. In the centre of his back, slightly to the left, protruded a large arrow, feathered with a short, harsh pinion from a raven's side. A steady stream of blood dripped down upon the steps.

Mara felt herself gently moved to one side and stood back, allowing Father Peter to approach the body. She felt her heart thud against her ribs and she took a couple of deep breaths.

'He's dead, poor soul,' said Father Peter, feeling the wrist, and then turning the white head gently to one side and placing a finger over the lips beneath the white moustache.

'Dead,' echoed the abbot, stepping forward and waving the others away with an impatient wave of his hand. The untidy huddle of brothers and laity stepped back and then parted, turning around to stare at the white-faced girl who advanced up through their centre with the bow in her hand.

'Well done, Ellice,' said Mara firmly. She averted her eyes from the body at her feet and looked keenly at Shane, now struggling to free himself from his father's embrace.

'Are you all right?' she questioned, noticing the trickle of blood from his neck that had already stained the top of his white *léine*.

'I'm fine,' he said, embarrassment flooding his face with crimson and then retreating to leave him unnaturally pale and shaking from head to foot. 'That was a good shot, Ellice,' he called, steadying his voice with an effort. 'That was *iontach*!'

No higher praise could be bestowed, thought Mara, trying hard to distract herself. Despite her brave words she, also, had begun to shiver. A feeling of sickness welled up within her and she hoped that she was not going to faint. She still kept her eyes from the body on the floor, clenching her hands so that the nails drove painfully into her palms. Her eyes burned with unshed tears and she breathed slowly and deeply, fighting for control as she turned to face Turlough.

'The boy had to be saved,' he said quietly, answering the unspoken appeal in her eyes as he grasped her hand in his large warm palm. 'It was the only way. No words of yours could have stopped him. He was a bitter and disappointed man who probably didn't want to live. Thank God Ellice had the presence of mind to do what she did.'

Mara nodded. He could have said nothing better to help her to regain control over herself. She looked lovingly across at Shane, now in Brigid's arms, and then at Patrick, standing there, eyes no longer hooded, but gazing intently at his youngest son. The whole church seemed filled with the relief of all. Everyone clustered around wanting to touch Shane, the women to hug him, the men to slap him on the back, even Frann and Banna were smiling at each other with relief. Conor proudly put his arm around Ellice

and she responded by moving closer to him. Even the carpenter,
a man who had worked side by side with Dualta, had given a
satisfied nod when Father Peter had pronounced the mason to
be dead.

'Put down that bow!' The abbot's fury-filled words erupted
from white lips.

Ellice turned to him in a puzzled way and then glanced down
at the bow that still hung from her right hand. Ardal courteously
took it from her and looked enquiringly at the abbot.

'You have profaned the house of God!' The words were spoken
quietly, but the whole church immediately fell silent. Brigid took
her arms away from Shane, turning towards the abbot, her freckled
face blazing with indignation, but no one spoke.

'Thou shalt not kill.' Now the voice rang out and reverberated
against the stone.

'This man had already killed and was about to kill again, Father
Donogh,' said Turlough mildly, but Mara felt how his hand had
tensed.

' "Vengeance is mine," saith the Lord.'

'That would not have been much consolation to us all if the
boy had been murdered as well as your own brother,' thundered
Turlough.

They faced each other like two bulls in the same field, these
two members of the O'Brien royal family, shoulders squared,
heads slightly lowered, eyes locked on eyes.

'All things, that are unjust in this world, shall be made right
in the next world,' said the abbot loftily.

'And yet,' said Mara, taking a step forward, 'you yourself said
that the man who killed your brother, Mahon O'Brien, should
be hanged.' It was time to put a stop to this. Turlough would not
fare too well in the swapping of pious quotations. The abbot
turned to her furiously.

'That is the law; ' "thou shalt give a life for a life, an eye for
an eye and a tooth for a tooth". So says the law, and the Church
espouses that law. But only the law can authorize that death.
Two wrongs do not make a right.'

'The Church may think as she pleases,' said Mara dryly. 'This
is the territory of the Burren and Brehon law prevails.' Has the
man gone mad? she wondered. Is this visit from the high-ranking

monk from Tintern Abbey of such tremendous importance to him that any threat to an orderly picture of praying monks and distinguished guests is enough to make him lose sight of reason? Was the prospect of being abbot of Mellifont enough to make him offend his sovereign?

'And you will impose a fine on this woman,' sneered the abbot. 'What is that in comparison with a God-given human life?'

'There will be no fine.'

He was silent then, gazing at her with his raven-grey eyes.

'If needs be, I will judge this case at Poulnabrone,' said Mara clearly, looking around to make sure that her words reached all ears. She looked away from the abbot and fixed her eyes on Ellice's thin white face. 'But I can tell you now, according to the best of my knowledge and recollection of the judgement texts, that no fine will be imposed; no crime has taken place. The law is quite clear; blood may be spilled in order to save a life. The boy was in grave danger; we all saw the knife and can, even now, see its track on his neck. Ellice deserves the thanks and praise of us all.'

'Well said,' burst out Turlough. 'She's a girl of high courage. We're all proud of her.' He dropped Mara's hand, enveloped Ellice in one of his bear-like hugs and then slapped Conor lightly on the shoulder.

'Lucky lad,' he said. 'If I wasn't going to be married to the most beautiful, most wonderful woman in the world then I'd be envious of you.'

There was a ripple of laughter at that and Mara hastened to put an end to it. There would be time for all of this afterwards; first Dualta must be given his due.

'Father Abbot, will you give orders for a grave to be dug in the cemetery; I know that you have a strangers' corner and this will be appropriate. Master Carpenter, will you be able to make a coffin; I will pay you for that work?'

'No need for that,' said the carpenter quickly. 'We worked together for many years, and when he could keep away from the strong liquor there was no better worker. I would do it at my own expense, but it happens that there is a rough coffin of soft pinewood ready; I made it so that Master Mason, may God have mercy on him, could use it as a guide for making the stone tomb. I'll take one of these young brothers and we'll fetch it.'

He touched Brother Melduin on the shoulder and they both disappeared.

'Will you give him absolution and anoint the body, Father Abbot?' asked Mara.

He hesitated, but he could not refuse this; the oils were fetched immediately by Father Peter and placed into his hands. Turlough knelt down and the others followed his example. Mara took a step back so that she was standing beside Father Peter.

'The grave,' she whispered.

He nodded in reply. 'Best get everything done quickly.' His voice was barely audible to her ears and he got to his feet as softly as any cat. Mara saw him touch the shoulders of four strong lay brothers and they all slipped to the dimness at the back of the church without attracting his abbot's attention.

There was a certain bustle, anyway, as the carpenter with Brother Melduin, now returned through the cloisters' door. They carried the makeshift coffin to the top of the church and placed it on the marble slab where, only a short time ago, the elaborate coffin of Mahon O'Brien had lain. Together they lifted the body of Dualta into it, turning him so that he lay on his side. Mara knew they did this so that the arrow would not need to be withdrawn, but she thought it gave Dualta an air as if he slept. Despite the widely staring eyes, there was something about him, now, that reminded her of the twenty-year-old when she had last seen him.

Brother Melduin withdrew, but the carpenter spent a few minutes bending over the coffin, straightening the legs and joining the hands together. Mara watched him appreciatively. Somehow his gestures spoke of a relationship, a comradeship between two people who worked together and who respected each other's skill. She wished now that she had said more to Dualta when they talked there in the church. She wished that she had shown her appreciation of his talents, of the heights to which he had attained in a profession that he had adopted as a second best. Perhaps if she had done that he would not have taken that final fatal step.

Now the carpenter had finished his work. He straightened up and glanced at her. Brother Melduin had returned carrying a large plank. They would use this as a lid.

'Wait!' Mara swiftly crossed over to the pier where Dualta had left his candle earlier and groped around until her fingers touched the tiny stone harebell. Dualta had been working on this, the last replacement flower for the circle of flowers above. If he had lived this stone blossom would have taken its place, beside the others, on the frieze that encircled the tall column. Mara picked it up and held it to the light for a second. It was quite perfect: the five star-like points pricked out with careful exactitude. She carried it across and placed it in the coffin beside the right hand of the man who had fashioned it. If, sometime in the future, the bones of Dualta were uncovered he would be known as the artist who had carved some of these wonderful capitals, which adorned the clustered piers at the north transept. Perhaps the fame of this work would endure when the work of Brehon lawyers had been forgotten. She nodded to the carpenter and then stood back. Now was the time to close up the makeshift coffin.

The carpenter took the large plank, covered the coffin with it and then, taking the iron nails one by one from his pouch, hammered it securely to the crude box which was to be the final resting place for that handsome youth, son of a wealthy mason from Thomond, who had come, full of ambition, to the law school of Cahermacnaghten over thirty years ago.

Then there was a pause. The abbot had not moved. With knitted brows and compressed lips, he was standing staring at the patch of blood on the ground. He had blessed the coffin in a perfunctory fashion, but was now obviously brooding on that challenge to his authority, when the Brehon had brushed aside any question that this bloodletting in church was a crime. Everyone waited for his instructions.

He lifted his eyelids and stared coldly at Ellice, and Mara noticed that the girl flinched at his gaze. Then he raised a long forefinger and beckoned to a couple of young lay brothers. Mara guessed that they were being told to carry the coffin, but she guessed wrongly. They both nodded their heads, looked quickly and furtively at Ellice, then went and stood by the door to the cloisters waiting while the abbot retrieved the keys and unlocked the door, jerking his head at Brother Porter to accompany them. Still no one in the church moved, though several looked inquiringly at each other. The presence of the porter seemed to show that these brothers were being sent on an errand outside the gates of the abbey.

A few minutes later, the porter was back, alone, whispering in the abbot's ear. Of course, thought Mara, Dualta had stolen the porter's key to the great front gates of the abbey. However, she decided to keep silent. Why disturb the coffin now – surely there were other keys.

With an expression of annoyance, the abbot detached a key from his own bunch and handed it over. Now Mara guessed what was happening. She stepped a little to one side so as to be nearer to Brigid and said in a low tone: 'See whether Brother Melduin knows where these two have been sent.'

By her side Turlough stirred impatiently. It was time for the dead man to be carried to the burial ground. The carpenter stood with one hand on the coffin obviously ready to take his share; but no man can carry a coffin on his own.

'Father Abbot,' said Turlough in tones which he strove to make sound low and reverential, 'will some of your young brothers carry the coffin?'

'I will ask no man to carry the body of a murderer.' The tone was low and almost neutral, but the glance that flashed around the clustering monks held the whiplash of authority in it. No brother, whether lay or choir monk, would dare to offer now.

Mara felt the tears well up in her eyes. This man was once her husband. If they had stayed together, even if his death had been so untimely, sons would have been born who would, by now, have been old enough to perform that last simple service for him. There would have been other daughters, too; sisters to Sorcha, and their husbands would have lent broad shoulders.

'I will carry the coffin, then.' As unassuming as any farmer, Turlough stepped forward and stood beside one corner.

'I will partner you, my lord,' said Teige promptly with a quick malicious glance at his priestly cousin.

'Come on, lad, match up with Master Carpenter; you two are much of a size,' said Turlough impatiently to Murrough.

'Garrett and I will take the head, my lord,' said Ardal, stepping forward before Murrough had moved and in a few moments it was all arranged with the four younger men at the corners and the two middle-aged cousins in the centre positions.

Dualta would have been pleased to know that royalty and nobility were carrying his coffin, thought Mara, looking affectionately at

Turlough. Cumhal, she noticed, was looking slightly shame-faced. However, he and Brigid had hated Dualta with a depth of bitter dislike which was in proportion to the height of their love for herself: she would not have given him an order to do what would have been distasteful for him. As it was, this was a princely cortège. Decisively she linked her arm to Ellice's and walked behind the coffin, noticing with pleasure how Banna and Frann, still side by side, followed her. Soon those two would be friends. Frann had an engaging way about her and poor Banna would probably soon find herself in the position of second mother to the coming child.

Coming out into the bright fresh air was a relief after the dark, dank heaviness of the church. A few late evening streaks of sunlight silvered the heights of Abbey Hill and illuminated a small pink herb Robert, blooming in the shelter of the stone wall around the graveyard as happily as it had done right through the summer months. The fractured rays of the winter sun gilded the rain-washed rocks and the silver carapaces of the carline thistles. Mara sniffed the air; the strong north-westerly wind brought the smell of the Atlantic ocean even to this enclosed ground. There would only be another couple of hours of daylight, the sun would sink down behind the mountains of Connemara in the north-west and then would come the night before Christmas, a night to celebrate the birth of Christ and the turning of the old year.

She turned towards Ellice, feeling her tremble, and whispered reassuringly: 'You did the right thing. None will blame you. You saved the boy's life in the only possible way that you could. Thank God that you were there and that you had the skill and the courage to do it.'

Ellice said nothing but a little colour came into her white cheeks. If the day had not turned stormy, thought Mara, if Ellice and Father Denis had managed to reach Galway they would now be on their way and he would be alive, but then perhaps Shane would have died. Perhaps God was watching over them and arranging everything better than any man could do it. Perhaps if Conor's health improved, he and Ellice would settle down to a happy marriage. The king should make sure that his son played more of a part in the governing of the kingdom and that Ellice,

also, would have her role. I'll talk to Turlough about this, she
promised herself.

The grave was just being finished when they entered through
the gate to the burial ground. The four lay brothers shovelled
out the last few sods of the light, friable soil and then climbed
out and stood with bowed heads. Father Peter, his grey cloak
fluttering in the stiff wind, came forward. He looked around
for the abbot, but, seeing no one, he himself began the service,
first in Latin, and then rather movingly in Gaelic, praying that
the man's sins be forgiven and that his crime be not remembered, but rather that the good he had done and the beauty
that he had created should live after the maker himself had
turned to dust. The figures around the grave watched with
solemnity, and in silence, until the coffin was lowered down to
its final resting place. Then Banna sobbed quietly and Shane
gave a sudden violent shiver and a loud hiccup. Up to now,
childlike, he had been almost elated by his escape and by his
admiration of Ellice's skill, but now the awful realization of
death had suddenly hit him.

'Take Shane over to the Royal Lodge and give him a hot
drink, Ellice,' whispered Mara. Brigid would have been delighted
to do this, but Mara felt that Ellice, also, should not be present
when the earth was shovelled down over the coffin of the man
she had killed. 'And Conor had better go too,' she added. It was
bracing, but cold, out in the fresh air, and the delicate Conor
would be better not standing around too long. In any case, in
caring for the boy the couple would find a closeness which might
otherwise be spoiled by mutual embarrassment. Mara's eyes
followed them with satisfaction. Ellice had an arm over Shane's
shoulders, but her other hand was firmly held by Conor.

Father Peter must have guessed her intentions, because he had
made a quick gesture to the lay brothers to stay their hand for
the moment. Once the three figures had gone through the small
iron gate, they began to shovel quickly and soon the hole was
filled with the fine-grained Burren soil.

I'll bring some harebell seed in the summer and plant the grave
with them, thought Mara, and then she blessed herself and turned
away. Turlough was talking to Teige O'Brien, so Mara went over
to Brigid.

'How did you manage with Brother Melduin?' she asked in a low voice.

Brigid's eyes twinkled. 'He was listening, of course,' she said. 'He's a man after my own heart; he always knows the latest news.'

'So, what's the story?' asked Mara lightly, borrowing one of Brigid's favourite phrases.

Brigid moved a little further away from the group and Mara followed her.

'He sent those two brothers to Kinvarra,' she whispered.

'Kinvarra?' Mara frowned with puzzlement. Kinvarra was only a few miles away from the abbey. It was not Burren territory, but neither did it have anything to do with the Galway city. It was part of O'Flaherty territory. 'That's all right, then,' she continued. 'I was afraid that he had sent them to Galway, though I did think it was a long way to go – it would be dark by the time they got there and then it's Christmas tomorrow.'

'Ah, but listen, Brehon,' said Brigid eagerly, 'it's not all right. It's not all right, at all. He sent them to Kinvarra because the sergeant-at-arms – Brother Melduin thinks that's a kind of Brehon – the sergeant-at-arms from Galway is staying there with his wife's family.'

'I see,' said Mara thoughtfully. She was very doubtful as to whether this sergeant-at-arms would bother disturbing his Christmas holiday to come and investigate a crime which was committed well away from the laws of Galway. On the other hand, he might be friendly with the abbot – otherwise how would his whereabouts for the festival be known – and he might feel that it was a good opportunity to extend the sway of English law and English customs. Undoubtedly nothing serious would happen to Ellice, but the abbot probably felt that he should make a show of maintaining discipline within his abbey. It was a risk that she was unwilling to take and instantly she made up her mind.

'Brigid, what are your stores of food like, back at Cahermacnaghten?'

Brigid, as usual, had followed her thoughts accurately and answered instantly.

'Plenty for all, Brehon; the sooner we go the better.'

'I was thinking that we could perhaps have our Christmas

festivities back at the law school,' said Mara, her eyes gazing
thoughtfully towards Clerics' Pass. How long would it take the
two brothers to ride to Kinvarra and then to return against a
strong headwind? Long enough, she decided. She looked back at
Brigid who was nodding her head vigorously and counting off
storeroom items on her fingers.

'There would be the king, of course, and the two bodyguards,
and . . .'

'And the lads and Shane's father,' finished Brigid. 'And perhaps
the king's son, Conor, and his wife?'

'And the O'Brien and his wife?'

'Plenty for all, Brehon,' repeated Brigid.

'And perhaps Father Peter?'

Brigid looked doubtful. '*He*'d never let him go,' she said.

'Who, the abbot?'

Brigid nodded.

'I think there is a rule among the Cistercians that they have
to lend their herbalist when there is need of his skills,' said Mara
thoughtfully. 'You and Cumhal go and load the cart, Brigid. Do
it as quietly as you can and say nothing to anyone. I'm going to
talk to the king, now.'

Turlough was chatting genially with Father Peter, but broke
off when she came to stand by his side.

'God bless you, Brehon. Isn't it good we had you here,' said
Father Peter, smiling his toothless grin. 'I was just saying to my
lord here that you always find the answer.'

'I think you helped me to find it, Father Peter,' said Mara
modestly. 'You told me that I probably knew the truth, that I just
had to look into my heart. It was true; everything was known
to me, I just had to fit the pieces together.'

'Well, it's been a sad and difficult time for everyone. I hope
the boy is all right.'

'That's just what I was going to talk to you about, Father Peter,'
said Mara quickly, seizing the opening. 'I'm a little worried about
Shane. I wonder would it be too much of a trouble for you to
go over to the Royal Lodge and have a look at him? Brigid is
there and she will get you anything you need.'

'What are you getting rid of him for?' asked Turlough with
an amused smile after Father Peter had scuttled away. 'No need

to raise your eyebrows so innocently at me, I know you when you are planning something.'

'I just want to get him out of the abbot's way until my plan comes to fruition,' said Mara. 'Turlough, do you remember what you said this morning, about spending Christmas at Cahermacnaghten? Were you serious?'

'Of course I was serious,' said Turlough emphatically. 'Let's go there now, just the two of us. After all, the murder is solved. I don't want any more boiled cod. We'll go, shall we? Just the two of us?'

'I think,' said Mara thoughtfully, 'some others must come, also. I'm a bit worried about a few things.'

'I thought it was too good to be true.' Turlough spoke in resigned tones, but Mara knew it was half-feigned. He was a sociable man who enjoyed the company of family and friends. They would have a good Christmas.

Nineteen

Uraicecht Becc
(Small Primer)

The honour price of an abbot depends on the size of the abbey over which he rules. The abbot must ensure that his monks are devout, honest and that the ordained clergy are properly qualified in the services of baptism, communion, celebration of mass, sanctification of marriage, requiem for the dead and preaching of the gospel.

If a church building is allowed to become a den of thieves or a place of sin, it can be destroyed without penalty.

'I fear that we must leave you now, Father Abbot. Father Peter is of my opinion that the young boy, Shane, needs to be taken away from the place where his life was threatened. He is very shaken by the events. Perhaps in your kindness you will allow Father Peter to come with us and to stay until we are sure that the boy is well, again? His father, the Brehon from Tyrone, would be very grateful. I would not ask this favour were it not that Malachy, my own physician, has taken his daughter to Galway for the festive season.' Time enough, later on, for him to realize that the king, his sick son, Conor, and Ellice were all going to spend Christmas at Cahermacnaghten.

The abbot bowed graciously and then cleared his throat, a two-note sound filled with embarrassment.

'Of course, there is no reason now why a marriage service cannot be performed between yourself and the king, tomorrow morning,' he said tentatively. 'I'm sure that Father Richard Wyche from Tintern would be delighted to witness the ceremony.'

Mara shuddered slightly. An artistic shudder, she congratulated herself inwardly.

'Let's not talk of weddings on this sad day of burials,' she said gravely. She extended her hand graciously. 'We will meet again in happier times. And thank you so much for allowing your herbalist, Father Peter, to come with us in order to care for my young scholar.'

'And, of course, Banna, I will pay to you the fine that is due to you as compensation after the death of your husband.' Banna looked as if she were about to demur and then looked uncertain.

Mara hastened to reassure her. 'No, no, I would be uneasy if I did not take it upon myself to do this.'

Hopefully this would soften the blow when Banna found out that she had been disinherited by her late husband and that all of the wealth that was his to dispose of had been willed to his wife of the second degree, the fertile Frann, while his wife of thirty years was left with only a house and land fit to graze seven cows.

'Well, if you're sure that is the right thing, Brehon.' Mara felt a certain shifting of guilt from her shoulders when she saw the woman bow her head with acquiescence. Fortunately Banna knew little of the law and did not realize that divorce ended all liability, and, of course, even if Mara and Dualta had still been married there would have been no obligation. As Fithail put it: '*Marbhaid cach marbh a chinta* – every dead man buries his offences.'

'And what of yourself, Banna? What will you do now?'

'Well, I'll spend Christmas at the abbey and then I suppose I will go home,' said Banna with a weary sigh. She looked better today, thought Mara. The dramatic events of the last couple of hours seemed to have stemmed her tears.

'And you will go and see your late husband's Brehon on your return, won't you? Now I will wish you the best and may your sorrow become bearable in the months to come,' said Mara solemnly, with an eye on the sun which was moving into the south-west. They should be on their way as soon as possible to ensure that they reached Cahermacnaghten before sundown and there were two more farewells that she needed to make before departing. Across the garth, she could see that Murrough and Turlough had made their farewells and from the abrupt way that each man turned his back on the other, she guessed that it had not been an amiable meeting.

* * *

'So you are off again, Murrough? A long journey for such a short visit.'

'It was worth a gamble,' said Murrough with a shrug of his broad shoulders. He made as if to go away, but then turned back. Mara looked at him warily. He had his ingratiating, small-boy smile on his face and his green eyes appraised her carefully before he spoke.

'You're a woman of sense, I know,' he began.

'Thank you, Murrough.' Mara was amused, but willing to make an effort to part on friendly terms.

'I know that I can put my trust in your discretion.'

'I think you may,' said Mara warily.

'And you will try to make my father see the right way forward.'

'The right way?' she queried, raising an eyebrow.

'You know what I mean.' His tone was impatient.

'No, I don't,' said Mara. 'But if it worries you, I think I can assure you that your father will always take the right way – the honourable, decent way – without any advice from me.'

'Or from me, either, I suppose you mean,' he said, with an undercurrent of mockery in his voice.

'That's true. Surely it should be the other way around, shouldn't it? It's for a wise and experienced older man to give advice to a younger.'

'I bet you didn't think that when you were my age.' The sudden grin made him look so like his father that Mara could not resist smiling back.

'No,' she admitted. 'I don't suppose that I did. I suppose we all have to make our own mistakes and go our own way until we find wisdom for ourselves.'

They stood smiling at each other for a moment, while in the background the noise of the heavy cart with Cumhal and Brigid, surrounded with baskets and crates, trundling through the gates and down the paved road leading from the abbey died away. Both of them followed its progress with their eyes and then turned back to face each other. More needed to be said; Mara waited and saw how Murrough's face darkened.

'Well, everything has worked out well for you; you can get married now with the blessing of Rome on your union; I suppose I should wish you happiness.'

'Only if it comes from the heart,' said Mara indifferently and then, as he turned away, she called after him, 'Tell me something, Murrough, why did you come dressed as a pilgrim? What was the point of that?'

'I knew you would be against me.' There was a spurt of malice in his voice, the tone of the spoiled boy. 'I thought I would try to get my father on his own away from you; if I did that I might have a better chance of convincing him. I planned to get into conversation with him, still disguised.'

'And then came the news of the death.'

Murrough nodded. 'Actually, when I heard him announce the vigil the night before, I had planned the meeting. I thought that, first thing in the morning, in the church, alone, would be an ideal time to see him, but when it came to it, well, I didn't want to leave my bed. If I had done so, I would have been the first to discover the body and then you would have been certain of my guilt.' He laughed suddenly: 'Like father, like son,' he said. 'Both of us saved by laziness.'

'So why did you try to stop the marriage? Was it because you thought I might interfere with your plans?'

'Of course I had to try to stop that marriage.' Now his voice rang with sincerity. 'I suppose that was the real reason for coming. It would have disgraced my father to have married you, a woman lawyer – I could just imagine what they would have thought of that in London.' He gave a short laugh. 'They wouldn't be able to imagine such a thing as a woman lawyer; you would have been burned as a witch – and then you were a divorced woman! In England no woman could divorce her husband. You were no fitting match for a nobleman like my father. The Great Earl has a niece, a young girl of just fourteen; he would be pleased to give her to my father if he made obeisance to King Henry VIII.'

'Possibly your father does not want a fourteen-year-old given to him; perhaps he would prefer to choose his own wife,' said Mara mildly. She was getting tired of this egotistical boy; it was time to put a stop to this. 'Well, Murrough, you have chosen your path, tied your chariot to the wheels of the Earl of Kildare, and I do believe that you are sincere in your beliefs, so I will wish you a good future and may the road rise up with you, as the old people say. I must leave you now because I want to see Ardal O'Lochlainn before we go.'

'We're leaving now, Ardal. I want to get Shane away from the abbey as soon as possible.' It was always best, Mara thought, to keep to the same story. 'Would you like to ride with us and have a Christmas Eve supper at Cahermacnaghten?'

'You're very kind, Brehon.' His tone, as always, was full of courtesy, but his eyes went restlessly across to the doorway where Frann was demurely taking leave of the abbot. 'I have some business to attend to in Kinvarra so I thought I would escort Mahon O'Brien's widow to her home at Dunguaire,' he concluded.

'How very kind of you,' said Mara sedately. 'I'm sure she will appreciate your company.'

And they will make a handsome pair, she thought, looking from one to the other, Ardal with his red-gold hair and blue eyes and Frann with her alluring charm. What a pleasant Christmas they would have. And then she thought of her own plans for Christmas and smiled mischievously. She would not confide in anyone for the moment, she decided.

'She's a wonderful woman, that Brigid of yours,' said Turlough as they rounded the last corner before reaching Cahermacnaghten Law School. 'Look at that; there's smoke from every chimney and I swear that I can smell cooking already.'

'Well, she has Nessa full-time to help her these days; you remember Nessa from Kilcorney? That case we heard at Poulnabrone last Bealtaine? Nessa has had her instructions to keep the fires going until we returned; we had intended to do that tomorrow, anyway. We wanted to have everything to be warm and welcoming, then.' Mara surveyed her home with satisfaction. She had complete confidence in Brigid; no doubt, there would be a meal fit for a king served up at suppertime, but in the meantime, she herself had a few things to organize.

'. . . So would you and Shane cut lots of holly and ivy and decorate the schoolhouse, Fachtnan? I'll send Séan to help you,' she added as a shriek from the kitchen house warned that Brigid was already losing her temper with the slow-moving, slow-thinking Séan.

'Could I help, too? You'll need a rest, won't you, for a while.' Ellice turned her dark eyes on to her husband's weary, white face with an awkward semblance of wifely concern.

'Yes, you go along now,' said Father Peter, 'leave the *tánaiste* to me. A rest for an hour or two and then a good supper; that's the best thing for you, Conor.'

'That's great, Ellice. You'll be able to show Shane and myself where to put the holly and ivy; we're neither of us very good at decorating,' said Fachtnan with his usual easy courtesy.

After speaking to Turlough, Mara crossed the yard towards the schoolhouse. It was now quite dark, but she found her way easily by the light from a candle that had been placed on the stone window seat by the unshuttered window. She pushed open the door and stood smiling with pleasure. The boys, assisted by Séan, had worked hard to bring the evergreens in from the little woodland next to the law school, but she guessed that Ellice had decided the artistic arrangements. Great branches of sweet-smelling pine and red-berried holly were tied with pink linen tape to the crossbeams and doors; windows and the wooden press were garlanded with long, graceful trails of ivy. The placid fire of slow-burning peat had been fed with discarded pieces of pine and the orange and crimson flames leaped high into the chimney.

'That's perfect,' said Mara appreciatively. 'Ellice, could you just spread this linen cloth on my table and you others set out the benches. Arrange them in a semicircle around my table. That's right. Shane, run and get some cushions, Fachtnan, just go and see if there are a few snowdrops out there at the entrance to the wood.'

'Where will I put the mistletoe? Over your table?' asked Ellice.

'That would be lovely,' said Mara. She thought for a moment and then had doubts. 'No, perhaps better not. Tie it up over the door, Séan.'

There was a box of candles and some spare candleholders in the bottom of the press. Mara took them out and lit them, placing six on the snowy expanse of linen and crowding the rest on to the stone window seat. The room was filled with light, though nothing rivalled the dancing flames in the fireplace. She gazed around with satisfaction. The room looked beautiful, fit for its purpose.

'Are we going to eat in here, Brehon?' asked Shane, returning with an armful of cushions.

'No,' said Mara. 'We'll be in here first and then we'll go over and eat at the Brehon's house. Brigid is hard at work over there. Séan, you'd better go over and see if she needs anything. She had the two fires going in the kitchen when I looked in and she'll probably need some more wood soon. Oh, thank you, Fachtnan, I'll take the snowdrops; I'll put a few here and I want the rest of them for the table in the Brehon's house. You three carry on; you're making it look wonderful.'

She smiled sweetly at their puzzled faces and went across to the guest house where Father Peter was looking after Conor.

'So, how long have you been a priest, Father Peter?' Mara enquired. She spoke softly as Conor was dozing on a cushioned bench by the fire.

He meditated for a moment, visibly adding the years, checking them off on his fingers. He was a man whose thoughts seldom dwelled on himself, she guessed.

'It must be thirty-one years now.' His voice had a note of shock in it. He pondered for a moment and then added, 'Of course most of our order are brothers, but I wanted to be a priest from the start.'

'You had ambitions to be abbot,' she teased.

Father Peter jerked his head back with a deprecating gesture that bared his skinny neck and his lips parted in a toothless smile. 'Ah, that wouldn't be me, at all,' he said gently. 'I'm happy to serve the Lord in any way that I can be of use. If Father Donogh, God bless him, moves away to become abbot of Mellifont, then the order will appoint a new man to our own abbey. I'm too old for anything like that now.'

'But you would have administered all the sacraments, wouldn't you?'

'I never baptized a baby,' he said sadly.

'What about marriage?'

'Nor that, either.' His voice was cheerful now. 'We get only one or two marriages a year at the most and, as they are mostly important persons, Father Abbot attends to them himself.'

'But you could marry a couple?'

'Of course I could; any priest can do that.'

'Well, Father Peter,' said Mara lightly, 'just get your prayer book out and have a little practice because in half an hour we are going to have a wedding in the schoolhouse.'

'What!'

Mara smiled blandly at him and waited.

'You and King Turlough,' he said after a minute.

'That's right. All the other adults here are already married.'

'Lord bless you, the abbot will have my life. I couldn't do that – marry the king himself here, in a schoolhouse, not even in a church!'

'Well, I have a problem, Father,' said Mara, a note of well-feigned concern in her voice. 'You see, what with you in one bedroom of the guest house and the *tánaiste* and his wife in the other, and the Brehon from Tyrone in the third, Brigid is going to have to lodge the king in my house . . . and, well you know what the Church says about avoiding an occasion of sin . . .'

'Lord bless us and save us, you're a terrible woman to be saying things like that to me, Brehon,' he said in a shocked tone, but his small grey eyes were full of merriment.

'So you'll do it?'

'Sure when you put it like that, Brehon,' he said in a resigned way, 'I suppose I can always say that you left me with no choice.'

'We'll tell the abbot that we tortured you!' whispered Mara. Conor's wide blue eyes were starting to open so with a quick smile she left them.

'Brigid, could I disturb you for a moment?' Mara put her head around the kitchen door. The scene looked relatively peaceful. Nessa and her mother were peeling vegetables, Séan was feeding both fires with alternate pieces of pine and lumps of turf, all of the iron pots were simmering, boiling or roasting and nothing seemed to urgently require Brigid's attention. Mara knew that Brigid liked to keep an eye on everything but, on the other hand, Brigid had looked after her since she was a baby: if anyone deserved to know her news first, it was Brigid. She beckoned to her then, and led the way upstairs to her bedroom, closing the door behind them.

'Brigid,' she said nervously. 'I'm getting married tonight.'

'What!' Brigid's jaw dropped and her pale green eyes widened and bulged like gooseberries.

'Well, I don't see why you are looking so astonished,' said Mara lightly. 'After all, I was going to be married tomorrow. This is only a few hours earlier.'

'Yes, but . . .' spluttered Brigid. 'Do you mean you are going back to the abbey, or down to Noughaval Church?'

Mara shook her head. 'I've decided not to bother about the church.'

'What!' Brigid's outraged and scandalized voice rose to an ear-splitting volume.

'But we will have a priest; Father Peter is going to read the service.' This seemed to bring approval. 'It will be so much nicer here with you cooking the wedding feast instead of us having to eat the food that the abbey offers,' she ended diplomatically and watched the red patches of indignation die down from Brigid's cheeks.

'Well,' said Brigid with a sigh, 'you always did go your own way and I suppose there is no one to stop you. The king, God bless him, is just like your poor father, always ready to let you do anything that takes your fancy.'

'What do you think I should wear, Brigid?'

The question, as Mara had intended, immediately distracted Brigid.

'What would you wear but your wedding gown,' she said immediately. 'Let's look at it. I suppose you haven't even bothered taking it out of the chest since Cumhal carried it up here. Crushed to bits, I suppose.' Still muttering she opened the chest and took out an elegant red satin gown frilled and embroidered with heavy encrustations and with it an elaborate veil. Her son-in-law, Oisín, a merchant from Galway, had brought the cloth over from France and the veil as well as the gown had been made and embroidered in Galway City.

'You're right, Brigid,' said Mara, filling her voice with penitence. 'Yes, they are too crushed. And the wedding is in half an hour; Father Peter is already conning the service.'

'They don't look too bad to me,' said Brigid, dubiously. She looked suspiciously at Mara but could see nothing but regret there.

'I think I'll wear this,' said Mara. Quickly she took from the wooden press a simple woollen gown made in the traditional Irish fashion.

'What! That! But you've had that for years!'

'The king likes this one,' said Mara serenely. 'He said the colour reminded him of hazel leaves in the spring.' That was not quite right, she had made the remark and he had nodded agreement, but it did clear the anxious look from Brigid's face.

Mara held up the gown. It was always a favourite with her. The skirt was made from twenty-four triangular pieces of fine woollen cloth sewn together and each one of the triangles was pleated into four and attached to a broad, waist-hugging band. The bodice was beautifully tailored, with darts at the front. It had a small high collar at the back of the neck, but in front it was cut low. Quickly she pulled a snowy white *léine* of bleached linen over her head, then slipped the gown over it, laced up the bodice and then turned to look at herself in the long silver-plated mirror. Yes, she thought, it looks good. The heavy tubular folds fell straight down over her slim hips, the laced bodice outlined her breasts and the white of the *léine* trimmed with delicate lace at the neck, cuffs and hem enhanced the cool green of the gown.

'What about the veil?' queried Brigid.

Mara shook her head. 'No, no veil, it wouldn't go with this gown. I like my own black hair as it is.'

Brigid's freckled face lit up with a loving smile. 'Well, you always had beautiful hair. You could see your face in it I used to say. You look lovely, *alannah*, he's a lucky man, king or no king.'

Everyone from Cahermacnaghten crowded into the schoolhouse; farm servants and the two scholars rubbed shoulders with the O'Brien royal family as they sat on the heavy school benches.

There was no singing, no chanting, no ceremony, just a simple exchanging of vows and a recital of the Latin service conducted by Father Peter with frequent references to his well-worn missal. Then when all was over he put away the prayer book and turned to face the small congregation and beamed his toothless smile on them all.

'Brothers and sisters in Christ, we are here today, on this Christmas Eve, to bear witness to the exchanging of marriage vows between King Turlough Donn O'Brien and Mara O'Davoren, Brehon of the Burren,' he said. He paused for a moment and then continued in a conversational voice. 'We all know this man, King Turlough Donn, the worthy descendant of Brian Boru. We have all lived under his benign rule and we have all prospered. I am an old man and I have seen troubled times where neighbour killed neighbour and there were widows and orphans starving after bloody battles, but for the last ten years, since our king, God bless him, has ruled over these three kingdoms there has been peace and plenty for all.'

He paused for a moment looking kindly on the faces around him and then his eyes rested on Mara.

'Our Brehon, may the Lord make her burdens light, has reigned over us like a queen for even longer than that. It's hard to believe it when I look at her and see her like a girl before me, but she took on the task of Brehon of the Burren over fifteen years ago and since then has kept the peace between families and friends; she has seen into the human mind, unravelled all crimes, made the rough ways smooth and the brethren to dwell together in unity. The heart of every man and woman in this kingdom will wish her well as she is united with her noble husband.'

Then the old priest raised his right hand in solemn benediction, saying, 'Now may God Almighty bless the union between this man and woman and may they go through life helping each other to bear the heavy burdens of their sacred offices, may they go on doing the Lord's work for many years to come and may they be blessed in their children and in their children's children.'

Mara and Turlough bent their heads for the blessing and then exchanged the formal kiss. The others crowded up to congratulate them and Mara found her eyes wet as first Conor and Ellice, then Teige and his wife, her two scholars and then the farm workers, encouraged by Cumhal, poured blessings and good wishes upon them both. Last of all she found herself in Brigid's arms and felt her tears mingle with the tears of the woman who had been a mother to her for all of her life.

'The Brehon, God bless his soul, would have been a happy man today to see his daughter married to the king,' said Brigid, eventually, mopping her face with a large square of linen.

Then the wedding was over and by the light of the stars they all walked across to the Brehon's house.

'I wonder what they are eating at the abbey, now,' said Teige, helping himself to some more duck from the platter in front of him.

'Salted cod,' shouted Turlough, raising one of Mara's precious Venetian glasses in a salute before emptying the dark red burgundy in one long swallow. 'Come on, everybody,' he added, distributing the wine with a liberal hand, 'let's not forget the salted cod. I give you a toast to its memory.'

Patrick chuckled quietly, adroitly removing the cup of burgundy from in front of Shane and substituting some small beer.

'Oh, Lord tonight,' said Father Peter, his small white face creased with consternation, 'it's Christmas Eve and I should be fasting.'

'Not on my wedding day,' said Mara firmly, rescuing the last of the duck from Teige and sliding it on to the monk's platter.

'Nor on mine,' roared Turlough, tilting the flagon of wine over Father Peter's glass. 'You just obey your king, my lad, and forget about the abbot. No one will carry tales.'

'Well, I suppose I did take vows of obedience to my superiors,' murmured Father Peter with a resigned smile. His kind old eyes were watching Ellice and Conor, shoulder to shoulder on the cushioned bench. Ellice was feeding her husband pieces of duck from the point of her knife and he was chewing them hungrily.

'The lad's looking well, isn't he?' said Turlough in Mara's ear and she nodded happily. Conor, she thought, was looking better than he had for the last six months. Perhaps there was a chance that he might recover, after all.

'Our bridal night,' said Turlough with deep satisfaction. 'Well, with a feast like that and such good company it will be a night to remember. Just look at those stars out there!'

'I think we had our bridal night three months ago,' Mara said, but she wasn't really listening to him. She lay back on the bed, her face preoccupied and one hand on her stomach. There it is, again, she thought. For a while she had thought that she must be wrong; it was, after all, twenty-one years since she had felt this movement, but now she knew that she had made no mistake. She leaned out of the bed, took a piece of pink linen tape from her pouch beside the bed and turned to her new husband with a smile.

'Slide off your ring, Turlough,' she said. 'I need to borrow it for a moment.'